THE EMBROIDERED SUNSET

The Embroidered Sunset

Joan Aiken

1970
Doubleday & Company, Inc.
Garden City, New York

Library of Congress Catalog Card Number 77-116180
Copyright © 1970 by Joan Aiken
All Rights Reserved
Printed in the United States of America

This light romance is for Isabelle Taylor

THE EMBROIDERED SUNSET

I

If it had not been a pleasure it would have been a duty to hate Uncle Wilbie Culpepper. He sat blandly smiling upon his household, impervious to Lucy's malignant appraisal, rotund, tight-skinned, infinitely self-satisfied. There was not an atom out of place in Uncle Wilbie's universe; sometimes Lucy doubted if he could be a genuine member of the human race; he seemed too pink-cheeked and unwrinkled to be subject to regular human ailments and difficulties. It was more probable that he was constructed from plastic—unfadable, unmeltable, unshrinkable—and would last forever. A dismaying prospect.

"You mean there's no money left *at all?*" Lucy repeated, steadily encountering Uncle Wilbie's beaming regard. His eyes were opaque, like onyx-coloured marbles.

The charged quality in Lucy's voice caused Aunt Rose to come out of the fashion pages, and Corale to lay down a catalogue of Caribbean cruise wear.

Uncle Wilbie measured with his eye the dimensions of a large segment of chocolate layer cake, carefully bit off a third part, and masticated it.

"Yep," he replied concisely, when he had half consumed the mouthful. "I'm afraid that's about the size of it, Your Highness." It was one of Uncle Wilbie's pleasantries to address Lucy as Princess. "Your schooling at Cadwallader used up every red cent. *And* a bit over, if we must go into it," he added apologetically.

"It didn't occur to you," said Lucy with tight, cold control, "that it might be better to send me to a cheaper school, so there would be a bit of money left to train me for a career afterwards?"

"And have people say we sent Corale to a better school than you?" Aunt Rose began.

"Why, Princess!" Uncle Wilbie silenced his wife with a look. "Why, Princess, I'm surprised at you. It was the least I could do for your poor father's memory to see that you had a decent education." He took another large, squashy bite of chocolate cake, and passed his cup to Aunt Rose. "More coffee, please, Rosie-Posie."

"I doubt if father would have considered it needful to send me to one of the most snobbish schools in the world," said Lucy, grimly recalling her sufferings over the last six years; remarkably high-priced sufferings, it now appeared.

"Your father, my dearest Princess, was not the wisest of men when it came to practical matters. I think we are all agreed about that," said Uncle Wilbie with relish. He received his cup back from Aunt Rose and took a long, meditative swallow. My goodness, he is enjoying this, thought Lucy. "Not to put too fine a point on it," Wilbie added, replacing cup on saucer, "your father, Princess dear, was completely and utterly hopeless where money was concerned. He was a spendthrift. Unreliable. In fact a bum. A—a—wait"—he checked with uplifted hand the beginning of her indignant rebuttal—"I'm sure he seemed a hero to you, Highness, and that's very proper; we haven't wanted to do anything all these years to spoil his image for you." No, not until now, thought Lucy, her perceptions bright with rage, not until you could get the maximum satisfaction out of it. "But when you come down to brass tacks, that's all he was. A guy who could leave his wife and baby living on National Assistance in Liverpool while he went off to Canada on some crack-brained scheme."

"He wouldn't have left us if he could help it! It was because of my heart trouble, mother didn't think I ought to travel."

"*You* can't really know that," Corale pointed out with silky accuracy. "You were only two." She's loving this, Lucy thought, pointedly ignoring her blonde cousin. Only Aunt Rose looked distressed.

"No, you really *don't* know about it, dearie! A man who could leave his wife to die of pneumonia—"

"He didn't hear till it was too late."

"Now what makes you think that?" asked Uncle Wilbie, smiling. "Ah, I suppose little Minnie said so. Your mother's sister always thought the sun rose and set in him. Yes, with all his faults, Paul was a dear, lovable fellow—at least the *girls* loved him!"

Lucy ground her knuckles together. "Since Aunt Minnie's dead too—" she began. But then she changed her mind. She took a long, steadying look round Uncle Wilbie's famous kitchen; the quarter-deck, he loved to call it, in deprecating reference to his long-ago naval career. Everything was shipshape and shiny: steel, brass, mahogany, and dark-blue paint made an austere, masculine setting for Uncle Wilbie's famous tipsy-cakes, his clambakes and charcoal-broiled steaks. Aunt Rose, it was understood, operated in there only on sufferance and with extreme diffidence.

Let's not lose our temper, Lucy thought. That's what he wants. That's what he enjoys more than anything. That's what he's trying for now. I wonder why?

Raising dark-pupilled light grey eyes—her only good feature—she carefully surveyed her uncle. He twinkled back at her.

"So I'm afraid the princess will have to be a hard-working little princess from now on—unlike her lazy, no-good, layabout cousin there," he added, with a loving wink at his daughter.

"Dad! I work hard!" expostulated Corale, who donated her days to a charitable organisation, in whose offices she ate candy, read the glossy magazines, and used the telephone to arrange her dates.

"I haven't the slightest objection to hard work," said Lucy coldly. "Being a concert pianist must be one of the hardest jobs there is."

"Princess *dear*, we've been all over this once already. There just isn't the dough right now for such highfalutin notions—let alone going to London to train with some fancy-pants Roumanian maestro—"

"He is a Czech."

"Czech, Roumanian, what's the difference?" said Uncle Wilbie, who had put Europe behind him once and for all—except as a market—when he crossed the Atlantic from Liverpool to Boston twenty years ago. "Now, look, why don't you be a good little princess and find some nice sensible job—get one here in Boston, easy as falling off a brick—then in a couple of years you'll have saved enough, I daresay, to train with Comrade Pullover, or whatever he calls himself. After all, it's what most kids do—work to put themselves through college. It's what Corabella would have done if she'd wanted to go to college, isn't it, Bella?"

If she had been bright enough to go, Lucy thought.

"And," Uncle Wilbie went on in gentle remonstrance, "I don't like to labour the point, Princess dear, but it is just a *little* bit ungrateful of you to act this way; after all, if we hadn't sent you to Cadwallader, where, as well as having family connections through Aunt Rose and Corabella, you got the chance of a first-class musical education, you wouldn't even have *known* about your gift for piano, would you? Just remember that before you blast off at your poor old well-meaning uncle for not making a few thousand dollars stretch twice round the *world!* After all, two years isn't so long to wait, dearie, not at your age."

He smiled forgivingly at his niece. Her pale freckled face remained unresponsive.

"Two years will be just a bit too long in this case, I'm afraid, Uncle Wilbie. Max Benovek is dying of leukemia; he has only a couple of years to live. If that."

"Bit of a crazy choice for a teacher, then, isn't he," Uncle Wilbie said genially. "Better think again, Princess, and pick out some guy who's likelier to last your time out; no point sinking your savings in a fellow who's going to die on you! Besides, if he's as sick as that, the chances are a thousand to one against his taking on new pupils."

"Mrs. Bergstrom thought there was a chance he'd take me on."

Wilbie heaved a martyred sigh and looked at his wife with ruefully raised eyebrows. "Sometimes, Rosie, I almost wish your great-aunt *hadn't* been the founder of Cadwallader! If our little princess hadn't gone there and been jacked up on all these high-flown hopes by Madame Bergstrom, just think how much easier our life would be now!"

Aunt Rose looked apologetic and alarmed, her usual reaction to Uncle Wilbie's fun.

"I—I'm sure I never— If I'd ever thought—after all, *Corale's* perfectly—"

"That Mrs. Bergstrom's nuts, anyway," put in Corale. "She couldn't ever see anything wrong with her favourites. Nobody who had sense took her seriously."

Lucy and Corale exchanged measured, inimical looks.

"So, Princess, I'm afraid you'll have to put Commissar Thingovitch out of your mind. Heck, this country must be crawling with exiled Czechs and Hunks and Polaks, anyway, if you really must have a foreigner!" Wilbie glanced at the watch on the table in front of him which, according to habit, he had unbuckled from his wrist so as to be more relaxed while eating. "Well, well, time the old breadwinner was on his way, or there'll be tight belts in the harem soon!" He jumped up, wiping a stray chocolate-cake crumb from his smiling little mouth, walked round the table, and kissed his daughter. Corale never lifted her eyes from the catalogue. "So long then, harem, be good girls. What's my long-stemmed American beauty doing today?"

"Doing over the attic," said Aunt Rose wanly. "The Korean girl just called up to say she's not coming any more."

"Oh, too bad. Maybe our highness here could help you—if her heart permits. Well, have fun!" He kissed his wife, who, being some eight inches taller, had to incline her handsome, haggard head towards his husbandly peck; this she did with an anxious air, as if continually afraid that Wilbie might take her extra height for a piece of presumption. And he, as usual, with a malicious grin, made much of the disparity; grasping his wife's shoulder with a heavy hand he stood on tiptoe in his thick-soled shoes to salute her cheek.

" 'Bye, Princess dear. Forgive?"

Lucy neatly bypassed her uncle's kiss. Aunt Rose, wincingly noting this piece of rashness, wondered on whom the subsequent retribution would fall. Wilbie never let a debt go unpaid.

"Adios, girls!"

He was gone, a plump, smiling little man, bustling away from Belmont in his big car, in to Boston where the money rattled and the wheels of commerce went round. Uncle Wilbie, like another hero before him, had made a fortune from marketing a small domestic article, and since fondness for cash grows with its acquisition, he was now busy increasing his pile.

Corale languidly dumped the breakfast dishes in the dishwasher and then went off to her charitable work.

"I'll help you with the attic, Aunt Rose, of course," Lucy said.

"Oh, thank you, dear. I'm sure—your uncle didn't mean—that is—well you know how he—"

Despite the fact that they had lived together for six years, Rose was nervous of her niece and placatory when they were alone together; almost as placatory of Lucy, indeed, as she was of her husband. In spite of her small size and pallor there was a kind of indomitability, a stoic quality about Lucy which had this effect on some people.

"Yes, I know how he is," echoed Lucy, absently watching Aunt Rose don a pink-flowered smock, above which her beautiful, characterless, defeated face looked more natural than with her more usual matinee or cocktail rig. Uncle Wilbie saw to it that his wife engaged in an active social round; there is no point in possessing a trophy if you keep it shut away in a closet where nobody can see it.

"I'll take those," said Lucy, and grasped the duster and vacuum cleaner that her aunt was clumsily trying to manoeuvre up the polished pine stairs.

"But—Lucy dear—is it all right? What about your heart?"

"Oh shucks."

"Dr. Woodstock—"

"Dr. Woodstock's an old fusser. If I hadn't any other reason to be glad I'd quit that school, I'd be thankful to be rid of him."

"Lucy, *why* didn't you like Cadwallader?" Aunt Rose asked, following with a cobweb broom and can of moth spray. "It seems so queer. Coralie just adored it all the time she was there."

"Corale and I are just different," Lucy said, pausing in the large, airy second-floor hallway to give her troubled aunt a look that was half sardonic, half tolerant. "You hadn't noticed? Besides, they didn't go for my Liverpudlian accent at Cadwallader; thought it was common. Ee, they reckoned I was joost a gootersnipe!"

"Oh, what nonsense, dear! You don't have any accent. Besides, Coralie's cousin—" Aunt Rose began flusteredly.

"Being Corale's young cousin didn't help a bit. She's big and beautiful and outgoing and good at athletics and crazy about boys and dancing; oh, just naturally one of the gang! Whereas, look at me!"

On the third-floor hall where they were now, the girls had their rooms and bath; there was also a sewing room with a long mirror set in its open door. Lucy paused in front of this and nodded ironically at her undersized reflection. "No, I can tell you, they were quite as glad to see the back of me as I was to get out of there. Only, I'm just sorry to discover that my education there used up every last penny of Father's money."

"Lucy—if I can—" began Aunt Rose. Then she stopped and bit her lip. "I believe I can hear the phone ringing," she said. "Excuse me a minute. I'll just put these here and be right back. Oh, here's the attic key; you know how your uncle is about keeping the door locked."

Lucy did know. During the last six years she had not set foot in the attic more than three times, and she now went up the last flight, opened the door, and gazed about her with frank curiosity. The room was large, stretching the whole length of the big, old-fashioned house, and it was crammed with the accretions of nearly twenty years. Trunks, tennis rackets, old porch furniture, stacks of newspapers, discarded games, bundles of curtains, bicycles, were all jammed together in grimy confusion. Yellow curled-up photographs spilled out from dusty albums. A tangle of sports equipment, surfboards, scuba gear, fishing-rods, guns of various calibres, bore witness to Uncle Wilbie's various phases of activity; any sport, for Uncle Wilbie, represented a means to an end and was therefore pursued for a set period with single-minded devotion; the end, of course, being a useful enlargement of his social circle.

Plugging in the cleaner, Lucy set to work with a brisk efficiency that—though she would have rejected the thought—was inherited from her uncle. Starting at one end of the long cluttered room she moved and restacked everything, cleaning as she went, folding clothes, piling furniture and boxes more neatly, shaking and shuffling papers into tidy piles.

Aunt Rose, reappearing apologetically after twenty minutes, gave a gasp and exclaimed, "Mercy, what a lot you've done already. Do take care, dearie, don't overtire yourself."

"Oh, I'm fine," Lucy said absently. "Don't you worry about me,

I'm enjoying myself. Aunt Rose, who in the world did these marvellous things?"

"Which, dear?" Rose replied in a vague tone, glancing at her watch.

"These pictures over here."

Five small dormer windows gave light to the attic. Lucy had dragged an old wicker couch in front of the middle window and propped three canvases against it.

"Honestly, Aunt Rose, they are the most amazing things I ever saw!"

The three pictures all represented biblical subjects; in one a top-heavy ark was on the point of sliding into the flood as two giraffes leapt hastily aboard, last of a procession of animals disappearing over the deck; in another Absalom hung by his hair from an ilex tree while his horse galloped into a background where a wild battle raged, and overhead a portentous thunderstorm darkened the sky; in the third, tiny Samuel in a white nightgown stood riveted, listening, in the bottom righthand corner while the immense, rich, dusk-filled temple loomed around him.

"*That* one!" said Lucy. "Look at the way he's *listening!*"

As she considered the infant Samuel her too-thin, closed, wary face softened into a tender and amused expression which, insensitive though life had obliged Rose Culpepper to become, yet struck her with an obscure pang. I've never seen Lucy look like that before, she thought.

"Who did them, Aunt Rose? Do look at that colour—the lightning flashing on Absalom's hair, and the white horses galloping against those dark-green hills. And the ark—all that red and prune and ochre and charcoal. Oh, I know they're primitives, but they're astonishingly subtle too—whoever did them knew exactly what he meant, and had a sense of humour into the bargain. Look at Mrs. Noah coping with the cobra. And Samuel's *feet!*"

Aunt Rose was quite bewildered. "But Lucy—art isn't your subject—"

Lucy's ironic expression returned. "You mean, what right have I to be so enthusiastic? Can't I even be allowed to recognise a work of genius when I see one?"

Poor Rose peered, straining her beautiful short-sighted eyes.

"*Those* funny old things? Why, they're all flat—what's the word? —two-dimensional? Everything kind of shoots uphill."

"Yes, that contributes to the sense of movement and humour. They're really very complex."

"Why, Lucy! I never heard you talk so—"

"No? Maybe you never heard me talk at all," Lucy said not unkindly.

"It seems so strange—! Why, they're not even all paint; there's bits of cloth, and bottle-tops, and wool, and embroidery stuck all over. Wilbie just laughed at them when she sent them. A regular old maid's jumble, he called them."

"He would," said Lucy. "But where did they come from? Why haven't I seen them before?"

"Oh, I guess they arrived some time when you were away at school or camp. Two or three years ago, it would have been. Wilbie thought people would laugh at them; he told me to write a letter of thanks—well, I would have done that anyway, of course —and put them up in the attic. She'd never know."

"Who would never know?"

"Old Aunt Fennel."

"Aunt Fennel?"

"Fennel Culpepper. Your great-aunt, I suppose she'd be. Your Uncle Wilbie's aunt."

"Father's aunt, then, too?"

"Why, yes, I guess so. *Mercy*, look at the time!" Aunt Rose exclaimed, recollecting herself. "Lucy dear, don't trouble any longer about this stuffy old attic. What I came to say was that the Bankses have invited me round there for lunch and bridge, so I'm afraid I can't help you any more right now, if I'm to have my hair done first. In fact, I ought to be on my way this very minute. So let's lock up and I'll finish off in here another day. I'm sure you've done as much as you ought."

"No, honestly, Aunt Rose, I'm fine. I might just as well finish, now I'm started. It won't take more than another hour or so."

"Well, but—the thing is—I don't know if your uncle—"

"Oh," Lucy said with an unerring guess at the real reason for her aunt's fluster, "I'll be finished long before Uncle Wilbie gets home. He needn't know I've been up here on my own."

"Why, Lucy, that wasn't what I meant!"

"Never mind," said Lucy, not unsympathetically shooing her aunt out of the room. "You go play your nice bridge. You know how I am at always putting the worst constructions on things. Oh, what shall I do about all these old papers?"

She indicated a pile of the *Kirby Evening Advertiser and East Riding Gazette.*

"Oh, just leave them," Aunt Rose said hastily. "Wilbie hates anything to be thrown out."

Lucy put them in a corner, wondering why her uncle bothered to subscribe to an English small-town paper. Then the name Culpepper caught her eye in a tiny paragraph: ". . . funeral of Miss Beatrice Howe, who for many years resided at Appleby with Miss Fennel Culpepper and was a well-known contributor to our columns on herbal and wild-flower lore . . ." Presumably that was the Miss Fennel Culpepper who had done the pictures? But there was nothing more about her in the news item.

Contrary to his usual custom, Uncle Wilbie did in fact reappear in the house at noon. By that time, however, the attic was tidy, the door relocked, the key back in Aunt Rose's bureau drawer.

As was his wont, Uncle Wilbie stood just inside the front door and bawled:

"Rosie! Where are you? *Rosie!*"

There was no reply. Becoming irritated at once, he bustled off to the music room, where Lucy was sternly slicing her way through the slow movement of Beethoven's Opus 109.

"Hey, what goes on around here? Where's your Aunt Rose?"

Apart from an organ, unplayed and hopelessly out of tune, and the Knabe which he had acquired secondhand from a business colleague when he still had hopes of Corale's turning out musical, Wilbie had never done anything much about furnishing the music room. It looked north on to a dustbin area at the side of the house, to conceal which Aunt Rose had provided net drapes. Corale and her friends occasionally overflowed in here when the TV room proved too small for their parties, otherwise Lucy had it to herself. The walls were white, the floor bare polished pine, the acoustics good. A plaster bust of Beethoven (thrown in along with the piano) made clear the room's cultural function. Lucy kept the piano tuned but had made no attempt at embellishing the room until today.

Beethoven and Lucy wore identical scowls as she raised her face from the keyboard to meet her uncle's eyes.

"Sorry, what did you say, Uncle Wilbie? Oh, Aunt Rose? She went off to lunch and bridge at the Bankses'."

"She shouldn't have done that," Uncle Wilbie said, annoyed. "Just taken a couple of contracts away from Banks's firm. Their prices aren't competitive any more."

"Shall I call up and tell her to come home?"

"No, never mind," he said, missing the sarcasm. "I just wondered—but if she's at the Bankses' it's okay. I guess she went off quite a while ago. Didn't have time for much else?"

"Not much," Lucy answered impassively.

Uncle Wilbie suddenly became gay.

"Here's the poor old breadwinner, toiling away downtown, and what does his harem do? Tinkle all day long on the piano or gad off playing bridge! Oh well, back to the treadmill for us workers, hey, Russ?"

For the first time Lucy noticed that Russell McLartney, one of the brighter young men from the office, had accompanied her uncle and was waiting in the hall. Russell, thickset, thick-haired, and self-confident, had been for several years now the favourite aide of Uncle Wilbie, who paid unusual attention to his opinion; Lucy suspected that Wilbie had him scheduled as a possible successor in the firm, and that Russ had himself scheduled as a possible mate for Corale; though when Lucy once suggested the latter possibility Wilbie flew into an unexpected rage; evidently he had more ambitious plans for his daughter. Meanwhile a formal escort relationship existed between Russ and Corale, and a strong hostility, tempered by unwilling mutual respect, between Russ and Lucy.

"Hi there, Lucy," he said, strolling in. "Still giving the classics a beating?"

"Hello, Russ," Lucy said coldly. She sat waiting for them to go. Sensing this, Uncle Wilbie chose to remain; he began to bounce a little on his thick rubber soles, expanding with the bonhomie that came out in him on such occasions.

"We've been visiting the Tintax works," he explained to Lucy, who remained impassive at this piece of information. "So on the way back into town I stopped off to pick up my watch. Left it at home this morning." He walked over to the piano and inspected the album on the music rest.

"What's this, eh? Strauss? Friml?"

"Beethoven." Inexpressively, Lucy watched as he flipped over the pages.

"Wonderful how she understands it all, ain't it, Russ? Mysterious-looking stuff! *Andante con moto*—what language are those words in, Princess?"

"Italian."

"Greek to me." Uncle Wilbie laughed heartily. "Why can't they put it in English? Beethoven wasn't Italian, was he? What's this one, *vol—volti subito?*"

"Turn over quickly."

"As the actress said to the bishop! That's a handy one, Russ! We must remember that if we ever make a business trip to Italy. More to this music than meets the eye, if you ask me . . . oh well, better be on our way. The Princess isn't a bit pleased to have us interrupting her labours." Bored with Lucy's lack of response to his needling, he turned towards the door and stopped abruptly.

"Why," said Russ, "you've put those pictures up at last. Has the old lady passed over, then?"

He moved forward to admire the three primitives which Lucy had hung on the wall facing the window. Against the bare white background they glowed like stones in ultra-violet light. "Amazing things, aren't they?" he said with satisfaction. "I told your uncle they'd be worth a fortune some day, and I bet I'm right. All they want is a bit of PR work, you wait and see."

"How did those get down here?"

Lucy could tell that Uncle Wilbie was furious. He had gone very quiet and pale, never a good sign. The geniality dropped from him like ice from a defrosted freezer.

"Aunt Rose said you didn't care for them, so I thought you wouldn't mind if I put them in here," Lucy replied calmly. "I found them when we were tidying the attic."

"He didn't care for them?" Russ said. "You've got to be kidding! Why, when I told him—"

"Quiet, Russ! Aunt Rose made a mistake," Wilbie said shortly. "I'd like them to go back in the attic, please."

"Very well." Lucy stood up, but before she could touch the pictures, Uncle Wilbie, recollecting himself, added, "Russ will take them up."

Wilbie himself was extremely strong; like some dreadful little ant, he could carry about four times his own weight, but it was a matter of protocol never to do so.

"Sure, I'll take them." With obliging rapidity, Russ scooped the pictures off the wall and bore them upstairs. Lucy heard their voices faintly, then the slam of the attic door, presently steps descending again.

"So long!" Russ called politely. The front door slammed in its turn, and Wilbie's Cadillac started up in front of the house. Lucy recovered her place in the music but did not immediately recommence playing; with her elbows propped on the keyboard lid she rested her chin on her fists and brooded.

At supper Uncle Wilbie was his gay self again.

"Such a project I've got for our Princess!" he announced jubilantly, when he had divested himself of the striped blue and white butcher's apron which he wore tied round his plump body during the preparation of his famous rice dish while Aunt Rose, who had put in a couple of hours beforehand chopping and assembling the ingredients, hovered anxiously nearby in case of last-minute requests. "Bridge all afternoon and then she gets her dinner cooked for her into the bargain!" he chided her fondly. "And there's Corabella tired out and yawning from reading the comic strips all day; little Lucinda and I are the only guys who do any work around here, hey, Princess?" He directed a loving look at his daughter and one full of malice at Lucy. "Bella, quit slouching and take your hair out of the horseradish! Look how nice and straight Lucy sits to eat her supper!"

"Project for Lucy? What do you mean, dear?" Aunt Rose inquired nervously.

Lucy's pale eyes met her uncle's little twinkling ones. "Thank you for the kind thought, Uncle Wilbie," she said, "but don't trouble to find any jobs for me. I'm going to work my passage to England as a stewardess, and then try to get to see Max Benovek; if I could talk to him I'd know where I stood."

"Well, and isn't that just what I was going to *suggest?*" Wilbie cried triumphantly.

"A *stewardess?* Lucy, dearie, the work would be far too much for you!"

Lucy waited, looking at her uncle, her expression one of total suspicion.

"You see, Princess, I've been worried for quite some time about old Aunt Fennel Culpepper—the one who did those pictures you're so sold on." The pictures, Lucy thought; I knew there was something odd going on. It really threw him off balance for a moment this afternoon to find I liked them. But why should that suddenly make him agree to my going to England? Or is it that he just wants to get me away from here? It was certainly true, she thought, catching her uncle's eye for a flickering instant, that their mutual antipathy had intensified of late.

Aunt Rose looked as if she wished to speak, but one glance from her husband was enough to abort the impulse.

"I thought Russ said Aunt Fennel died?"

"That's just what we don't know." Uncle Wilbie carefully loaded a fork with rice, prawn, chicken, pimento, and pine kernel, transferred the load dexterously to his mouth, and chewed with relish. "Used to write every so often," he presently said. "Village news, you know. Sent pictures, few years ago. Then—no more letters."

"How old is she? Where does she live?"

"Oh well on; in her late eighties, isn't she, Wilbie?" Aunt Rose put in. He nodded.

"Lives in England—little village in northeast Yorkshire. Appleby-under-Scar—pronounce it Appley. Whole family came from round there once. Thing is, she doesn't write any more, but she goes on getting her annuity from the firm. Paid into bank account in York."

Lucy began to guess the cause of Uncle Wilbie's discontent. To a man so mean that he urged his family to have cold showers rather than hot, and went around switching lights off behind them, the thought of this perpetual trickle from the firm's resources must be a constant annoyance.

"She invested in your firm, then?"

"Oh, years back," he said, as if all obligation had long ago been cancelled. "What I'm beginning to wonder is, if she's dead, who's getting the dough? Should cease at death."

"I don't see why she's got to be dead," Corale said, yawning. "There's other reasons why she could have stopped writing letters. Maybe no one answered them."

"Or her eyesight may be failing," said Lucy. "Think of all that fine embroidery and close work on the pictures."

"That's so." Wilbie nodded again thoughtfully, as if the idea had not occurred to him before. "Yep, that *might* be the reason. On the other hand, there might be a bit of skulduggery going on somewhere."

Trust you to think that, Lucy reflected. A mind as devious as yours would naturally look for double-dealing in others.

"But surely," she said aloud, "it's not so easy to draw someone else's annuity? There'd have to be signatures, and proof of identity, and so forth?"

"Sharp as a little needle, our Princess, eh? But it's not all so plain and simple as you might fancy. Old Aunt Fennel never married—lived with another old lady for the last God knows how many years—name'll come to me in a minute—so what's to stop the other old dame claiming the cash? Easy to forge signature of someone you've lived with for last forty years."

"But, good heavens—" To Lucy the idea seemed wildly far-fetched. "There'd be no end of complications—death certificates, insurance policies—people would know at once, surely?" Old ladies are just not likely to embark on a course of wholesale fraud, she would have said, particularly immediately following the death of a dear friend. But in Uncle Wilbie's book this was evidently just the sort of behaviour to be expected from old ladies.

"Who's to tell one wrinkled-up old girl from another?" he demanded. "I bet even their doctor didn't know them apart! Never had the doctor, anyway—all these herbal remedies. No, if you've decided to go over to England, Princess, that couldn't be handier. Minute you get there, you nip up to Yorkshire—I'll pay your train fare, hey?—and spy out the land a bit, will you?"

"But how would *I* be able to tell?" Lucy was not at all enthusiastic about doing this private-eye job for her uncle. "I've never even *met* Aunt Fennel, so far as I know. Have you a photograph of her?"

"Might have one somewhere, have we, Rosie?" Rose looked doubtful. "Anyway, if there's anything going on that's not strictly on the up-and-up, the arrival of a bona-fide great-niece would be enough to scare whoever's doing it and put a stop to the business, don't you see?"

"I don't like it," said Lucy.

"Oh, come on, Princess, what's the harm? And if it's the real Aunt Fennel, you'd like to meet her, wouldn't you? Sweet old lady, just your dish, I'd have thought, brewing up her herbal remedies and doing her embroidery; why, if you were so crazy about those ones up in the attic, think of all the other pictures you'd have a chance to see."

"Has she done such a lot?" In spite of herself, Lucy's curiosity was pricked by the thought.

"Hundreds, by all accounts. Whole house full of 'em, I guess, by now. Come to think, that's another thing you could do while you're there." Lucy shot a narrow glance at her uncle. The increased airiness of his manner warned her that now they were approaching the nub of the whole business.

"Well, you know how young Russ thinks those pictures might prove quite a hot selling property. Daresay the boy's dreaming, but he says there's a fashion right now for primitives and stuff —naïve art, he calls it. We're all plain folks round here, we wouldn't know about that, eh?" For once, the look he directed at his daughter was less proud than impatient, but she merely yawned again. "Seems wild to me," Wilbie went on, "but we still don't want to pass up a thing like that if there is a chance of realising a bit on them, do we?"

"I see," said Lucy coldly. "You want me to collar all the pictures before somebody else does?"

"Well, damn it, they're family property, ain't they? I'm her next of kin. No sense in letting some stranger cash in. She's probably given them away all round the village, that's what worries me—"

"Why don't you go, if you're so anxious to buy them back from all these unsuspecting strangers?"

"Now, Lucy! You know how busy your uncle always is!"

"Sure. Much too busy to go to England right now. I wish I'd had time to nip over when I was in Stuttgart last summer, but there wasn't a minute."

"It would only take a week-end, if you flew."

"Uncle Wilbie hates planes—you know that," Aunt Rose said reproachfully. "They upset his digestion for *days*."

"Anyway," Wilbie said, "if an old businessman like me was to go snooping round collecting pictures—supposing Aunt Fennel's dead, that's to say—people would get wise to what was going on in no time. But if *you* were to do it, Princess—innocent young chick like you—you could give any old reason, memorial exhibition, sentimental wish to get hold of as many as possible—heck, you're crazy about them, you said so your*self!* It would be as easy as winning the kids' crossword!"

"I don't like it," Lucy said again. "I'd feel sneaky."

"For Pete's sake! Who's getting done? Nobody. Tell you what —I'll pay you a commission on every picture you collect—might come to enough to pay your fees with whosis if you're still hell-bent on this piano business."

That did make Lucy pause. She pushed salad about her plate in silence.

"I must say, Princess," Uncle Wilbie said in an injured tone, "I do think you might show a little bit more sense of obligation to your aunt and me, considering all we've done for you. After all, we took you in and gave you a home all these years since your mother and Paul and Minnie died—gave you education, social background, the whole *works*—"

"You expect gratitude from Lucy?" Corale said. "What a hope! She hates our guts, every last one of us, don't you, Luce?"

Trapped, Lucy looked up in time to catch her aunt's expression of hopeless resignation to a situation beyond her control.

Chivalry was a very minor element in Lucy's tough, wary heart, but her aunt sometimes called it out; Rose's situation was so infinitely worse than any possible future one could imagine.

"Oh, all right," Lucy said at last, crossly. "If everyone's going to make such an issue of it, I'll try and locate the old girl."

II

Waking in the morning. Cold and dark. Bed's lumpy, must get Dill help me turn mattress, refill with new Ladies' Bedstraw blossom. New bag of bean flower to put under pillow. No, wrong time of year for bean flower, must be winter, so cold and dark. Seat feels cold in bed. Waking up a little more, would rather not wake, would rather go back to sleep. Happy dream, now I remember. Outside the cottage, High Beck, picking valerian off the front wall. Dill weeding the stone troughs, all blue with lobelia. Bees humming, old Taffypuss sunning himself on the doorstep. Taffy! He's purring. Dill picks bunch of sweetbriar—can smell it. Now she's climbed down the dene to get watercress. Careful, Dill! Birds are singing too loud, have to wake up. No birds really. Dream goes peeling, shredding away like burnt paper, oh, come back, come back! No, gone. Oh, Dill, oh, Taffypuss, I do miss you so. When will I ever stop?

Waking up. Cold seat. Must ask That One about good brushed nylon knickers. She *said*, sent to laundry, but gone for weeks. Queer sort of laundry. Can't trust anyone around here. Cold even in bed now. Mustn't get up, though. That One furious if people get up before breakfast. Not at her best in morning. Can't make breakfast, she says, if people downstairs underfoot. Well, I don't mind breakfast in bed. Would rather be up though, putting on own kettle, going to hen-house, collecting eggs, push hand under warm, feathery, grumbling hen, egg each for me and Dill

. . . No use thinking that way. Anyhow, breakfast here not bad. Porridge, toast, tea quite hot sometimes. Warms you up in cold bed. Breakfast is best part of life here. Not saying much.

Here comes That One upstairs now. Can hear her with clanking tray. How she doesn't fall and break her neck! Stairs so cluttered with that Venus statue at top, suitcases, boxes, and then the Hoover cord running from top to bottom; downright dangerous if you ask me with all these old people, mostly half blind. Have to grope your way like in a mine; I never let go of banisters. Funny, really, when you think. They say High Beck was dangerous for me and Dill, with the dene down below, said fall was to be expected. But if they could see this place! Far worse. And if there was to be a fire . . . trapped in tiny bedrooms full of furniture. But don't let's think of that. Here comes That One with tray.

Good morning, Mrs. . . .

Good morning, ladies. Lovely hot porridge.

Three in bedroom is wickedly overcrowded, specially such small rooms. Beds all jammed together, hardly room to open drawers. Only one wardrobe between three. Have to put trays on commodes, not very nice. No privacy at all. Just have to ignore others. One of them wants window open, one wants it shut. If shut, can't hear birds. But can't mention that. Because. So much to remember all the time. No curlews here anyway, no nightingales; only sparrows. Better half a sparrow than no bird. Dill would laugh, she always laughs at my jokes. Honestly, Daff, one day you'll be the death of me. But I wasn't. *He* was. That other one. Why did God have to let him do it? Dill was so good. Never harmed a fly all her life long. If she found a cockroach in the larder I was the one who had to get rid of it. All those birds with hurt wings, squirrel with broken leg. People's pets. She looked after them, every one so carefully. No one looked after her. There she lay, all night long, half in beck. Doctor said, must have called and called for help. No one heard, not even God. Maybe God did hear at last.

Clinking spoons. People eating porridge. Must sit up and have breakfast while it's hot. *Ah!* Rheumatism.

Queer, you lie in bed, thinking, remembering. You might be any age. Body feels light, relaxed. You don't feel old. But once you move—*ah!* pain in elbows, knees, back. Old age grips like a trap with teeth. Funny, they used to say High Beck bad for rheumatism, with the dene just below, but never any rheumatism there. Kept too active, probably. Hens, garden, milking Betsy, going to Cronkley Wood for herbs. Never had a twinge. But here! No chance of exercise, that's why. Sitting about in dark little poky parlour all day long. They call it lounge, but I say parlour. Old-fashioned is best. Daren't go out in street for fear of meeting That Other One.

Sitting up now. Get bed jacket from under blanket where keeping warm. Put round shoulders. Ah! Twinge. Carefully put sugar on porridge. Not too much, jar has to last week. Porridge, lumpy, like bed. But hot. Not real porridge though, only instant stuff. Never cream, only milk and skim at that. Do you remember, Dill, Betsy's cream in the enamel pan, so thick you could crumple it like paper? Shouldn't talk to Dill, she's not here. Spread toast, butter tastes like marge, probably is marge. One of the others says she thinks it is marge. Beg your pardon, what did you say? I haven't put my hearing aid in yet. Sorry, can't put hearing aid in till ears washed. Drink tea. It's hot, that's all you can say. I just wish I could have a drink of camomile or melilot. Peppermint, growing in the stream. "I'll make us some peppermint tea," she used to say. Or lime-blossom. Raspberry leaf, wood betony. Hot and fragrant, like meadow on summer's day. This is like floor sweepings in hot water. "Tea begrudged, water bewitched," Dill would say.

Out of bed then. Put feet on icy-cold floor. Queer to see feet, so old and thin and bony. Never get used to that. Quick, put on brown slippers, coat. No room for coat *and* dressing-gown, That One says. So coat. Somebody in bathroom, have to wait. Should have more than one bathroom with so many. But That One says, lucky to have bathroom at all. No bathroom at High Beck, outside W. and kitchen sink, but clean and sweet. Only me and Dill. Can't say the same for here. Ah, she's out. Time, too.

Water's hot because washday. That One will be furious if use too much, but must have good wash. Good wash best pleasure now. Still have three tablets of lettuce soap, what will I do when it's finished? No use worrying yet, ought to last few weeks still. Someone banging on door, hurry up whoever's in there, going to stay all day? Pretend not to notice. Ready to leave, got everything? Soap, flannel, powdered elm bark. Out into passage. Oh, so sorry, been waiting long? Apologies, but can't help it, can I, if only one bathroom among so many. Careful not to trip in dark passage. Trunks with metal corners. Hurt ankle bones. Wardrobe. She ought to find somewhere else to put them. Hoover leaning against wall. Don't grip it, would fall over. That was how old man with black patch over eye broke hip; ambulance took him to hospital. Now in geriatric ward, That One said. Please God don't let that happen to me. I know about those geriatric wards; they take away your spectacles. Say you're incapable of managing your own affairs. This place is paradise compared to them. Maybe the old man didn't go there. Maybe his relations came for him; took him to home with garden, terrace to sit in sun, own big room, grandchildren to chat and run little errands.

Now, getting dressed. Washday, so clean vest. Take off dirty vest. Take clean one from under pillow where warming. Keep coat over shoulders, turn back to others. *Ah!* twinge. Coat keeps sliding. If only I had room to myself. If only I was ever alone.

No good thinking that way.

Struggle. Struggle.

Well, almost done. Vest on, liberty bodice on, stockings on, two pairs of knickers on (must ask about good brushed nylon ones again). Tiring. Must sit down and rest, but first change over little cloth bag. Unpin from inside of dirty vest, pin to inside of clean vest. Safety pins are stiff. Fingers getting weak. Suppose they get too weak to manage safety pins? What will I do then? If I could get some powdered seaweed to soak hands in. Or celery tea. No use asking That One. Little bag feels scratchy on chest. Pin not properly fastened. That's better. Only safe place to keep the wealth.

Dress, cardigan. Brush hair. Arms are stiff. Damp lumpy bed, what can you expect? Tired, breathing not good. Sit on bed for minute. Tray on commode. Put in hearing aid. First clip battery case on cardigan. Clip very stiff, fingers very weak. Fiddle. Fiddle. Shall I help you, Miss Culpepper? That One's come back, has she? Wants to make bed, I suppose, that's what's behind helpful offer. Grabs it from me, clips on wrong side. Dreadful breath, like drains from a brewery. Can you wonder? Never mind wrong side. Change it downstairs when she's not looking.

Right. Now cord round back of neck, under bun, poke plug into ear. Difficult. Very difficult. Fiddle. Fiddle. That One standing watching, impatient. Fiddle. Poke it in anyhow for now, wait till downstairs, or she'll offer to do *that*. Right, Miss C.? Got your carrier bag? Off you go downstairs then. The lounge is nice and warm.

That's as maybe.

Handkerchief, comfrey tablets. What you want to take all those tablets for, can't do you any good. Mustn't let her see me taking them, she gets offended. Isn't the food you get here good enough then? Frankly, no, it isn't. Couldn't say so to her face though.

Down the stairs, hold on to banister all the way. Watch out for Hoover and cord. Watch out for statue of Venus. Indecent thing, all bare, towel falling off stomach. Having no arms doesn't make it any better. Dill would laugh at me and say it was famous art, but I say inconsiderate. Who wants naked female smirking at top of stairs every time they go past to bathroom? Top-heavy too. Dangerous. Might easily fall on someone. Who wants Venus falling on them? Who's that at foot of stairs? Dreadfully dark in front entry, stained-glass window panes in door, grandfather clock, umbrella stand, That One's bicycle right where can't help falling over it.

That you, Miss Culpepper? Can I help you down last few steps?

It's the old man, Mr. Thing, always very polite. Never could fancy a beard and his all dirty, yellow with tobacco, disgusting. Won't do not to be polite back though. Thank you, Mr. Thing, the eyes *are* very dim today, can hardly see at all. Could you kindly pass white stick out of hall stand? (That One won't have white sticks upstairs in bedrooms, says people might trip over them at night. As if there weren't plenty else to trip over.)

Into parlour. Six people there already, sitting. Nobody speaking.

Nice and warm, she said. Humph.

Is it a fine day, Mr. Thing? somebody says after five minutes. Mr. Thing goes down to paper shop for papers, that's his little job.

Grey, says Mr. Thing. Cold. Not raining. That's about all you can say for it.

Would be a good day for collecting lichen. Or willow bark along the river bank. No use thinking that way. If only I dared go out though. Just to pick a few dandelion leaves. Maybe in public gardens? No, too far. Would not dare. Must ask Mr. Thing when he will next be going to chemist.

Is anybody looking? Don't think so. Fix hearing-aid plug in safer with bit of tissue. Better. Now sit. Ear very sore.

What time is it, Mr. Thing?

Half-past ten, Miss Er.

Cup of tea in half an hour. Lunch in two hours. Tea in six hours. Supper (not supper really, just Bovaltine) in eight hours. Bed in twelve hours.

Another dreadful day begun.

III

Max Benovek sat in his balcony looking down at the view below. He sat there resentfully, because he was too tired for any other occupation, and he looked down with a sort of angry apathetic compulsion, as somebody might who, having waited forever in a dentist's anteroom and seeing another eternity in prospect, cannot in the end resist picking up the one magazine on the table, however crucifyingly dull its pages.

The Queen Alexandra Sanatorium was vast. Sheer size alone would have suggested its institutional nature, but the dreariness of its architecture made this a certainty. The beholder's first idea was that it must be a prison or workhouse, but the design did not seem quite right for either: built fifty years earlier, in a period when fresh air was considered essential for chest illnesses, it carried the maximum number of balconies and consequently looked like a huge yellow brick waffle standing on edge amid the Surrey pines. All the ironwork of balconies and fire escapes was painted a durable red; the waffle appeared to have been smeared with jam.

On the first floor, directly over one of the main entrances, Benovek had his large private room. It had originally been intended as a matron's office; even the most expensive private patients' rooms were less than half the size, but the name of Benovek and the fact that his piano would not fit anywhere else except in the operating theatre had decided the matter. He found the situation distractingly noisy and almost daily declared that he could not stand it and must be transferred somewhere, anywhere else, but the impossibility of resiting the piano always, when it came to the point, constituted an insuperable difficulty. When he lay awake at night one of his principle pastimes, or tortures, depending on his physical state, consisted of trying to find somewhere else to put the piano.

The view commanded by his balcony was in fact quite a pleasant one: across the large, institutional, but well-kept garden, across a valley filled with beechwoods, to the north downs. Benovek, however, impatiently ignored the distant prospect, and looked at the closer one only when he could not avoid doing so; dozens of times every day a horrified fascination drew his unwilling eyes to it.

As now.

A young father with two small children had come to see his wife who was dying of emphysema. Children were not allowed inside the hospital, therefore it had been arranged that the mother should be taken outside in a wheel chair for a couple of hours; the husband had wheeled her to and fro along the gravel paths while she held the younger child in her lap, and the elder one, who was probably no more than three or four, trotted alongside. Every five minutes or so, in the course of the afternoon, Benovek's eye had been reluctantly drawn back to the group as they went up and down the paths, encased in their little capsule of solitude. He did not think the parents spoke to one another at all; occasionally the walking child asked a question, which they appeared to have difficulty in answering. Now it was time for the visitors to leave: a nurse had emerged to wheel the patient inside, and the father had taken the baby from its mother's arms. But the older child, hitherto quiet and docile enough, at the prospect of leaving his mother yet again was suddenly transformed into a desperate creature. He screamed, he sobbed, he clung to her, he kicked out at the nurse and at his father when they tried to detach him from the woman in the wheel chair. The father, handicapped by the baby he held, was unable to take any effective action; the nurse, who was young and inexperienced, seemed totally at a loss. The group was now directly below Benovek's balcony and the child's reiterated, sobbing, frantic plea—"Let me stay with

Mummy. *Please* let me stay with Mummy," rang in his ears and on his nerves and could not be shut out.

"Dee," he called restlessly. "Are you there? Help me inside, would you?"

But there was no answer; Dee Lawrence, who came every day to write his letters and do other secretarial jobs, had left the room to collect his tea tray. Max grasped the arms of his chair, summoning all his will to move. At this moment, however, the scene taking place below was deflected by an additional character; a girl had been walking up the long approach to the sanatorium and was now close enough to take a hand.

Benovek heard the young father, his voice ragged with strain, call out, "I say, could you hold the baby a moment while I get my son into the car?"

The girl, evidently grasping the situation, seemed unperturbed at having her help thus enlisted by a stranger.

"Is that your car over there?" she said. "Why don't you strap the baby in first while I hold the little boy."

"I doubt if you'll be able to—*Barney!* You *must* let go of Mummy. She's ill—you'll make her worse!"

It was unlikely that this argument would have had any effect on the distraught Barney, but the girl, with one calm forceful movement, detached his grip.

"Now *you* make a quick getaway," she muttered to the nurse, who took her advice and rapidly whisked the wheel chair indoors.

While the father slotted the baby into its car seat, the girl squatted down beside Barney in the middle of the gravel sweep; her grip on him, and her entirely concentrated attention, appeared to carry comfort as well as authority, for his exhausted hysterical sobs died slowly down to an occasional hiccup of "Mummy—Mummy"; Benovek could hear the girl talking to him in a soothing incantatory murmur.

"Yes, I know. Yes, I *know*. It's bloody unfair. But that's the way life is, Barney. They just hand you out the tough stuff, and you might as well get used to it. Yes, I *know* you want to stay with her. It's just a rotten deal, poor old Barney, and we can't do a thing about it. Not a single thing. That's what's so tough—just having to put up with it. It's a bloody awful shame, I know. But you'll feel a bit better by and by, I promise. Yes, you really will.

I *know*. There'll be tea, and sand castles, and your birthday, and Christmas. It's just as bad as can be *now*, I know; that's why things have got to get a bit better. See? For instance we can blow your nose, that'll help. Right?—blow, then. That's the boy. Again— grand. Okay, and now, look, your Dad's waiting for you. Want to get in the car?"

"Come on, Barney," said the father. "Let's go home and see what Granny has for tea." To the girl he said, "Thanks, you were a big help. You certainly know how to manage children. Got any of your own?"

"Heavens, no," she said. "I don't think I ever met one before."

"Well, thanks again. Say goodbye, Barney."

"Don't want to go home to Granny," muttered Barney, but without conviction, allowing himself meanwhile to be strapped into the front seat. Then he looked out of the car window and said to the girl, "What's your name?"

"Lucy," the girl called as the car reversed and moved away. She waved, then turned and vanished below the front portico.

Max let out his breath. Next moment the inner door burst open and Dee Lawrence elbowed her way in with the tray of tea. She was big, buxom, and pink, her flaxen hair done in a classic knot; she had looked after all his physical needs for the last thirteen years.

"Sorry to be so long," she said, kicking the door to behind her. "Those fools in the kitchen! Ginger cake again; you'd think they'd know by now you hate it. I had to go all the way down. Want to move inside?"

He had intended to but now changed his mind.

"No, I'll stay out here. It's still quite warm."

"Better have your rug then," said Dee, and brought it with his cup and plate. "Here's the letters to sign; I'll put them on the table till you're ready. Regent Television rang; they want to know if you'll appear on their Sunday night charity spot and make an appeal for the United Kingdom Cancer Research Fund."

"No," he said, and then, "no, wait. Tell them I'll think about it."

"Hobson rang to say he'll be here tomorrow for the last Forty-Eight recording. Half-past eleven. And the tuner's arriving at nine. That's all."

Somebody knocked; Dee opened the door and moved quickly out into the passage, pulling the door to behind her. Benovek heard indistinct voices. Presently Dee returned.

"Another of these girls hoping for piano lessons. Honestly it really is extraordinary the way they track you down. Little ghouls—"

"What did you say to her?"

"The usual thing. I can't think how she got past the porter's desk," said Dee vexedly. "I said you were a sick man and hadn't the strength to take on any new commitments. After all, why should you?"

"Why indeed?"

"Well, good heavens, you wouldn't have wanted to, would you? After all, we don't know a thing about her."

"Who was she?"

"Oh, somebody's star pupil, as usual. Might have been American, from the accent."

After a pause he said, "I mean, what was her name."

"Who?" Dee was checking through his engagement diary. "Oh, that girl? Culpepper."

"No, her first name."

"Her *first* name? Why? I'm not sure. Does it matter?"

"I just wondered."

"Now I come to think, I believe she said it was Lucy."

"After all I might as well see her," said Benovek. "Would you mind going after her? I don't suppose she will have got very far."

Dee was puzzled and more than a little affronted. "You're crazy, Max! You really can't afford to scatter your energy like this, you know. What's the idea?"

"Call it a whim, my dear Dee. I just happen to like the sound of her. Lucy Culpepper. A pretty name, don't you think?"

"*She's* not pretty," said Dee shortly. "As you'll see. Oh well, have it your own way."

She left, with something of a flounce, and returned after about five minutes, preceding the girl.

"Miss Culpepper to see you," she announced brusquely, and, to the girl, "you'll be careful not to tire him won't you, Miss Culpepper. He's a very sick man, remember."

"All right, thanks, Dee," said Max. "I'm not sure that you need keep reminding us. Sit down, Miss Culpepper. Dee, I've signed these letters. Would you be an angel and take them down with you—I'd like this one to catch the five o'clock post."

Dee left, battening down her exasperation.

The girl sat, without saying anything. Benovek studied her. Over her high forehead fell strands of lint-pale hair, very different from Dee's corn-coloured abundance, and she certainly was not pretty; Dee had been right so far. She was undersized and puny, but her hands, Benovek noticed, were good: long, strong, flexible fingers. Her face was too thin, too pale; the sprinkle of freckles on her nose looked almost black in contrast with its wanness. But the mouth was wide and firm. Not a particularly prepossessing girl, but there was something tough, wary, and resourceful about her. She looked steadily back at Benovek, waiting on his mood.

"How old are you?" he said at last.

"Eighteen."

"Who has taught you?"

"Mrs. Bergstrom. At the Cadwallader School in Boston."

His expression became a little less detached.

"Hella Bergstrom? Good heavens, is she still alive?"

The girl smiled at that, looking up at him through her forelock; the smile revealed slightly crossed incisor teeth which made her resemble a squirrel, Benovek thought. Squirrels are manic creatures and have no sense of humour; this girl had little, he suspected, but the capacity might be there. When she smiled her eyes tipped up at the corners.

Come to think of it, he reflected, he had very little sense of humour left himself.

"Yes, she's alive. Live and teaching."

"And she told you to come to me?"

"She gave me a letter for you."

He skimmed rapidly through the note she handed him. It was warm, grubby, and slightly convex from having been carried in her trouser pocket all the way from Boston.

"Hard up, are you? How did you get over from America?"

"Worked as a stewardess."

"*That* won't have done your hands any good."

"They're okay." She flexed her fingers. "I used to play the piano in the tourist lounge at night."

Benovek shuddered.

"And then you made your way here . . . It was pure chance, really, that you got in to see me. Miss Lawrence generally guards me like a bulldog."

"I would have managed to see you in the end," she said with calm certainty. "I would have taken a job here as a ward maid."

"To earn enough to pay my fees?"

She made no answer to that. It was interesting, Benovek thought, how much communication seemed to pass between them without the need for speech.

"I'd better hear you play, hadn't I," he said. "Help me inside, will you?"

It was like being helped by a mouse, or a leveret; he could feel the bones of her arm, brittle as charcoal, under his hand.

"What shall I play?"

"Bach, of course."

"I don't play Bach at all well."

"Naturally not."

She played the preludes and fugues in C and C sharp major and minor, then several pieces by Couperin.

"Now some Chopin," he said.

"*Chopin?* Why?"

But he did not answer, and she played the sonata in B minor.

"Okay," said Benovek when she had finished. "That's enough."

"'You play a *little*, I see; perhaps rather better than some, but not well.'"

"I did not say so?" For the first time she had surprised him.

"Nor did I; it's a quotation." Playing seemed to have liberated something in Lucy; she turned on the piano stool and linked her hands together, waiting, looking at him attentively.

"So; all right; I'll teach you. You have a lot to learn."

"I know. I know I have." Now she was subdued, but it was, he understood, by the thought of what lay ahead of her, not by his reputation or gesture. She had a right to learn from him, and they both knew it.

"What about fees?"

"Never mind them. And you are not to go taking some stupid

job that will ruin your hands. Besides, you are going to need most of your time for practice. I will arrange an allowance for you."

"I don't like charity—" Lucy began.

"Don't be silly, please."

"No. I'm sorry."

"Money is not an object. I am very rich, as it happens, and I am dying, as you probably know," he said irritably. She nodded. "But I still—believe it or not—have a strong urge to impart as much as I can of what I know before it is too late. And I think—I think you and I have qualities in common that would make you a suitable choice. But there is not much time, and what there is must not be squandered on idiocies. You can rent a room in the village and come here every day."

"Why did you make me play the Chopin?"

"I will play it for you now; listen."

She helped him to the piano stool and he played it; by the time he finished he was very pale and sweat was trickling down his concave cheeks.

"Now then: you see the difference? You see why it is?" He moved heavily back to his armchair.

"I see *what* it is, but not *why*."

"Who is it that you hate so?"

This was so unexpected that she stared at him, quite silenced.

"Well, it is so, isn't it?" said Benovek. "What ought to be free and running in you is all tied up in a knot. And that is because of this strong hate, which is using up nearly all of your energy. As for love, where is it? You have the capacity, no doubt; anybody who can hate can love also; but you hardly seem aware of it. You are all tense, like some creature at bay; I tell you, you will never play the piano properly until you have your emotions more in equilibrium. And for the hate, chuck it out. Hate is no good; it is a self-destructive emotion."

"Well, but supposing the person you hate *deserves* to be hated?"

"Ah, so you admit it. Who is he, then?"

"My uncle."

"The wicked uncle." Benovek lay back in his chair and looked dreamily at the ceiling. "Let me see now. He has embezzled all your fortune, seduced you when you were twelve, forced you to marry your illegitimate, mad half-cousin, and now he is attempting to murder you. Am I right?"

She gave a reluctant grin. He caught the flash of the crossed incisors.

"I can't *prove* that he has embezzled all my money. But he says horrible, untrue things about my dead father. And he's trying to swindle my poor old great-aunt out of her annuity."

"Ah, so, who cares? Just forget it all. Clear it out of your system. Or if you can't do that, then you will just have to quickly prove that he has committed all these crimes and see that he receives his deserts. But that might take too long, and I want you to start lessons on Monday."

"I shan't be able to start quite as soon as that."

"Why, pray?"

"I promised my uncle that I would go and visit my great-aunt. He has even given me the fare, so I must. He wants me to find out if she is still alive, or if some other old lady is impersonating her in order to draw the annuity. And he wants me to beg or buy up cheaply all her embroidered pictures because he believes they might soon be worth a great deal of money."

"Indeed?" said Benovek. "What sort of pictures are these?"

"Oh, *beautiful!*" said Lucy. She described them; the crossed teeth flashed again. Benovek listened absently, lying back in his chair; a vague pageantry of biblical figures moved like the Bayeux tapestry across his mind's eye.

". . . sort of village wise woman, too, I guess," Lucy was saying. "She collects herbs."

"Herbs and simples. What is a simple, tell me?"

"I think it's a plant used for medicine, as opposed to a kitchen herb," said literal Lucy.

"Disappointing. I had hoped it was a kind of one-shot panacea, a cure-all. Do you suppose your wise great-aunt could put me on my feet again?"

Lucy bit her lip.

"No, you are right, she could not. Never mind, you will go to this village—"

"Appleby, pronounced Appley."

"You go to Appleby, you unearth the great-aunt, or uncover the fraud as the case may be. That should not take very long."

"No, it shouldn't. But I'd like to find out, too, if she remembers anything about my father."

"A very natural wish. So as to give the lie to the wicked uncle's calumniating accounts."

"Yes."

He looked at her thoughtfully; she was squatting now, like a gargoyle, on the piano stool, knees under her chin, her hands clasping her crossed toes.

"Might not that be a mistake?"

"Why?" The pale forelock fell back raggedly as she looked up at him.

"Suppose your uncle told nothing but the truth?"

"That man never told the truth in his life," said Lucy with bitter emphasis. "Unless it was by accident."

"It is useless to warn children," mused Benovek. "In any case you are tough, I can see; unwelcome disclosures should not throw you off course."

"No, they shouldn't," agreed Lucy. "But why should there be any?"

"Because events never turn out as simple as one would wish. Not even with the herbal grand-aunt. You should smile, I have made a pun."

"Hardly? Also, I want to make sure the old girl is comfortable and well looked after," pursued Lucy. "After all, she's about my only relation, apart from Wilbie's lot."

"Another wish most natural and proper. Good. I will expect you back, then, in, say, one week. That ought to give you time for these various purposes."

Lucy nodded.

"It should be enough. I'd better go, then; I'm afraid I've tired you."

"Wait." He was reluctant to have her leave, and said, "How do you propose to get to this Appleby?"

"Hitchhike. Uncle Wilbie's given me the train fare, but I'm going to keep it for food and lodging."

"Not a good plan," pronounced Benovek. "No, no, I am not worrying about whether you are raped or not," as she opened her mouth to protest. "It is merely that people who pick up hitchhikers are generally the worst drivers. I don't wish your hands to be injured at this juncture in some stupidly avoidable car smash. Better go by train or car—do you drive yourself by any chance? Have you a licence?"

"Sure; international; we had an all-round education at the Cadwallader."

"In that case take this blank cheque which I made out to Simon Goldblossom; you will find his car show-room up behind Goodge Street; mention my name and he will see you get something with the brakes and big end intact that will take you to Yorkshire at not too ruinous a price."

"But—" said Lucy. "I mean, you needn't really—" A faint pink tinge coloured her pallor and then receded, leaving the freckles even darker than before. She looked doubtfully at the cheque, rubbing her prominent cheekbone with the back of one hand. "Anyway, how d'you know *I'm* not one of the worst drivers?"

"Then when you come back," Benovek went on, disregarding her, "the car will also prove useful, for you will need transport from the village to here every day; needless to say the bus only runs once a week."

"Oh well, in that case—thanks. It's very kind of you," she said gruffly. "I can't think—no one's ever—"

"Yes, you can think. I give you lessons because you should have them. That is clear."

"But a *car*."

"Oh well, say that it is because you make me think of a Poe tale."

She looked puzzled.

"I'll explain another time. You had better go now; I really am rather tired. Wait, though—"

She paused again in the doorway, looking at him inquiringly, and he said quickly, "Write to tell me how you get on in your researches."

"Yes—okay!" she said, rather astonished, went out and closed the door behind her.

Benovek lay back, more exhausted than he had been for weeks, and stared at the ceiling.

"H'm," remarked the medical superintendent, Dr. Rees-Evans,

when he came for his usual evening chat, "pulse slightly better than usual. What have you been doing today?"

Benovek said, "The walls of my prison have expanded to take in a persecuted orphan, a wicked uncle, a village witch, Great-aunt Moses, I should say, and a collection of Three-D Bible pictures."

"I beg your pardon?" said the medical superintendent.

When she left the hospital, Lucy walked quickly down the long drive until she was out of sight round a bend, then turned aside into the thick, unpruned shrubbery, flung herself down on the ground, and cried as if her heart would break.

But she soon jumped up again, having failed to notice that the undergrowth she had cast herself into was thickly interwoven with nettles.

Misfortunes of this kind constantly occurred to Lucy.

IV

Lucy travelling north: rediscovering England, as the stubby little A.30 vibrated along second-class roads through the shires; she had no intention of trusting herself on motorways yet awhile. So she battled up hills and down; along the crests of ridges where on either side extended a limitless view of elm-fringed, church-studded plains; through tidy red-brick villages and small manufacturing towns, famous for pies, boots, or fox-hunting; and as she advanced the names of places on signposts rang their mnemonic chimes; it was like leafing through a dictionary of quotations.

Ride a cock horse to Banbury Cross; Battle of Naseby 1645; Sherwood Forest, carrying its echo of Robin Hood; Gainsborough, Hatfield, Pontefract—

"Pontefract Castle, call they this at hand?" No, that's wrong, it was Barkloughly Castle. Pomfret was where they finally did him in. Poor Richard II, but he was a drip; Lucy could not feel total sympathy for him. Acaster Malbis, Marston Moor, Thornton le Clay; it is impossible to drive through England without remembering how thoroughly it has been battled over by Romans, Normans, Yorkists, Lancastrians; time it was invaded again, maybe that is what is the matter with it. Uncle Wilbie would say so; he has no patience with England nowadays, a lot of idle playboys speaking in effete London accents. They don't know how to work hard any more. Uncle Wilbie certainly works hard: obsessively, frenziedly hard, in his office from eight-thirty till seven-thirty, driving himself and everybody else, piling up more and more millions as if to prove—what? That it is so easy anyone can do it with a bit of application? Or that it is so difficult we should all admire him more than we do?

She stayed at York, but the Minster was a disappointment; stuffed with scaffolding so that it was like a forest inside a church; impossible to admire the Seven Sisters, people kept wheeling barrows over her feet.

She also visited the Lancashire and West Indies Cotton Bank, repository of the annuity paid to Great-aunt Fennel by Uncle Wilbie's firm.

"Miss Fennel Culpepper? Yes, I believe there is an account under that name."

The bank manager plainly was not impressed by Lucy's threadbare duffel coat and jeans. She felt humble—a dusty field mouse that had somehow insinuated its way into an enormous polished mahogany coffin. She wished she had thought of asking Uncle Wilbie for a note.

"May I ask what you wish to know?" the bank manager asked. He was soft and downy all over; if you prodded him, the hole would stay, instead of filling out, Lucy decided, peering at him through her fringe of hair. His voice was downy too.

"Miss Culpepper's my great-aunt," she said. "I want to locate her."

After her cash without doubt, the bank manager's pale eyes commented. Another of these *students*. Won't work, refuse to learn, all they want is to grab a bit of money off someone who has worked hard all their life.

"I'm afraid we can't in any circumstances divulge our clients' addresses," he said smoothly.

"Well, can you tell me if she is still alive?" Lucy asked bluntly.

"Dear me!" He gave her another condemnatory glance. "The account still stands, let me put it that way. Does that satisfy you, young lady?"

"You don't think someone is forging her signature?"

"Well really—good heavens!" He drew himself up. Lucy realised that she had shocked him deeply by calling the acuity of the

Lancashire and West Indies Cotton Bank into question. "What —if I may say so—what a very improper suggestion!"

"It would be even more improper if someone were *doing* it."

"I can assure you there is not the remotest chance of such a possibility."

"How can I get in touch with my great-aunt? Can you tell me if she is still at Appleby?"

A totally negative expression closed over his face.

"I'm afraid the only thing, Miss—"

"Culpepper—"

"—Miss Culpepper—" he pronounced the name with scepticism, "is to write to her in care of this branch and we will, of course, undertake to see that the letter is forwarded—"

"But if she doesn't answer?"

"That, I am afraid, is not our responsibility. We can do no more than forward your communication." He began to move papers about his desk in a dismissing manner.

"You do have a *real* address for her, do you?" said Lucy. "I mean, not just a post office box?"

"That, I am afraid, I am not at liberty to say." He jabbed his gaze decisively into the *Financial Times*.

Lucy stood up. "You're a real red-tape addict, aren't you," she said. "Nothing matters to you so long as your gilt-edged double entry accounts balance, does it? For all you know that poor old girl is lying dead somewhere, stuffed inside a safe-deposit box, but that wouldn't worry *you!* I sure am glad I don't have your mentality."

She swung out of his office, the dignity of her departure marred by an unexpected marble step on which she stubbed her toe.

After she had gone the manager sat in shocked silence for a couple of minutes. Then he called in the chief cashier.

"Nugent, I wish you'd just check over an account—let's see, what's the name? Culpepper, Miss Fennel Elizabeth Culpepper—"

"What's the trouble, sir?"

"No, on second thoughts, don't bother." The manager, embarrassed and irritable, was already regretting his impulse. That girl's suggestion was too impossible to take seriously.

"Students! I'm glad my Maureen is going straight into the bank."

Lucy passed the night as cheaply as possible in a bed-and-breakfast place populated by students and commercial travellers; the students all disappeared to work, the travellers sat in a fumed-oak lounge where television roared non-stop, so Lucy went early to bed, longing for her car radio.

Dear Max Benovek, how can I ever possibly thank you? To be given a car is astonishing enough, but to have a radio specified as well raises generosity to the most rare pinnacle of consideration.

"Ah yes, from Max Benovek, how is he? He rang me up, but he will never talk about himself; look out for a girl like a chipmunk, he tells me, see you don't sell her a pup, Simon, she is the coming pianist of the next generation. But don't give her anything too fast, mind, I don't want her speeding and breaking her neck, none of your souped-up minis; a decent little car with good brakes and it must have a radio so she can listen to the music programme, they are doing my Forty-Eight recitals every day next week, those she must certainly hear. So, very well, how much are you prepared to give, I say, decent little cars with good brakes are not to be found lying about under every bush on Hampstead Heath? Simon, you are my friend, he says, we were boys at school together in Brno and I trust you; I have sent her with a blank cheque. So what can you do with a man like that? It is enough to break your heart."

Mr. Goldblossom himself was not unlike some lovable inmate of a Disney zoo; he had large rolling black eyes under pouched lids, the aristocratic nose of a guinea pig, and a heart-shaped smile of immense charm; in repose his face was sombre, but when he smiled it lit up like the beacon on a breakdown wagon.

"So here I have just the thing for you; take no notice of the colour, it has belonged to one of those Third Programme poets who suddenly wrote a play; he turned this in for a Jag, but there's nothing wrong with this little job, does forty to the gallon and she'd take you across the Sahara. For his poetry I say nothing, but that man really did know how to look after a car; kept the engine tuned like one of Max's Bechsteins. Radio, heater, seatbelts, windscreen washer; in her, you need not be ashamed to drive round Buckingham Palace."

"Inside or outside?" inquired Lucy.

"Mazeltov! You are too young to have such a sharp tongue."

"How much is this miracle going to cost Mr. Benovek?" Lucy asked, studying the little Austin, which was painted a feverish plum colour. She often wished later, after hearing the BBC Third Programme, that she knew which poet had been her car's previous owner.

"You think I would do down my friend Max?"

"I don't know," said Lucy truthfully. For the second time in her wary life she found herself utterly unable to make head or tail of a character. She handed over the blank cheque and added rather doubtfully, "I suppose I shall simply have to trust you."

"I should be so trusting!"

"I don't want to use Mr. Benovek's money badly."

"Don't worry your precious head about that," said Mr. Goldblossom, suddenly dead serious. "Anything I can do for Max, I am proud to do. You just jump in this lovely little job and buzz up to Harrogate to visit your Granny."

He gave her his heart-melting smile again and slipped away to the small, oily office at the back of the showroom; Lucy, glancing through the window a moment later, could hardly believe her eyes. She was almost sure she had seen him tear Max Benovek's cheque in half and make as if to throw it in the fire; then, arrested apparently by a second impulse, he tucked the two halves together and slipped them tenderly into his wallet. Lucy hastily climbed into her plum-coloured auto and with considerable caution manoeuvred it out into the London traffic.

Dear Max Benovek, I guess I liked your friend Goldblossom, though he seems an unexpected schoolmate for you. And the little car I love with all my heart, dear little PHO 898A; even if it doesn't quite do his forty to the gallon it chugs reliably on its way, mile after mile, hill after hill. How can I ever pay you back? That is a stupid one-sided view of the matter, you do not need to be paid back. But I need to pay. No one ever gave me a present before.

In her mind's ear she heard Benovek:

"What, never? No birthday, no Christmas? The whole family are as wicked as the wicked uncle?"

"Oh well, of course they went through the motions; duty presents, probably bought with *my* money: scarves, stockings, booktokens, record-tokens, because everybody knew I liked reading and music, but nobody knew what, nobody gave a damn."

"Did you give a damn about them?"

"No, and why should I? All they cared about was money and their deadly social round."

"Maybe you could have showed them something better?"

"Now look here, Benovek, you're supposed to be teaching me piano, not morality."

She switched on the car radio.

". . . Andrew Haskin with the nine A.M. news summary," said the announcer. "An Iraqi tanker is on fire in the English Channel; tugboats are standing by. In the South Molton by-election the Conservative candidate has been returned with an increased majority. A report on a new anti-measles vaccine suggests that it may have serious effects on heart sufferers; supplies are being withdrawn. A long-term prisoner has escaped from Durham jail. A painting thought to be by Hieronymous Bosch has been discovered in a crypt at Norwich. The dry, windy weather will give way to local thunder showers . . . That was the news and weather, it is now four minutes past nine. Each day this week the pianist Max Benovek will be playing Bach's Forty-Eight preludes and fugues . . ."

Music spurted from the radio like a series of audible equations. Lucy's heart rose, the accelerator went down under her foot, and the car sprang forward on to the first slopes of the Yorkshire wolds.

The dry windy weather had not yet given way. A buffeting gale pushed the little car from side to side on the exposed road; heavy dark summer trees thrashed in the river valleys, endless ripples moved sweepingly over silvery dry grass on the chalk uplands. Birds in dissatisfied flocks kept circling across the inexpressive grey sky; here and there big stone farmhouses hunched snugly among their trees and barns, like cats tucking in tails and paws against a draught. And the road climbed and climbed; down across a valley but always up again, more and more steeply.

This must be ancestral country now. On her map she saw the

name Wilberfoss, origin, presumably, of the forebear after whom Uncle Wilbie had been named. Strange to think of grandparents and great-grandparents buried in these dry, blond hillsides. Dear Max Benovek, thank you for giving me a chance to see this country at my own pace, instead of from a hitchhiker's perch. Are you fond of England yourself, or do you regard it as merely a refuge?

Moors loomed ahead, disappointingly grey, not purple in the deadpan light, but empty and wild; the wind here, she thought, smelt of roots and herbs, aromatic and teasing. At regular spaces along the roadside were little stone constructions like sentry-boxes for midgets: what could they be? Snow shelters? Individual sheep pens? Shrugging, she abandoned the puzzle and consulted her map again. Over to the right the moor reared up sharply; beyond the ridge it must drop even more sharply to cliffs and the North Sea. To her left, twenty miles of empty land was threaded by no more than a scanty parallel system of cart-tracks and streams, cutting north and south; ahead, the little single-track road ran steadily on for another twenty miles, but somewhere, halfway across the moor, she might expect to find a crossroads: Grydale Moor Cross. And from that an even smaller road diverged northeast over bits of land called Scroop Moss and Black Gill until it reached a tiny bunch of dots labelled, in barely legible script, Appleby-under-Scar. A symbol like a moustache on the map was presumably the scar in question. Northeast again lay Appleby High Moor and beyond that the coast curved round: more cliffs and more North Sea. Also, ten miles farther north, what looked like a fishing-port, jammed uncomfortably in a millimetre of green between cliff and shore: Kirby-on-Sea. Kirby would represent civilisation for the village; presumably the nearest hospital, supermarket, fire-station, library—but there seemed to be no connecting road. However, perhaps the map was out of date; very likely a road had been made since its publication, though this would plainly necessitate quite a steep hill down from Appleby High Moor.

Having halted to map-read, Lucy decided that she might as well eat her lunch before entering Appleby. She had bought at a cooked-meat shop in York an anonymous-looking article the size and colour of a much-used baseball, called a Claxton Pudding; eating it brought no greater enlightenment as to its contents but a stuffed sensation as if she had indeed swallowed a baseball. She took some deep breaths, started the car, and drove on.

Grydale Moor Cross was no more than a heather-tufted mound supporting a signpost, one arm of which did, rather to Lucy's surprise, say Appleby. She drove on, feeling like Shackleton, like Nansen, like Livingstone. Was it possible that in half an hour she might be sitting in front of Aunt Fennel Culpepper's fire drinking tea? Herbal tea, no doubt; even so, the idea seemed too improbable to entertain seriously. She passed a stone ruin and realised with dismay that it was probably the inn marked with such confidence on the map; still, no doubt Appleby would offer some kind of accommodation.

Ahead now she began to see trees and houses: square grey granite cottages and leaning wind-shredded beeches. A black-and-white sign presently announced that here began Appleby-under-Scar.

Lucy had been so preoccupied with map-studying and sense of achievement that she had ignored the darkening sky; a splatter of rain on her windscreen and a rumble of thunder awakened her to the fact that one of the promised local storms had caught up with her. Entering Appleby the road took a right-angled bend round a farm with an enclosing wall, and then came abruptly into a wide open space where it divided to encircle a village green. As Lucy drove round this corner the sky opened and solid water descended; a sudden swash of lightning baptised all the little stone houses in silvery light. Then they were veiled behind sheets of rain. Lucy, finding that she could not see more than a yard ahead, pulled up.

In five minutes the downpour diminished to a moody patter which might go on for hours. Not a soul was to be seen; hardly surprising in view of the climatic conditions; Lucy decided that her first impression of a village that was only half populated had probably been misleading; smoke trickled from at least four chimneys and in a couple of windows a dim gleam was visible.

Deciding to reconnoitre on foot, she pulled on the navy duffel coat she had bought second-hand in London, left the car on a wide grass verge, and started along the green to where a telephone box made a cheerful splash of scarlet against the prevailing grey-green. A telephone probably meant a post office, and a post office would be able to tell her where High Beck cottage was located. "Old Miss Culpepper's?" Her imagination ran ahead. "Nay, you can't miss it, luv, past t'houses, up yon hill . . ."

Uncle Wilbie had been vague on the subject of the cottage's location, and yet Lucy gathered, or thought she had, that he had been here. Surely he must have? On some return visit to relations, though she knew his youth, like her own, had been spent in Liverpool. But there had been some remark—"Quaint little old village green, Princess, whole graveyard full of Quaker ancestors, don't tell me you're not wild to see it?"

Quaint, Lucy thought, looking round her, was not precisely the adjective she would have applied to Appleby-under-Scar; the stone houses were too impassive and flat-faced; slap on the sidewalk except in a few cases where they were enclosed by stone walls; far from welcoming, they kept their own counsel. A school and a chapel, built in the heyday of nineteenth-century gothic, faced each other inscrutably. No children? No congregation? Midweek, of course, holiday time; perhaps the children were away at the sea. Perhaps there were no children. This might have been inferred from a wayside pulpit notice outside the chapel which observed gloomily,

"Rid and deliver me from strange children—Ps. 144. 7."

Another, by the telephone kiosk, retorted,

"Woe to him that saith to the wood, awake; woe to women that sew pillows to all armholes; woe to them that join house to house."

Why? Lucy wondered. What harm? Some of the houses in Appleby main street were joined together; others brooded apart among their cabbages and runner-beans.

The telephone box bore a sign: OUT OF ORDER. The post office was shut, implacably shut and locked. Searching among a wealth of written and printed notices in its windows Lucy presently located one that told her today was early closing. Another announced that the thirtieth of last month had been the final date for the registration of village greens by those interested. Had somebody registered Appleby Green, she wondered. Or did nobody care? And if nobody cared, what happened now? It seemed hard to imagine some rapacious real-estate firm acquiring the land

for speculative building. Several of the houses were plainly
derelict.

Where now? A brook in a deep gully bisected the village green
and was bridged on either side; remembering the name High
Beck, Lucy looked upstream and saw the church, above and to
one side of the village on a steep knoll. Beyond the church a tree-
hung cliff led up to what was presumably Appleby High Moor.
A church meant a rectory or vicarage; the vicar, surely, would
know the whereabouts of all his parishioners. Taking a footpath
which followed the bank of the stream and led past a red-brick
municipal convenience, Lucy climbed up to the church. In front
of it a war memorial commemorated the deaths of four men from
Appleby in World War II.

The church, which had an apse at one end and Norman arches,
was undoubtedly old, but, somehow, rather ugly; Lucy scanned
it uncertainly. It had the air of an elderly, dentured lady who
knows that nobody is going to admire her and keeps her ironic
gaze fixed on distance. The Victorian vicarage beside it, though
hideous, looked well-found and inhabited. Lucy pressed the bell-
push. After an immensely long wait she banged the brass knocker
and the door instantly flew open.

A short, red-faced man stood in front of her. He was certainly
not the vicar; his shirt was hanging half out of wrinkled, very
dirty trousers, his fly-buttons were undone; he wore no tie, the
cuffs of his tweed jacket were fringed with age, and his white
hair bristled in an aureole.

"Yes?" he said sharply. At first Lucy thought he was smiling,
then she saw this was a rictus of impatience, or perhaps deafness;
he leaned slightly forward, inclining his head to one side.

"I'm very sorry to bother you, but can you tell me where Miss
Culpepper lives?" she said slowly and clearly.

"Eh? What's that? Speak up, can't you!"

Deafness, then.

"Can you tell me where Miss Culpepper lives?"

No answer. She repeated her question a third time, even
louder.

"Oh, go to hell!" he exclaimed suddenly and savagely. She had
just time to snatch her fingers from the jamb before he slammed
the front door with violence.

Retreating, somewhat discomfited, to the footpath, Lucy surveyed the solitary cottage that lay twenty yards higher up, past the vicarage, perched on the steep bank above the tumbling stream and approached by a footbridge. High Beck? It could be. But at a nearer view from the bridge, the cottage was plainly deserted; two of its windows gaped, glassless, and the little front garden was rank with weeds. A gaunt tabby cat eyed her alertly from a bramble-covert and whisked out of sight when she snapped her fingers. No point in going on. She returned to the village green, stopped at the first cottage—it was one of those with its small front garden bounded by a wall—pushed open the gate, walked up a stone-paved path, and knocked.

A suspicious voice called out, "Who's that?"

Since it was pointless to give her name, Lucy merely knocked again. After a moment the door opened slowly. Lucy found herself being scrutinised by a tall girl who might be four or five years older than herself. It was hard to be sure; the girl was in the last stages of pregnancy. Her face was pale, haggard, and dirty; her uncombed hair had been stuffed indifferently into an elastic band; she wore slippers on bare feet and a grease-spotted, sagging brown jersey dress which dangled irregularly round her bulging figure. She seemed quite unconcerned about her own appearance, but studied Lucy with composed hostility.

"Well?" she said. "Which department sent you? What do you want?"

Her accent was not, as might have been expected, broad Yorkshire. It was not broad anything. Lucy had not suffered for six years at the Cadwallader without becoming tenderly familiar with the upper-crust accents of almost every country in the world; in the tones of this slattern she recognised what had long been recorded in her mental notebook as P.B.A., Pure British Aristocracy.

"Keep your skin on, pal," she therefore replied with equal composure, peering up at the girl through her fringe. "I'm not from the welfare. I'm a stranger here—just called for some information. Can you tell me where in the village I can find an old lady called Miss Fennel Culpepper?"

"I'm afraid I haven't the remotest idea," the girl said coldly. "The village is full of old ladies."

"This one lives in a cottage called High Beck."

"Sorry; can't help."

She was retreating, about to shut the door in Lucy's face, when they were interrupted from the gate by a delivery van driver with a bit of paper in his hand, who called,

"Can you tell me where Mr. Carados lives?"

Plainly irritated and put out, the girl hesitated and at last said, "Here. Why?"

"One baby's cot, one pram, one baby's bath. Right? Strewth, had a job to find this place. I'll just bring the van a bit nearer."

The van which Lucy had vaguely noticed cruising up and down the village street as if searching for some elusive goal, was now parked two houses away. On its side it bore a severely plain sign: RAMPADGES, LONDON. The driver presently extracted three enormous objects, anonymous under layers of expensive packing.

"Oh God; leave them here. I'll take them in presently," Mrs. Carados said, looking at them with dislike.

"You didn't ought to be carrying weights, matey, pardon me, not in your condition," said the van driver. "You just tell me where you want them put, I daresay this young lady won't mind giving me a hand."

"Of course," agreed Lucy, poker-faced, concealing her amusement. "I'll tell you what, too," she went on calmly. "Why don't we take off all these wrappings out here, you won't want them cluttering up the place indoors. Can you spare another five minutes?" she said to the driver.

"Blimey, yes, considering how long it took me to get here! I'm not supposed to, but I'll take the packaging away too, if you like; bet you don't have dustbin collections more'n every month of Sundays in a frontier post like this."

He produced a knife and slashed with rapid dexterity; in a short time an amazingly opulent bassinet came to view; it was tucked and rucked, squabbed and frilled, lavish with satin and lace, the sort of article one might expect to see in a ducal nursery. Again Lucy repressed a grin.

"Best get it indoors, mum," the driver said. "Still spitting with rain. Where'll we put it?"

"Oh, anywhere upstairs," Mrs. Carados said impatiently, hardly glancing at it.

"Sure you can manage?" the driver asked Lucy.

"Good heavens, yes."

The cottage stairway, facing the front door, led straight up; Lucy, going backwards with her end of the bassinet, snatched a quick glance into the rooms on either side, one an indescribably cluttered kitchen, the other a glum living room. The two rooms upstairs were almost equally untidy, but as one was almost entirely filled by an unmade double bed it seemed best to put the cradle in the other. In due course a pink and gilt bath was added.

"What about the pram, missus? Where'll you have that?"

The pram was about four feet high and four long, sprung like a perch-phaeton, glossy as a battleship.

"Oh Christ—*I* don't know. Stick it in the coal shed," Mrs. Carados said, eyeing it with loathing. Lucy wondered if she should remind Mrs. Carados that the man ought to be tipped. It was not delicate feeling that held her back, but reluctance to part with her own scanty cash if Mrs. Carados had none.

"Are you going to offer him a cup of tea after all his trouble?" she finally suggested.

"God, no. Here—" The girl fished an elegant suede wallet from under a crumpled heap of newspapers and took out a pound note. She gave it to the driver as he returned from the coal shed. He hesitated, looked as if he might refuse, finally shrugged and accepted.

"Tata, then," he said, and drove off.

"Can you tell me," said Lucy, just before she was shut out for the second time, "where you got the picture hanging over the fireplace in your living room?"

"Picture?" The girl looked at her vacantly.

"Picture," Lucy repeated with patience. "Adam and Eve and the serpent. Half embroidered, half painted."

"Oh, *that* funny old thing."

"Where did it come from?"

"God knows. I suppose Ro—my husband picked it up somewhere. I really couldn't tell you, I'm afraid."

It was plain that she could hardly wait to be rid of Lucy. Why? Just natural antipathy?

"Oh well, thanks." Lucy shrugged, and was retreating to the gate when a car pulled up outside with a screech of brakes. It was a white Mini. A man leapt out of it, exclaiming, "Fiona, sweetie, I'm *terribly* sorry I couldn't make it sooner—"

"Oh, hullo," said the pregnant girl, unsmiling. She submitted to his kiss. He was in his forties, short, fair, with pale-blue eyes and a bright blue suit. He cast an inquiring glance then at Lucy, who was standing her ground.

"Yes?" he said civilly. "I'm sorry, I didn't—? Is there anything—?"

"Only if you can tell me whereabouts in the village old Miss Culpepper lives."

"Terribly sorry, we're strangers here ourselves," he said quickly.

"Or where you got the picture you have hanging over your mantelpiece?"

"It's rather divine, isn't it? I've no idea who did it, I'm afraid; part of the furnishings that came with the house. Local produce, I suppose. Well, we mustn't keep you—" He gave Lucy a rapid, meaningless smile and hurried his wife indoors, shutting the door briskly behind him.

Dear Max Benovek: I had a little trouble locating Aunt Fennel. English villages aren't the cosy welcoming places full of smiling dairymaids and joking yokels that they are represented to be in the tourist literature.

Rejoining her original course, Lucy proceeded along the village green. The sky was still dark and thunder grumbled somewhere; the red pantiled roofs shone wet. She went up to the next cottage with a light in its window and knocked. Nobody answered, so, after repeated bangs, deciding she could not make herself more conspicuous than she already felt, Lucy peered through the window, since this was one of the houses that fronted directly on to the footpath.

She was looking into a tiny, dim front room, lit only by a log fire. A dark, clotted-pattern wallpaper absorbed most of what illumination there was, but Lucy gained a vague impression of tight-packed furniture, brass oil-lamps with fluted shades, and a lot of little pictures in oval gilt frames. Over the hearth hung a larger picture cast into shade by the shelf below it. When a log broke with a splutter of flame, light, reflected from the ceiling, suddenly threw into relief a large indigo whale, springing out of a sequinned ocean in which every wave was as regular as the tiles on the roof above.

"In fact one can see where she got the idea," muttered Lucy. "Lord, has she given pictures to the whole village?"

Moving on, she heard a regular creak and rattle; some human activity must be taking place.

Round the corner of the next cottage she found an elderly man drawing a bucket of water from a well.

"Good afternoon," Lucy said. "I wonder can you tell me where Miss Culpepper lives?"

"Eh?" He straightened. "Speak oop, I canna hear you."

Is everybody deaf in this village, Lucy wondered, putting her question again two tones higher.

"Miss Culpepper!"

"Miss who? Niver 'eard o' her."

"Miss Fennel Culpepper."

"Oh, *her*. Why didn't you say so first off?" He repeated the name pronouncing it quite differently. "T'owd lady, eh? There was two on 'em, two owd bodies lived together oop at High Beck. One on 'em died, t'other moved away."

"When?"

"Oh, I don't call to mind; last year, year before, 'appen. They kept themselves to themselves, I keep myself to myself; folk round this way don't bother each other wi' nosey-parkering."

"Which of them died and which moved away?"

"Oh, ah, I dunno. Two on 'em there was, like as two peas in a pod. An' which was which, who's to say?"

Was the old boy a bit simple, Lucy wondered. He tipped his cap forward, scratched at his gingery stubble-hair, and gazed past her with abstracted blue eyes.

"Well, can you tell me where the one who moved away went?"

"Eh?"

"The one who didn't die—where did she go? What is her address now?"

"'Ow should I know? She dunnot write to me!"

"Well, can you tell me anyone who would know?"

"Reckon Mrs. Thwaite at t'post office 'ud be able to tell 'ee; aye, she'd be the one to ask." He picked up his bucket.

"But the post office is shut."

"Oh, aye, Mary Thwaite'll be down visiting her daughter-in-law at Kirby. You'll have to wait till tomorrow, then, lass."

"Isn't there anybody else who might know?" Lucy asked crossly, reflecting that for somebody who kept himself to himself he seemed well primed as to Mrs. Thwaite's movements.

"Nay, I dunno. Folk here keep—"

"—Themselves to themselves. So you said."

"Tell tha what!" he said triumphantly. "Why dunna you go and ask t'matron oop at t'owd folk's home? 'Appen she'd know. A right busybody *she* is, allus poking her nose in things what's no affair of hers, asking about folk's jobs an' who's kin to who. You do that, *she'll* put you on t'right road." He stumped off with his bucket, muttering, "An' if she don't, it's all t'same to me."

"Well, where is the old folk's home?" Lucy called after him.

"Oop at top o' village, o' course! T'owd hall . . ."

Rain was setting in harder again. Lucy ran back to her car. If she was going to visit Appleby Old Hall she might as well do it in style. Then a hopeful thought struck her. If the Old Hall was now an old folk's home, perhaps Aunt Fennel was actually *in* it; had decided to leave her lonely cottage for the comfort of expert care, and company . . .

Something failed to ring true about this theory though, she decided, pulling the starter. Individualists like the embroiderer of that whale do not take readily to institutional life; besides, if Great-aunt Fennel had moved no farther than Appleby Old Folk's home, surely the man would have known about it?

But still, there would be no harm in asking.

On her way down the village she made a needful stop at the red-brick public convenience. This was a cheerless, functional structure, embellished inside with the usual graffiti. "I love Sam Crossley." "Where was Lenny Thorpe on Friday night?" "Ellen Dean is a bad girl." "What happened up at High Beck?"

Well, what did happen? Lucy wondered, escaping from the damp and ill-equipped place with relief. On her way out she noticed a newly-painted sign: THIS CONVENIENCE NOT TO BE USED AFTER DUSK. BY ORDER. CLERK TO THE PARISH COUNCIL.

Why not? Was the place being used for marijuana parties? For orgies? It seemed highly improbable, but no other suggestion came to mind.

Dear Max Benovek, do you suppose there is an active local coven at Appleby-under-Scar? Shall I have to join before I get news of Great-aunt Fennel?

The Hall lay at a suitably seigneurial distance west of the village along a single-track but metalled road. Lucy took this at a cautious pace and it was as well she did for, rounding a bend, she was signalled to a halt by a black-cassocked figure waving at her urgently from the middle of the road.

She braked hard, then saw with dismay that what appeared to be a corpse lay on the tarmac beyond the man who had stopped her.

She got out of the car. The black-cassocked man grabbed her arm.

"Do you know anything about first aid?" he demanded. "They've gone for help, but we should do something—I'm sure we should do something—one feels so wretchedly inadequate on occasions such as this—but surely there must be something, *something* we can do for the poor fellow? Oh, these drivers—I know you are one yourself but *really*—to knock the miserable man off his bicycle and go on without stopping is utterly inexcusable, utterly monstrous—oh, my goodness, here I stand talking while we should be attending to poor Clough, but I'm so upset I hardly know what I am saying! Do, do look at him and tell me what you think should be done!"

He delivered all this at speed in a high-pitched nervous voice; he was an extremely thin, elderly man, very pale, obviously in the grip of shock. Lucy gently detached herself and moved on towards the seeming corpse, trying to suppress a feeling of terrified inadequacy.

To her relief she realised that the prone man was not dead, though certainly unconscious. Nor could she see any blood or obvious sign of injury apart from a swelling on his bald head. He lay on his back, a few feet away from a battered bicycle. He was a weather-beaten, gnarled-looking individual; his clothes and his hands were stained with earth and he gave off a powerful reek of chemical fertiliser.

"Poor, poor Clough," twittered the cassocked man. "The most harmless, innocent fellow—such a thing to happen! Such a sudden way to go!"

"Well, he hasn't gone yet," said Lucy. "His heart's still beating. You say someone has sent for help?"

"Yes, yes! They are telephoning for Dr. Adnan. But should we not do something in the meantime—undo his garments?"

"I don't think we ought to move him," Lucy said doubtfully. "They always say better not, in case of internal injuries. I've an old blanket in my car—we could cover him up."

She did so, muffling the injured man up to his chin, while the priest anxiously dithered about, getting in the way.

"Did you see who knocked him off his bicycle?" Lucy asked.

"Alas, no! These wretched automobiles go at such a pace! I heard the motor, saw a flash of something white, but arrived too late—ah, thank goodness, here come reinforcements."

Lucy was somewhat taken aback by the reinforcements, which consisted of half a dozen more aged priests, who came flocking out from a gate on the right like a covey of rusty old crows. One of them hastily knelt down by the recumbent man, anointed him with something pungent and sticky from a small gold receptacle, and exclaimed in a loud voice,

"Absolve, we beseech thee, O Lord, the soul of thy servant Samuel Ebenezer Clough from every bond of sin, that being raised in the glory of the Resurrection he may be refreshed among thy saints. Grant, O Lord, that while we lament the departure of thy servant we may always remember that we are most certainly to follow him! Give us grace to prepare for that last hour, that we may not be taken unprepared by sudden death, but may be ever on the watch . . ."

Rather a selfish prayer, Lucy thought.

"'Ere," said the man on the ground suddenly, "what t'flamin' 'ell's goin' on? What's to do?"

He struggled to move underneath the blanket; his eyes rolled frantically.

"Lie still, poor fellow! Help is on the way." Several of the old crows held him down vigorously; the scene was a macabre one. An incisive new voice broke into it.

"For heaven's sake! Will you have the goodness to move aside, please, so that I can see what is the matter?"

Somewhat reluctantly the old priests moved back from their object, who now lay quiescent, blinking in a dazed manner.

"What day is it?" he muttered to himself. "'Ave I gone daft? It canna be Sunday?"

The latest arrival, plainly a doctor, knelt down beside him and felt his pulse.

"What is your name?" he asked authoritatively. "Can you tell me what happened?"

"Eh, booger me, 'ere's another on 'em. Right lot o' carrion crows."

"Answer me, please!" repeated the doctor briskly. He turned up the man's eyelids, then opened a flat black bag and pulled out a stethoscope. The patient's eyes moved past him indifferently; he made no direct reply. "'Appen I'm in bed an' dreaming," he muttered to himself.

Impatiently the doctor peeled back the blanket, listened to his breathing, and started feeling him for broken bones. This made him writhe and giggle hysterically.

"Eh! Leave off ticklin' a chap, cansta!"

His struggles revealed one reason for his previous lack of response: a hearing aid which had evidently been dislodged from his ear by the accident, rolled out from a fold of the blanket. Annoyed, the doctor stuck it back in his ear.

"*Now* perhaps we shall get some sense out of this business. Well? Can you tell me your name?"

"O' course I can! It's Sam Ebenezer Clough, as onybody could tell thee."

"What happened to you? Did you see who knocked you off your bike?"

"Nay, I niver. Coom out o' drive yonder, an' next thing I knew, I was on my back in t'road."

"Well, Sam Clough, there's not much the matter with you except for a bang on the head."

"Did I ever say there *was* owt the matter?" demanded Clough ungratefully, scrambling to his feet. "'Stead o' makin' such a clapper, it'd be more to t'purpose if someone 'ud help me wi' my bike."

In guilty haste the old priests rushed to his assistance. Several of them pushed the cycle, which proved to be mobile, though bent, while others supported the impatient Clough.

"Better come back to the Grange, poor fellow—cup of tea and

a lie-down will be best—perhaps he should stay the night?—Yes, yes, Father Prendergast will certainly be able to arrange it—somebody can take a message to his family—doubtless you would not mind doing so, Dr. Adnan?"

With unexpected despatch the black procession of priests, bicycle, and injured man vanished through the hedge and along a gravel track which led to a largish building, half visible among trees.

Lucy and the doctor were left facing one another.

"Well!" he said briskly. "That was a great piece of nonsense about nothing and a waste of my valuable time. It was lucky that I was in the neighbourhood in any case and had not to come far. Who covered him up?"

"I did."

"Stupid of you not to check on the hearing aid first, wasn't it? That would have saved me some trouble."

"Look here!" exploded Lucy, suddenly at the end of her temper. "Who the blazes do you think I am? Florence Nightingale? I'd never seen him before—didn't know him from Adam. How was I to know the guy wore a hearing aid?"

"Was it you who knocked him down? I shall have to make a report about this to the police, you know."

"No, it was *not*," said Lucy furiously. "If you had any sense you would have noticed that my car is twenty yards off, facing this way. I was going to Appleby Old Hall when the priest flagged me down—"

"All right, all right, there is no necessity to get so het up," said the doctor calmly. "If it was not you who knocked him down, then you must have been passed by the vehicle that did." He spoke with a slight, unidentifiable foreign accent.

"Well, I'm afraid I wasn't."

"Really, you are a singularly unhelpful young lady. Why are you being so obstructive? In general I have found Americans to be most courteous and obliging."

"I am not an American."

"Ah, then perhaps that would account for it."

He began fitting the stethoscope back into his case, while Lucy struggled with about three different retorts which had bottlenecked in her mind.

"No matter. As you are going to the Hall, you will not object to taking me back to my car, which is still up there? I was at the gardener's cottage when the message came, so it seemed simpler to cut across the garden than to go all the way back and round."

"Certainly I'll take you," said Lucy stiffly, deciding that it would be more dignified to ignore his previous rudeness. When they were in her car she asked, "Do all those old clergymen come from the Hall?"

"No, there is also a hostel for retired priests over there at Thrushcross Grange. The Hall is a residential home for elderly persons of both sexes. Not a bad place; understaffed, as all such are."

"Do you look after the inmates when they get sick?"

"Why, yes," he said, raising his brows as if he found her question inquisitive. "It is my privilege to do so."

"Sarcastic so-and-so," thought Lucy, jamming down the accelerator in her irritation.

"I would not drive so fast," the doctor said calmly. "There is quite a severe bend coming shortly."

Gritting her teeth, Lucy braked.

"Do you," she asked, having carefully negotiated the bend, "do you happen to know if there is an old lady called Miss Fennel Culpepper resident at the Hall?"

"Not among the patients I have attended," he said without hesitation.

"Are there many residents?"

"Not a great many, no; fifteen, perhaps twenty; it has not been open for very long, only a few months."

"I see." Aunt Fennel might have moved away, in that case, before the home was opened. "You don't have a patient of that name anywhere else in the district?"

"I do not, no. But I live, and have my main practice, in Kirby, which is a town of some ten thousand inhabitants; it is possible that I might not have come across her if she were there."

"I suppose it is *just* possible," Lucy agreed coldly. She glanced sideways, hoping this shaft had struck home, and saw that he looked amused. He was a stocky individual not short but thickset and dark-eyed, with curly dark hair, rather dandyish sideburns, and a lavish Edwardian moustache that shaded off into gunmetal-blue unshaven haze round the jaw-line. He wore a plummy-dark suit, tailored very narrow, and a brocade waistcoat.

"Through these gates here on the left," he directed, and asked, when Lucy had made the turn on to a gravel drive which swung in a curve round a windbreak of pines, and a newly painted sign: WILDFELL HALL RESIDENTIAL HOME, "Why are you searching for this old lady?"

"Family reasons," Lucy replied shortly.

"Ah, I see." He added, after a moment, in a disparaging tone, "The Anglo-Saxons seem to lose track of their relations so very fast. It is a curious phenomenon. Now in Turkey (which is where I come from) it would be an almost unheard-of thing, to lose an old lady. She would be being cared for by her family. So much more civilised. No need for all these institutions, your so-called residential homes which abound over here."

Without making any reply, Lucy brought the car to a stop on the gravel sweep in front of Appleby Old Hall.

Dr. Adnan jumped out almost before the car had come to a stop, called a brief thanks over his shoulder, and made off at a rapid pace towards an Alfa-Romeo which was parked beyond the front door. On the point of getting into it he was intercepted by a woman in a dark-blue uniform who had evidently been waiting inside the door. The matron of the home, Lucy guessed, thirsty for information about the accident. While she plied the doctor with questions, Lucy got out of her car and stood somewhat detached from the pair, making it plain that she wished to speak to the matron presently. Meanwhile she gazed aloofly at the facade of Appleby Old Hall. Not so old as all that, in fact; the Hall was built of mustard-coloured stone faced with brick in a style that suggested the 1860s. A pillared portico protruded up to second-floor height in the middle of the front. The house was rather too high for its width, the chimneys too scrawny, the slate roof too flat. The third-floor windows were set in pairs and had round arches, which may have been intended to give a classical effect but succeeded instead, for some reason, in making the house look very like a station hotel. The balcony topping the portico was set about with large stone balls.

A retired wool magnate's residence, Lucy guessed; the proud achievement of some nineteenth-century Uncle Wilbie.

Tiring of the Hall, not an attractive structure, she turned for a dispassionate survey of the doctor, who was fidgeting and glancing impatiently at his watch. He did not, to Lucy's eyes, look like a Turk, but she had no preconceived notions of what a Turk should look like. Were they all so self-satisfied and impervious? As if sensing her criticisms, he looked up, met her eyes, and gave her a sudden smile, showing very white teeth. The matron glanced sharply over her shoulder.

"So that is all there was to it," said Dr. Adnan, briskly rounding off his report. "And now I really must be off."

"Just a moment, Doctor! The crutches you promised to take back!"

She vanished into the porch while the doctor shrugged expressively, casting up his eyes. Lucy remained unresponsive.

"Here they are! Mrs. Bantock has quite finished with them. Will they go in your boot?"

"I daresay." Looking put out, he opened the boot, rapidly fitted in the crutches, slammed the lid, and made his getaway.

"Yes . . . ?" the matron said, turning to Lucy. "Can I help you?"

Her tone was not exactly impatient, but not far off it; nicely gauged between summary despatch of Lucy's errand—probably in the highest degree unimportant, her expression indicated—and awareness that there might be, after all, a fee-paying elderly relative somewhere in Lucy's background.

Calmly sustaining the matron's assessment of her puce auto and shabby duffel coat, "I shan't need to keep you long," Lucy said. "You're in charge here?"

"Yes. I am . . . ?"

Lucy had a profound scorn for the autocracy of matrons, but there was no point in offending this one. And indeed, apart from a slight air of self-consequence, she seemed innocuous enough: a slight, pale-faced, thin-featured woman with fine brown hair drawn plainly back under an elaborate white-frilled muslin cap. Her pale grey eyes had the slightly opaque look that is sometimes caused by contact lenses.

"I wondered if by any chance you had an old lady called Miss Fennel Culpepper living here?"

The element of sharpness overcame the reservations in the matron's expression.

"No, I'm afraid I can't help you," she said briefly and began turning on her heel. "We have nobody of that name here."

"She used to live at Appleby but moved away last year," Lucy went on, undeterred. "There's no chance that you'd have any information as to her whereabouts?"

"My dear girl, I'm afraid I've never even heard of her! I only came here myself quite recently, I know very little about the neighbourhood."

Doesn't quite match what the old boy with the bucket said, Lucy reflected.

"Is that so?" she answered politely. "Well, so long as I'm here, I wonder if you'd mind telling me what your terms are? Miss Culpepper is my great-aunt, you see; I'm anxious to make sure she is being properly cared for. And do you have any vacancies?"

"Our terms are fifteen guineas a week." And that almost certainly disposes of *you*, young woman, the expression said. "As to vacancies, well, we *do* have a couple of beds, but our main difficulty is staff; we don't really have the help to cope with any more residents at the moment. So I'm afraid I must say no."

"However, I suppose your residents do occasionally move away or die?" Lucy said calmly. "Do you have a waiting list? Maybe I could see over the place, just on the chance?"

"It would be rather a waste of time." The matron gave her an acid smile.

"Still, I'd like to! And perhaps you'd give me your brochure?"

"Oh, very well!"

Lucy followed the matron's annoyed back through the eight pillars of the portico and into a highly-polished hall.

"Here is our leaflet." The matron reappeared from a small office just inside the front door and gave Lucy a shiny folder. It was headed Wildfell Hall Residential and Convalescent Home. Matron: Mrs. Daisy Marsham. Doctor in Attendance: Dr. Adnan Mustapha, M.B. etc. etc.

"Now: I'm afraid I can't give you more than five minutes; it's nearly the residents' tea-time."

Lucy glanced round at the mustard-emulsion walls and smiled her cross-toothed smile.

"Five minutes will be just fine," she said.

V

Mrs. Marsham watched the girl's shabby pink car until it had vanished round the corner of the drive. Even then she went on staring with a kind of unfocussed hostility as if she expected to see the car shoot impertinently backwards into sight once more and stop in front of her.

What with one thing and another it had been a tiresome day. One of the old ladies had cut herself quite badly on a cough pastille tin, so that the doctor had had to be summoned; two more had almost come to blows over whether their bedroom window should be open or shut. And the television had gone wrong, which always gave rise to a stream of complaint, as none of them could believe that anyone else had adequately reported the matter. Particularly tiresome when there were new arrivals. And then this fuss about the man getting knocked over . . .

A large, grossly fat, and rather dirty ginger cat emerged from the laurestinus by the front door and rubbed against her legs. She fondled it absently. "Who's Mother's boy? Who's Mother's lovely boy, then?" The cat pushed its great head violently against her ankle, almost turning upside down to do so. It was a repulsive beast, with a thick coarse coat, short stubby tail, and a disproportionately large, almost human-looking pink mouth from which protruded a triangle of pink tongue giving it a witless air enhanced by its large, pale, wild eyes.

After a while Mrs. Marsham went back into the house. By

now several elderly persons were slowly moving about the hall, some of them feeling their way by means of a rail set along the wall at hand-height.

"When will it be supper-time?" demanded a small wrinkled man hopefully.

"Not for another hour, Mr. Parsons," the matron said, looking at her watch. She shut and locked the door of the office, and walked through to the dining-room where the cook, Nora, was laying a dozen small red-plastic-topped tables for high tea. Nora was forty, plump, suffered from varicose veins, and was little better than simple-minded. However, as she lived in the village and needed the money to support her twelve-year-old illegitimate daughter, she could be relied on to keep turning up, which was more than you could say of some of the flighty girls who came and went. Furthermore she had persuaded her elder illegitimate daughter to come and help.

"You're putting too much butter on the plates," Mrs. Marsham said. "They'll eat all you put out. They're as greedy as children."

Nora made no reply except to stick out her lower lip. Mrs. Marsham took no notice. "There'll be two more for tea," she said. "Upstairs. I'll take the trays up."

"Oh? First I've heard of it," grunted Nora. "No one tells me anything."

"I'm telling you now," Mrs. Marsham said controlledly. "I've made their beds. They'll be on the top floor in number nine. Bed cases. One of them won't be able to eat anything solid for a few days. Now I'm going over to the annex to see what Dr. Adnan said to Clarkson about his arm. If there are any phone messages, write them on the pad."

Nora grunted again. Mrs. Marsham compressed her thin lips and went on, through the kitchen, out of a back door, and along a path that crossed a stretch of rough grass. The path led through an untended shrubbery of rhododendrons and araucarias. Beyond the shrubbery, in the hungry 1840s, a sort of earthwork had been thrown up to employ idle hands in the village, and the path ran under this in a tunnel set about with ornamental stonework to give it the air of a grotto. The tunnel led to a cobbled yard with a stable and sheds on one side, a large glasshouse on the second, a walled kitchen garden on the third, and three small cottages on the fourth. Beyond the kitchen garden was a back entrance to the road where Clough's accident had occurred. Smoke issued from one cottage chimney, and an aproned man was just closing the door behind him. He was too short-sighted to see Mrs. Marsham until she was directly in front of him.

"That you, missus?" he said then, peering. "I was just going to bring t'beans up to t'house and see you. Doctor said my arm's to be fomented three times daily; an' he's given me some stuff to take."

"All right, I'll foment it now as I'm here," the matron said. "I daresay you've got a kettle boiling in your cottage? You can take the beans to Nora afterwards."

When she had dealt with Clarkson's arm he went off up to the big house. Mrs. Marsham waited until he was out of sight and then let herself into one of the two empty cottages.

The three men in an upper room stiffened, hearing her key in the front door. Then one of them said, "It's Mother," and the other two relaxed. One of them, who was lying on a surgical couch, rolled sideways and vomited a mouthful of blood onto the polythene sheet that was spread under his head.

His pallor looked habitual but was at present accentuated to cod-fillet colour; his hair was a dead-white stubble. Large pink ears stood out from a face shaped like an indented oval; the absurdity of the ears did not suit the rest of him; his appearance at any time, whatever he was doing, suggested a hungry purpose, a kind of chronic anger.

The man who stood beside him was short, with a chubby pock-marked complexion, round dark eyes, and stiff dark hair. Although he looked tough, and as if he might have an ugly temper, he behaved in a curiously affectionate, protective way towards the man on the couch, and once even patted his head, as if to assure him that the worst of his ordeal was over; but he did it in a nervous, hasty way, like somebody taking liberties with a dangerous dog.

The third man, much younger than the others, was ginger-haired and thickset and had on a white lab coat. It was to him that Mrs. Marsham spoke when she came in.

"Did you put the car in the shed, Harold?"

"Do me a favour. Of course I did."

"Good. How's Harbin?"

"He'll live," said Harold laconically.

"No trouble?"

"Nope. Goetz helped me."

"All right, are you?" she inquired briskly of the man on the couch.

"Pain. Painful," he mouthed with difficulty, dribbling more blood.

"Give him a lump of ice to suck. Has he had codeine? He could have a couple more. You'll feel better in an hour or so," she said to Harbin. "You can come over to the house as soon as it's dark and have something to eat. That'll do you good."

He shuddered. Goetz, the third man, looked amused.

"Same old Linda," he said. "I could almost fancy we were back on the Hong Kong run, handing out paper bags and chewing-gum."

"Well, we are not," Mrs. Marsham said shortly. "And you'd better not forget it."

"What about Adnan?" Harold asked his mother.

"No trouble there." But Mrs. Marsham looked as if she were withholding volumes of adverse opinion. This was one of her strengths, and the three men eyed her uneasily.

At this moment the cat, which had followed her into the house, sidled round the door and rubbed against her legs, then jumped, with a sort of uncouth agility, onto the couch beside Harbin. He let out a bubbling yell, and spat more blood.

"Ge' that' 'amn 'at ou'a here!" he mouthed frantically.

Goetz grabbed at it and dumped it, none too gently, outside the door.

"Careful! You'll hurt him!" snapped Mrs. Marsham.

"Well you don't want him getting septicaemia or cat-bite fever, do you?" Goetz said. He dusted his hands together, looking at them distastefully; Harbin's glance crossed that of Mrs. Marsham. After a moment she turned on her heel and left the room, saying, "I'll expect you in an hour or so, then. Come in at the side door. Harold will show you."

"You want to watch it with that cat," warned Harold in a low voice. "Ma's crazy about the fat, overfed thing."

The other two men were silent.

Harold put his head round the door and called cautiously down the stairs.

"Hey, Ma!"

Mrs. Marsham was about to let herself out. She turned, key in hand.

"Well?"

"I thought I heard another car, after the doctor?"

"Oh, it was nothing," his mother said. "Some tiresome girl, looking for her great-aunt."

"Great-aunt? One of your old things?"

"No, nobody we've ever heard of," said Mrs. Marsham.

Now what are we going to do? Nearly out of tooth powder, need more cuttlefish bone. Ounce of cloves too. Also, not much oil of rosemary left. Old Mr. Thing would buy cloves, sweet oil, at chemist when he goes to cash cheque; old Mr. Thing very obliging, grateful for poppyhead lotion rubbed on gouty toe. Poor old Mr. Thing. But no use asking him look for rosemary or cuttlefish bone; wouldn't know one from the other. Rosemary grows in public gardens, or used. Remember exactly where, at back, against wall, behind benches, under plane trees. Remember seeing it when Dill and I used to come for seaweed. Not hard to pick a few sprigs; say after tea, when nobody much about. Cuttlefish bone on shore, used to be lots. Used to bring home for birds, too. Taffypuss used to get excited and roll on it. Oh, Taffypuss.

But would I dare go out? Hat with veil, green eye-shade? Might attract attention even more? Hard to know what to do for best. Long way to public gardens, even farther to shore, and steep climb back again. Take long time. Legs not what they were, due to lack of exercise. Could walk ten, fifteen miles, few years ago, out in all weathers, heather on moor, ransoms in Cronkley Wood. Much healthier. Not enough fresh air now, can't even walk about in house, all that furniture. So, long, slow journey through streets. Suppose That Other One in town, waiting, watching? If I knew child, could send child for cuttlefish bone. Used to send children for lichen. But don't know any child now. Wonder what happened to Paul's little one, Shrimpy he used to call her. Long ago.

All right, all right, just coming out of bathroom, have to have good wash don't I, nobody likes living with people who aren't properly washed. Several in this house could do with more. Not my fault only one bathroom.

Dressing. Fingers getting weaker. If went to shore for cuttlefish bone, could get seaweed too. Dry in back garden? Maybe That

One wouldn't mind hanging over kitchen stove; kitchen smells terrible anyway. Would be wonderful to stand on shore again, hear gulls, smell sea.

Brush hair, roll up bun. Arms tired already, only ten o'clock. Could do with sea air. Put on hearing aid.

My goodness, what was that? Sound came from stairs. Someone called out, then awful crash, then called out again. Footsteps running. Should go and see? No, better not. One of the others puts head out of door. Somebody fallen? Yes, someone fallen downstairs. Not surprised with Hoover cord trailing down like that. Only surprised more don't. Who fell then? Can't see, down at bottom, people there, but dark in front hall.

Better keep out of way, better not go to see. That One can be very sharp when there's trouble. I'll thank you ladies not to come running out like school-kids just because there's been a slight accident.

Slight? That didn't sound so slight.

Front door banged. Someone running on pavement outside. Going for doctor?

Voices muttering, voices chattering. Nearly time for morning cup of tea, probably late today. Possibly no tea at all.

One of the others gone down now, to see what's happened. Shan't go, shall stay here sitting on bed. Hands trembling, accidents frighten me. Can't help remembering Dill always. Oh Dill. But she's safe now, she's happy. Should be happy for her. But supposing she misses me?

Here's somebody coming back now.

What happened, who was it? Somebody fell downstairs? Old Mr. Thing? Tripped over Hoover cord? Not surprised, always have said—

Taken off in ambulance for X ray?

Suppose *he* stays in geriatric ward?

Who will I get to cash my cheques now?

"Humph," said Rees-Evans. "Not quite so good today. What have you been doing with yourself?"

"Waiting."

"Well, better stop waiting and do something else."

The two men looked at one another sympathetically. It is harder to bear another person's knowledge than one's own.

"I'll drop in for a game of chess later," the doctor suggested. "Shall I?"

"That would be very enjoyable."

"Got plenty of reading-matter?"

"Plenty." Benovek did not look at the triple stack of glossy new books on the window table.

"Well—" said the doctor, rather helplessly. He moved towards the door. "See you later then. Oh, I nearly forgot. Letter for you —your secretary asked me to give it to you. One of your fans in Yorkshire."

The door closed behind him.

"Dear Max Benovek:

I am truly sorry to be so slow in locating my great-aunt. I have written to her at her God-awful bank but she doesn't answer; I begin to wonder whether she doesn't *want* to be found. If she's alive. I'll give it another week and then come south. I've located plenty of her pictures, simply by looking through windows; almost every cottage in Appleby seems to have one, except the Old Folk's Home. But people don't know, or won't say, where she's gone. I don't know if I'm imagining it, but there seems a funny atmosphere about it all. And—this you'll hardly believe but I swear it's true—you remember I told you about that crazy notice on the public convenience that said it wasn't to be used after dusk?— well, when I asked about that at the post office, I was told *quite seriously* that people had complained it was haunted, and the Council wouldn't hold themselves responsible. So haunted by what? I asked. Well, no one would say anything much, but it was in some way connected with the death of old Miss Howe, who fell down a sort of cliff into the brook last year and died of exposure. Miss Culpepper's friend. Now she's supposed to linger near the spot. How's that for the growth of local folklore? Meanwhile the Council have fixed for a temporary loo to be put at the other end of the village; such things exist, it seems.

No, I haven't bought any of the pictures yet. Well, I'm not terribly keen to, till I know what's happened to Aunt Fennel; Wilbie said I could go to twenty dollars apiece and he'd send more

cash when necessary, but it doesn't seem right. He'll get mad
soon, I expect; that doesn't worry me a scrap. Anyway, the first
picture I buy is going to be for you. I know you'll love it. Why am
I so sure? I just am.

I couldn't find anywhere to stay in Appleby, so I'm in Kirby-
on-Sea, the nearest town. By road it's a long way but there's a
shortcut over the moor, very steep, a sort of watercourse. Your
beautiful little car, dear little PHO doesn't mind going *down*,
but up mightn't be so easy. In winter I guess it's a glacier. There's
a reservoir and a dam at the top, that's why they don't make a
road; something to do with vibrations. Anyway, no one wants
to go to Appleby.

Failing Aunt Fennel I'll describe Kirby-on-Sea for you. It's a
fine town. Two piers like lobsters' claws enclose the harbour, and
just as well; this is really a fierce coast, all cliff on either side, brown
and steep like the shoulders of the sphinx. The waves come rolling
furiously down from the north pole, grey as ink, and crash up
against the cliff, even on a calm day. What it must be like in No-
vember! There's a swing bridge and signs saying 'The public are
not allowed on these dolphins'. I thought there must be some kind
of zoo-aquarium with maybe dolphin performances, so quite right
not to allow the public, but no: it's something to do with the
bridge. There are trawlers and timber ships. The houses are
stone, rising up the steep cliff in tiers, and they have those red
pantile roofs, marcelled like mother's hair in old photographs;
smoke rushes hastily from the chimneys, there's always a strong
wind blowing, and the gulls never stop making a row. They sound
like school kids at recess. The air smells of kippers. There are
hundreds and hundreds of little shops selling them—oak-smoked
kippers, they are very good. There's also a fun fair and amusement arcade. But in spite of these gaieties this feels like an old
people's town, Max; all the bingo hall signs say Come and Join
Us, as if they were beckoning to the shy and lonely.

I must stop now and go out and have another hunt for Aunt
Fennel. I've tried the post office, public library, citizens' advice
bureau, women's voluntary services, and hospital; none of them
were a bit helpful. Trouble is, this town is just full of boarding-
houses just full of elderly people; they are always shifting about,
they move inland in summer when prices go up, they don't have

regular doctors, they live by selling their watches and rings. There are scads of second-hand shops. It's almost impossible to keep track of people. But I haven't given up yet. I'm going out and try all the drugstores and wool shops next, because old ladies use those a lot.

I don't keep thanking you for what you are doing for me because that would be boring, wouldn't it. But I don't forget it, not for an instant. I listened to all your Bach recitals and all the other things on the music programme. What do you think of Barenboim? Of Ivan Davis? Never mind, tell me when we meet. I wish you were here, though—the bracing air of this town would surely do you good.

I can't begin to express how much I'm looking forward to my lessons.

Love from Lucy

In my next letter I'll tell you about the candy-stores; they need a whole letter to themselves."

Kirby municipal gardens lay on four different levels, terraced up the cliff. Day trippers never bothered to go beyond the bottom layer which contained the showier blooms, beds of geranium and lobelia laid out in patterns, tulips, polyanthus, roses, according to season. On the higher levels more durable shrubs were planted. Up here, too, were the benches. Elderly permanent residents who lived in the criss-cross of late-nineteenth-century streets above the gardens would terminate their faltering descent here and sit looking down at the harbour's pincer-arms, the red-and-white lighthouse, and the expanse of North Sea, generally a surly slate-grey. Nobody stayed long, though; shrubs, however securely planted, continually trembled and winced in the relentless north wind. There were always vacant seats. But if it was cold up here, it was safe; the long-haired, arrogant teen-agers who swept in unpredictable droves along the streets round the harbour, arriving and departing with the random abruptness of migrant birds, never bothered to climb up. There was nothing for them at the top; it was cold and quiet and boring and the benches, backless and short, were unsuitable for love-making.

Lucy had had a migraine headache all day. Usually when this

happened—which was every two or three months—she went to bed and slept it off, having learned that there was absolutely no other way of alleviating the condition. But she could not bear to spend her time in Kirby so uselessly, and had been roaming the streets all day, staring into the faces of old ladies in a way that filled them with disquiet and alarm. In point of fact, Lucy could hardly see their faces; her vision was blurred, sometimes double, and she felt simultaneously hungry and sick; noises rang in her head with the ominous and shattering intensity of electronic music. At last, hopelessly aware that she was achieving nothing by this meaningless patrol, she started up through the gardens, proposing to go back to her boarding-house in Redcar Street and lie down for an hour. But the boarding-house, the cheapest she could find, would still smell, she knew, of the huge greasy breakfast which was pressed on all inmates; and the landlady's children, home for the holidays, would thump and rattle up and down the flimsy stairs, and the dog would howl in his kennel and Radio One would bawl from the kitchen . . . She turned aside and sat on a bench, resting her head on her hands.

Almost at once a woman came and plumped herself down at the other end of the bench. Lucy would have ignored her, but the woman instantly burst out, as if she had been hunting for an audience all day and could wait no longer, however unpromising Lucy's attitude and appearance.

"I'm just *so* angry," she declared. "I don't know *what* to do! I've been to the estate agents and to the citizens' advice bureau *and* to the post office—none of them would tell me anything sensible. I just don't know *what* to do," she repeated.

"Oh?" Pushing aside her forelock, Lucy squinted sideways and got a blurred, two-dimensional impression of a red hat set with quills and a pair of resentful eyes in a much-powdered face.

"I've tried mentioning the matter politely in the street, I've sent a note, I've sent *several* notes," the woman went on rapidly, looking through Lucy rather than at her.

"What's the trouble then?" Lucy croaked, finding her voice with difficulty. She moved her head cautiously, looking for a spot where she might go to be sick if necessary.

"It's this man who has moved into the house next door. Goodness knows what he *does*—looks like one of these commercial travellers! He's away half the time. And for reasons *best* known to himself he's changed the name of his house; it used to be *The Nook*, a perfectly respectable name, and he's changed it to *The Laurels*, which is the same as *my* house! Well, I ask you! You can't have two houses called The Laurels in one street, it leads to endless confusion. I get his bills, he gets mine. I asked him, I said, 'Why did you change the name of your house?' He said he didn't like The Nook. Well, really, I think he must be mad, I really do. What a ridiculous reason to give. I've sent notes, I've rung him up, I've asked the post office, they say we must settle it among ourselves. So I went to see him *again* and he said, 'Mrs. Truslove, do please stop bothering me. Why don't you change the name of *your* house?' Honestly! What a thing to say! And nobody has been at all helpful. Do you think I should go to the police? Or a lawyer? What do you think I ought to do?"

"I should change the name of your house," Lucy articulated carefully.

"But that's giving in to him! He must be mad, you know, that must be the explanation."

"Very likely."

"I shall go back to him again," declared the woman. "I shall say, 'Look here, Mr. Vanson, this has got to stop. If it doesn't I shall get a lawyer, I shall have to inform the police.' That's what I'll do."

She rose as if she intended to do it at once. Lucy peered up, uncrossing her eyes with an immense effort.

"Mrs. Truslove. Did you say that was your name, Truslove?"

"Yes, that's right," the woman said, faintly surprised at having her own identity suddenly put before her.

"Mrs. Truslove, don't go back to that man. He's unbalanced, you said so yourself. If you go and fuss and shout at him he's liable to get violent. He'll hit you with a h-hammer or something, he's just waiting for an excuse—"

"Well, *really!* What a very extraordinary thing to say!" For the first time the woman looked at Lucy full. "What an extraordinary way to talk! You want to watch your tongue, young woman, or you're going to land yourself in trouble, you certainly are!"

"I—was only—warning you," Lucy said with difficulty. "When I have a migraine—like now—I sometimes have—a sort of insight into how people will act."

"Well you can keep your insights and your warnings to yourself!" Mrs. Truslove said, and marched off, exclaiming audibly to herself as she went, "Drunk, I suppose, or under the influence of drugs. Really these teen-agers are quite out of hand!"

Lucy stood up carefully. Then she pushed her way behind a rhododendron bush abutting on the back wall of the garden and vomited; this relieved her, but not much. She sat down on the bench again, holding her head hard with both hands to prevent the top falling off. Dear Max, do you feel as terrible as this all the time? Did you feel like it when you played Chopin to me? I bet you did.

Somebody else sat down on the bench. Please, not Mrs. Truslove again.

No, not Mrs. Truslove. A gentle, threadlike voice said hesitantly, "Are you all right, my dear? You don't look very well."

(Oh, do go away.) Without raising her head, Lucy managed to articulate, "Yes, I'm all right, thank you, I just have a migraine."

"Oh, you poor child. They are terrible afflictions. I know. I had a dear friend who suffered from them."

Well, then, leave me alone, can't you.

But the old lady was rummaging in her waterproof carrier-bag. "Let me see, what would I have . . . raspberry leaf tablets . . . You are not pregnant, are you, my dear?"

"No," Lucy said faintly.

"Not raspberry, then. Ah! comfrey. Swallow one of these, love, it will do you a great deal of good."

"I'm terribly sorry," Lucy said. "I really don't believe I *can* swallow right now."

The old lady reflected. Swivelling her eyes together, Lucy decided that she resembled an otter; no, a beaver. She had that oddly topless look; benevolent but topless; grey hair drawn back under a white linen hat; for some reason she wore a green eyeshade.

"Streamlined ears," Lucy muttered.

"I beg your pardon, my dear?"

"Nothing." Trying to recall why the beaver-face was familiar, where she had seen the old lady before, Lucy thrust her fingers hard against her temples, then remembered: it had been earlier that afternoon at a drugstore where she was dazedly waiting to buy aspirin. The old girl had been collecting a prescription, or something of the kind, at the counter ahead of her. With clockwork accuracy the conversation came back:

"It's an old gentleman that usually comes in with this, isn't it?"

"He won't be coming any more, he's had a bad accident."

"Dear, oh dear, I'm sorry to hear that. Is he badly hurt?"

"Very badly hurt."

When the old lady turned to leave, her face as it swam into Lucy's field of vision seemed charged with tragic significance, but it was hard to decide if this had any objective reality or was merely in context with the words *bad accident* which reverberated like an iron clapper in Lucy's skull. The effect of migraine was rather like alcohol: things overlapped and time often seemed to function retroactively.

"Ah, I know! The very thing! How silly of me not to think of it at once. Here, my love, just sniff this."

Something tickled Lucy's nose; a cool aromatic scent gradually crept up her nostrils to her brain and made a little pocket of peaceful emptiness there.

"That is certain to do you good. Just hold it in your hand and keep sniffing. Now I shan't bother you any more. Poor dear, I hope you'll soon be better. Good-bye."

Her voice had been so soft, her departure so mouselike that it took Lucy a few minutes to realise she had gone. Solitude, thank heaven, silence, and this nostalgic scent which is finding its way into my frontal lobes and through my cortex . . .

Rosemary.

She opened her eyes, focussed without difficulty, and looked at the sprig that she held clenched between her fingers. Greener and stiffer than lavender; needlelike aromatic leaves with silvery underlining.

Going to church with mother and two old ladies. We had spent the night with them; they had a cow called Blossom, and a cat; I slept in a little room up a ladder. On Sunday we all walked to church and carried sprigs of rosemary in our handkerchiefs.

Lucy got to her feet and began to run, stumblingly at first, then faster, for her headache was clearing.

"Stop!" she called. "Oh, please stop! Just a minute!"

Dusk was beginning to settle; one or two street lamps blossomed among the plane trees overhead. Which way had the old lady gone? Uphill, certainly, but here the path branched into three, winding off circuitously among bushes. Up, down, along. Impossible to guess which one she had taken.

Lucy even called, "Aunt Fennel! Aunt Fennel!"

But the old lady had quite disappeared.

Lucy's mind was not yet completely engaged; she stood for a moment emptily staring at the divergent tracks. Then her inductive faculties returned and she ran downhill, back towards the town centre. Which drugstore? It had been a small one, on a corner, opposite a bank. A sign in the window said Health Foods and Natural Remedies. But would it still be open? She looked at her watch as she ran: twenty past five. The town was changing over from daytime to evening activity; food and commodity shops were closing, cafés and amusement spots were filling up. The harbour was almost silent but St. Bernard Street, leading up from it, blazed with mineral-coloured lights and juke-box sound.

A second street, a third: Woolworth's, Marks and Spencers; no, it had been in a quieter part of the town, a narrower street with more vocational shops, a saddler's, a shipwright's, windows full of tools, ropes, shoes to be mended. Blue cobbles underfoot. Ah! There was the saddler, Thos. Oakroyd. And here was the drugstore, no, chemist, with his old-fashioned retorts, one full of red liquid, the other full of blue; surgical appliances, sunglasses, and sponge-bags. Still open, but a girl in a white coat was just coming to bolt the door.

Lucy gulped air, slowed her pace, and walked in a split second before the girl got there.

"Did you want something quick? We're just closing really."

"It's only—I wonder if you can help me." Supporting herself on the door handle, Lucy took some more breaths. "I was in here earlier today, there was an old lady getting a prescription filled. She said somebody had been badly hurt."

The girl's face took on the mulish, abused expression of somebody who has finished thinking for the day and does not intend to begin again; an elderly man who had been tidying the counter peered disapprovingly round a display cabinet full of cosmetics.

"She was talking about an old gentleman who'd had an accident."

The chemist primmed his lips together.

"I'm afraid I really can't—"

"No, no, it's not that, it's just that I want to find the old lady. Can you tell me where she lives? The thing is, I believe she's my great-aunt."

The chemist and his assistant exchanged glances; their reluctance to be involved was obvious. The man was thin, dyspeptic-looking and suspicious, the girl a plump, cowlike blonde.

"Well—I don't know—"

"Look," Lucy said. She dug in her hold-all and found her passport. "My name's Culpepper, see? I've come from America looking for my great-aunt. She used to live in Appleby but she moved away from there—can you tell me if by any chance she's now living in this town? A Miss Culpepper?"

The chemist eyed Lucy's passport doubtfully as if he deplored such melodrama; however at sight of the name Culpepper his face did clear a fraction.

"Well," he said unwillingly, "we *do* have an old lady, a Miss Culpepper, who has dealt with us for many years. I believe she used to live in Appleby."

"And now she's in this town? Was she in here this afternoon?"

"I'm afraid I couldn't say. We have a great many customers."

"Do you have her address?"

They shook their heads; they seemed greatly relieved at being able to deny Lucy this information.

"No address written on the prescription?"

"It wasn't a prescription," the blonde said. "It was a cheque we cashed for her."

The chemist frowned; it was plain he did not approve of giving out this piece of information.

"Does she come in often? Do you think she lives near here?"

"I have no idea, I'm afraid."

The English *love* not being able to help, Lucy thought furiously; it was the first time she had consciously dissociated herself from the country of her birth.

"I believe she keeps moving," the girl volunteered. "I've an idea she never stays long at one address." This earned her another condemning glance from her employer.

"I'm sorry we can't help you any more," he said in a final manner.

"Oh, but you can!" Lucy flashed a smile up at him through her fringe. "You can give her this, next time she comes in."

Dear Aunt Fennel, Do please get in touch with your great-niece Lucy, she scribbled on a leaf from her notebook, and put the Redcar Street address and that of Max Benovek.

"There." She handed it to the proprietor. "I'm not the Mafia, honest! Don't look so scared, I haven't the least intention of coshing her."

The man's face froze again, so Lucy quickly left before he could refuse to take the paper.

Little does he know I'm going to haunt his shop from now on.

But meantime, what was the best thing to do? Abruptly, Lucy realised that she had two ravenous needs: music and food. She was now back under the yellow sodium lights of St. Bernard Street; she had been automatically making her way back towards the harbour.

She looked into the window of the shop she was passing. It was packed from top to bottom with sugar confectionery: pebbles made of icing-sugar coloured pink, blue, and green: immense thick sticks and circular slabs of nougat with great candied cherries in it, the slabs cut open like Swiss roll to reveal pink and white stripes; fantastic varieties of seaside rock: rock shaped and coloured like fruits, like clocks, like kippers, like fried eggs, like fish, like horribly realistic false teeth; rock made into life-size pink legs wearing frilly garters. Gross chocolate-covered bars of coconut candy, mounds of chocolate drops, of peppermint cushions, of coloured fruit-drops.

The sight of so much sugar made Lucy gulp. She moved on to the next shop, full of little blown-glass animals and sea shells with painted mottoes. On again, to an open-fronted booth giving out a blast of hot, oniony air. *Try our fried bacon rolls!* it offered. A belt of teen-agers, three deep, lined the counter; calmly and purpose-fully, Lucy bored her way to the front, bought a bacon roll, bur-rowed back and made her way to a street barrow where she bought a bag of apples, then went in search of her car, dear little PHO.

During the day it was almost impossible to leave a car anywhere in the streets of Kirby. They were far too narrow, congested, and steep; local professional traffic edged slowly and riskily round sharp-angled bends and angrily through heedless crowds of pedestrian trippers; busy traffic wardens piled up fines to swell the municipal funds. Lucy had discovered at once that unless she wanted a two-mile walk uphill to her car, it was necessary to spend almost as much in parking fees as she paid for board and lodging. This morning she had left little PHO in the most accessible car park, a large subterranean one opening straight on to the harbour front. She hurried back there now, ignoring calls of "Hello, darling," from sailors lining the harbour wall, ran down the approach-ramp and plunged into the huge, echoing cavern. By day cars were jammed bumper to bumper like greenfly on an unsprayed rose; after six P.M. the place gradually cleared. Little PHO was now in a deserted section and showed up as a bubble of rakish colour in the gloom. Lucy drove to the pay-booth, handed over the huge fee, accelerated up the ramp, and turned left immediately along the deserted promenade. She went on for half a mile below the cliff gardens, then turned, parked facing the beach, and switched on her radio.

". . . news headlines," said the voice. "No settlement in prospect for the strike of postal workers due to start next Monday. More warnings have been issued regarding the anti-measles vaccine. Police have moved in on rioting students and teachers at Salisbury University; there has been a breakdown in the Paris peace talks; still no news of the long-term prisoner who escaped from Durham jail last week; rain and gales are expected from the west . . . Now, a recital of eighteenth-century Italian music by the Colchester Chamber Orchestra . . ."

Music poured joyfully into the car while Lucy sat listening and thinking and eating apples. Outside, for once, the evening was calm; the distant grey sea crept slowly, muttering, up the empty shore.

Why would an old lady who had lived all her life in one spot suddenly move away, keep moving from one address to another, cash her cheques at the drugstore instead of opening a drawing account at a branch of her bank?

The thought of banks made Lucy count her money; there was

perilously little left. Any minute now it would be necessary to earn some if she wanted to stay on in Kirby. Not that she *did* want to; the thought of Max Benovek waiting to teach her was like an ache; but still, there began to be something mysterious and engrossing about this puzzle of Great-aunt Fennel. An old lady who had spent all her long life peacefully embroidering pictures and picking herbs . . .

While Lucy munched and brooded she had been absently following with her eye the erratic movements of a solitary figure far away on the twilit beach. The figure was too distant for its sex to be apparent; it progressed slowly and uncertainly along the sand with bent head, seeming to search—for shells, perhaps? Or some lost article?— The time and light seemed ill-chosen for such a quest, but of course the tide had been in earlier.

The figure had a stick and a largish bag; it appeared—though at such a distance one could not be certain—to have on its head something like a nun's coif tipped with green—

With an oath at her own stupidity, Lucy leapt from the car. The promenade was bounded by a concrete sea-wall; she climbed this and dropped on to the stones below.

It is not possible to run quietly over a shingle bank. Long before Lucy was anywhere near her quarry the distant figure had turned, let out a faint, anxious cry, and was flitting hastily away over the wet sand, going almost to the sea's edge in a desperate effort to escape. As Lucy broke into a run she could hear the fugitive giving piteous little panting whimpers.

"Please don't run away!" Lucy gulped, almost equally distressed. "Please stop! I only want to ask you—I only want to find out—"

But there is no reasoning with absolute terror. The old lady—for Lucy had now come close enough to be sure that it was the same one who had spoken to her earlier—fairly took to her heels. Next moment she tripped over her long skirt and fell headlong on the sand. After that she made no further movement at all but lay exactly as she had fallen.

"Oh God, suppose I've killed her?"

Girl student hounds old lady to death on beach.

With her heart thumping and fluttering like a tambourine, Lucy knelt down.

"Miss Culpepper! It is Miss Culpepper, isn't it? *Please* say some-

thing. Please don't just lie there! I didn't mean to frighten you—
I *promise* I don't mean you any harm! I'm your great-niece—I'm
Lucy. Do you remember, years and years ago, taking me to church
with a sprig of rosemary in my handkerchief?"

The old lady still lay with her face on her arm, motionless, but
the rhythm of her breathing slowed, as if she listened. But could
she, in fact, hear? Lucy was reminded of that other ludicrous episode in front of the old priests' home. Gently she removed Miss
Culpepper's white linen hat and eyeshade, cautiously turned her
and propped her into a reclining position.

Now—if only one regularly carried a flask of brandy—

But there was the old lady's carrier bag. Leaning forward, Lucy
stretched out an arm and just managed to reach it. Old ladies'
bags are notoriously crammed with restoratives and the essentials
for every crisis from childbirth to shipwreck.

A faint protesting moan came from the apparent corpse leaning
on her arm.

"It's all right, Miss Culpepper, honestly I'm not a highway
robber. Look, I'll put your stick in your hand so you can clout me
with it if you feel nervous. Would you like to sniff some of your
rosemary, it did my head an awful lot of good? And what'll you
take, comfrey tablets or raspberry leaf—what the hell's this, *seaweed?*" She pulled out a dank, odorous polythene bag. "Cuttlefish bone—humph. Aha, what's in this tin—gosh, ninety per
cent proof peppermints, by the smell. Here, Aunt Fennel, do, *do*
have a peppermint. May I have one too, to show we're friends?
And now, if I help you up, do you think you can walk as far as
my car? This beach is awfully wet."

Conveying Miss Culpepper across the sandy part of the beach
was hard enough, but scaling the shingle bank was a nightmare.
The old lady's flight seemed to have been a terminal spurt of
energy; she was now completely passive, obedient up to a point
but disastrously prone to collapse at any moment. Lucy thought
her state was not caused by weakness or injury, but simply due to
the fact that she was still at her wits' end with fright.

"Look, that's my car up there, you can just see it against the
cliff. There are some steps along here—thank heaven—d'you think
you can make it as far as that gap in the wall? Just keep putting
one foot in front of the other—grand! *Try* not to keep slipping

down. Now I'm going to put my arm round your waist and kind of hoist—okay? When I say *up*, you go up a step . . . Now do you suppose you can lean on the bonnet while I open the car door—?"

It was plain that Miss Culpepper had never been in a car before and, besides being still unstrung with fright, had not the least notion how to set about getting in. The first try ended with her back to front and upside down. Patiently Lucy started again, inserted her limb by limb, shut the door at last, and ran fast round to her own side. But Miss Culpepper seemed to have no more thought of trying to escape.

Switching on engine and heater, Lucy collapsed into her own seat. She had left her door open so that the inside light shone.

"I've put your stick in the back; do you want to put on your hat and eyeshade? Look, you can see yourself in the little mirror."

Obediently, without looking in the mirror, the old lady put on her hat; the shade seemed to be too much for her. Her hands trembled; her eyes had the fixed jerky movements of total apprehension. Quivers passed over her face.

"That's fine. Now, how about another of these marvellous peppermints? Or I've got some apples here—would you like an apple?"

Unexpectedly Miss Culpepper's eyes focussed on the apple. She put out her hand for it.

"Thank you, dear," she said faintly. "I've always fancied an apple—that looks like a Cox. Always used to have our own—never see one now. That One says they're too dear."

She bit into it.

"Do you like music?" said Lucy. "I always listen to music while I'm eating apples—it seems to make them more digestible—"

They sat side by side, eating their apples. It was hard to believe that five minutes before they had been engaged in that grotesque struggle across the shore, which now seemed completely dark, cut off from them by the windscreen.

"Why, hark," said the old lady. "I know that! It's a Strauss waltz—isn't it?"

"Yes, it is!"

Lucy noticed that her companion's apple was nearly finished. It seemed as if something would be lost when this point of rapport was eliminated.

"Would you like another, Aunt Fennel?"

The old lady shook her head doubtfully.

"Do you want to put your core in the bag?"

"Why do you keep calling me *Aunt Fennel?* You've done it several times." Suspicion was in her voice, and a quaver of terror.

"Aren't you Miss Culpepper?" Lucy said gently.

There was a long pause. Then the old lady said,

"Who are *you?*"

"Do you remember Paul? Paul Culpepper? Your nephew—your brother James's son? He married a girl called Ann Edwards—remember? I'm his daughter Lucy. So I'm your great-niece."

"Paul's daughter Lucy." The voice was completely detached, as if trying over each word separately for the first time. Another silence fell. But then she went on, very slowly, "Ann brought her over once or twice to see Dill and me, after Paul went to Canada. We used to call her the little shrimpy girl—funny little thing, so skinny and pale, and not a bit pretty, with those crossed teeth."

For once Lucy did not show her teeth. Instead she turned her face to the window.

"Don't mind me, Aunt Fennel, but I am crying a bit. I'm not used to having a great-aunt." After a pause she went on, picking her words with care, but resolutely. "That is—I hope you won't mind me talking this way, but you *are* Aunt Fennel, are you—Miss Culpepper? It was your poor friend Miss Howe who died, is that right? Please forgive my speaking about it—but nobody up at Appleby seemed quite clear which of you had died and which had moved away."

The old lady was silent. Little puckers and twitches ran over her face.

"Dill," she whispered at last. "Nobody knew how it could have happened. She'd gone to shut up the hens. But she did that every night of her life, never went near the edge of the dene before. Fell down, lay there all night. I'd gone to bed early with a headache. Knew nothing about it till next day. How could I have just slept, while she was dying? Dill?" She began to shake, more and more violently. "Dilly? Dilly?"

Lucy was horrified. "Don't—please don't, Aunt Fennel!" She worked an arm round the frail shoulders. "You've got to forgive yourself—*she'd* forgive you like a shot, wouldn't she now? She'd lived with you thirty years—she *loved* you. Hush! Stop crying now and tell me where you live, I'm going to drive you home. You're all cold and damp and upset—you ought to be in bed."

But the shaking did not immediately stop; Lucy heard a broken whisper.

"That's why I'm frightened, you see; how do I know it was her he meant to kill? How do I know he isn't going to come back and murder *me?*"

VI

Dear Uncle Wilbie,

I'm sure you'll be delighted to hear that I've found Great-aunt Fennel Culpepper alive and well. She had moved away from Appleby as she didn't like to stay on alone in her cottage after her friend Miss Howe died, and she has been living in a boarding-house in Kirby-on-Sea. It is a perfectly dreadful place, run by an old drunk called Mrs. Tilney; you never saw such a dark, cluttered hole in all your life. How they don't all break their necks every day, goodness knows. Well, one of them almost did the other day, I gather. I'm going to get Great-aunt F. out of there as soon as I possibly can. By good luck somebody—a Mrs. Marsham—has recently opened what seems to be a very decent private old people's home in Appleby itself and I think I can get the old girl in there; it would be much more suitable and she'd like to be back in her home village if properly cared for. I'll let you know developments. But a postal strike starts here next week, so you probably won't be hearing from me for a while. And it won't be any use your writing to me, as your letter wouldn't get through.

Please give my best to Aunt Rose and Corale.

Yours, Lucy

Lucy grinned her foxy grin as she stuck down the flap of the air letter, thinking of all the huge gaps she had left in it. The

main gap, of course, being that she still had no proof whatsoever
that Aunt Fennel was in fact Aunt Fennel and not Aunt Fennel's
best friend. But she was not going to say *that* to Uncle Wilbie.
Nor was she going to confess that the old lady was still far from
placing full confidence in Lucy—was still in a very strange state,
indeed, of alternating fright and affection, mixed terror, defiance,
and little impulses of trust.

It was like dealing with a badly disturbed child who had a high
IQ and no education at all.

Another subject Lucy had not touched on was the pictures.

After all, she thought, as long as Aunt Fennel's alive, Uncle
Wilbie has no claim to them—I'm damned if I'll help him get his
paws on them. And if my old girl is really Miss Howe, the chances
are that Aunt Fennel would have left the pictures to her, so he
still has no claim to them. I wonder if Aunt Fennel has ever
made a will? Wonder if old sourface in the bank at York would
say.

The third topic Lucy had not mentioned was one she had only
skirted around, even in her own mind. Why was Aunt Fennel—
call her that, till there's reason to do otherwise—just *why* was
Aunt Fennel in such a paralysis of fear? For there was no doubt
that fear had caused her to leave her beloved home and move
away from Appleby; fear had kept her on the move from one
shabby boarding-house to another, fear made her conceal her address and confuse her identity. And who was the person, alluded
to as That Other One, whom she suspected of having killed her
friend? Why did she plainly have every expectation that whoever
it was would follow up the first crime by trying to murder Aunt
Fennel herself? Was this just an old lady's dottiness? The para-
noia of old age? Or did she really have cause to fear? Who would
want to kill an old lady—a harmless old girl in a village at the
back of beyond? But then an old lady *had* been killed . . .

Let's not make mountains out of molehills, Lucy thought. Old
age is accident-prone; like it or not, old ladies do sometimes tumble into streams and die of exposure. It's probably all just a load
of baseless nonsense.

Yes? And what about the village gossip—the wailing ghost in
the glen calling for vengeance?

Nuts to the village gossip. When people live cut off by forty miles of barren upland, in a singularly unfrolicsome village, their only diversion is inventing ghosts and jumping out on each other. "Where was Lenny Thorpe on Friday night?"

Nuts to Lenny Thorpe too. Anyway the village superstitions and Aunt Fennel's fears were all subjective, whereas her peril at Mrs. Tilney's was *real*.

It had been perhaps half-past seven in the evening when they had arrived at the address in Reservoir Street which Aunt Fennel had at last, with considerable reluctance, divulged.

"Honestly, Aunt Fennel, you can't walk home, you're much too tired and upset. And all the streets in this town are just about vertical."

Reservoir Street turned out to be only two blocks away from Redcar Street.

"I might have come across you any time these last few days!" Lucy said.

"Oh no, dear, because I never go out. But I had to today, you see, to cash the cheque."

"I'd have found you sooner or later," said Lucy.

Mrs. Tilney's, number nineteen, was a two-storey terrace house. Its tiny front garden was almost entirely filled with junk: old coal-scuttles, marble-topped wash-stands, curtain poles, and defunct standard lamps. An agile person could just scramble through. Lucy wondered how they managed about deliveries; perhaps nothing ever was delivered here.

"We'll have to ring," Aunt Fennel said.

"Doesn't she give you latch keys?"

"Oh no, dear."

Lucy began to wonder if the bell worked, but at last the door flew open and a small, print-overalled, white-headed woman stood blearily regarding them.

"Oh, it's you," she said at last recognising Aunt Fennel. "Where the heck have *you* been? You'll get no supper now, you know; it's all over and done with long ago. Well, come on in."

"Are you Mrs. Tilney?" Lucy said.

The small woman's eyes swivelled round to take in Lucy. She had a pronounced cast, so that her eyes looked in disconcertingly different directions; Lucy addressed herself to the right one.

"Yeah, I'm Mrs. Tilney; who the devil are you?"

"My name's Culpepper; I'm Miss Culpepper's great-niece," Lucy said dispassionately observing the felt slippers, headscarf over curlers, and a sour-sweet waft of gin.

A bleary civility replaced Mrs. Tilney's aggression.

"Oh, pleased to meet you, luv. Do you want to come in and have a dr—a cup o' tea? Have to sit in the kitchen, I'm afraid; all the old dears are watching telly in the lounge, there's no room in there."

No room anywhere, Lucy thought, edging her way incredulously through four foot square of lobby crammed with bicycle, grandfather clock, umbrella stand, and twelve coats; getting a glimpse of the tiny front room filled to capacity with a huge TV set and what looked like a number of corpses sitting elbow to elbow.

"I guess my aunt ought to go straight to bed; she's very tired. Do you think I could heat her up some milk?"

"Oh yes, certainly, luv, if we've got any milk, that is. If not I'll just pop round and borrow a cupful from Mrs. Holbrook."

The kitchen smelt of stale grease and contained four chairs, each occupied by a fat scurfy animal. "I love cats and dogs," said Mrs. Tilney, surreptitiously helping herself to a teacupful of Booth's Dry. "They say it's a sign of a soft heart, don't they?"

"Oh yes?" Lucy found an egg and broke it into the pan full of blue milk.

"That's right, luv, make yourself at home; you'll find a cup somewhere . . ." Mrs. Tilney swayingly made her way to a chair, tipped off the occupant and sat down. "I get so tired, evenings, after looking after the old dears all day . . ." Her eyes closed.

Lucy washed a cup, found a hot-water bottle, filled it from the boiling kettle, and made her way upstairs. She managed not to trip on the trailing vacuum-cleaner lead, dodged round the statue of Venus (who in God's name had ever brought *that* into the house?) and wardrobe blocking most of the upper hallway, and prospected on towards a dim light. She found Aunt Fennel struggling to undress by the glimmer of a candle in a small room containing three beds, three commodes, another wardrobe, and a large chest of drawers.

"Here you are, Aunt Fen; I've brought you a posset. Let me

give you a hand; that's the way. Oh, you want your corsets under the pillow?"

"Yes, always, dear."

"Okay; now hop into bed quick and drink this while it's hot. There's a bottle for your feet."

"Oh, dearie!" Aunt Fennel took the cup in trembling hands and sipped; a tear slid down her cheek. "Nobody's looked after me like this since Dill died."

"Well, they're going to from now on," Lucy said grimly, looking at the hank of towelling which dangled from a nail in the wall two feet away from the flickering candle. "How you haven't all been burned in your beds I can't imagine. And as for that old gin-pot downstairs—"

"Oh, Mrs. Tilney isn't too bad," Aunt Fennel protested in an anxious whisper. "I've been in far worse places than this, dearie! She has a kind heart, you know."

"Kind or not," said Lucy, "I'm giving her a week's notice tomorrow."

No, there wasn't the slightest doubt that Great-aunt Fennel would be far better cared for in Appleby Old Hall; hideous it might be, and Mrs. Marsham was not Lucy's personal cup of tea, but it was clear that she was an efficient organiser and the place was clean and decently run.

Lucy grabbed her hold-all and ran down the stairs of her own boarding-house.

"I shan't have time for breakfast this morning," she announced gladly, putting her head round the dining-room door and getting a great greasy waft of bacon, "I want to get to the doctor's surgery at nine."

"Bottom of Knapp Street, last house on t'right. Something the matter, luv?"

"No, it's not me, thanks, it's my aunt."

One of Aunt Fennel's random impulses of confidence had caused her to disclose to Lucy that she often suffered from toothache which her herbal remedies, strangely enough, did little to alleviate; Lucy was determined that before they left Kirby she would find a reliable dentist and have the poor old lady's teeth set to rights, even if this meant dragging her bodily to the dentist's chair. Drunken Mrs. Tilney had of course forgotten the name of any dentist but thought her doctor had a list of them up in his surgery.

The last house at the bottom of Knapp Street had the well-worn look that doctors' houses acquire; following a sign that said SURGERY, Lucy went down a side path to the back. Passing a window she automatically glanced through and saw a sitting-room furnished with a bizarre but pleasant mixture of skeletal modern furniture and opulent oriental draperies; on the walls hung at least eight of Aunt Fennel's pictures; more, probably, Lucy thought, pressing her nose against the glass in a vain effort to see round the corner. Somewhere not far off she could hear a piano being played rather well and a male voice singing.

She went on to the waiting-room. Nobody else was there but the door had rung a bell; as Lucy looked round her for a list of dentists, Dr. Adnan came briskly in.

Today he was wearing a lemon brocade waistcoat over a flowered needlecord shirt.

"Are you the only patient?" he began, and then recognised Lucy. "We meet again! How delightful. I hope that you have some disease I can cure?"

"I think it highly improbable," said Lucy coldly.

"Oh, too bad; you are so young to have already an incurable ailment."

"Look here," said Lucy, "why did you tell me such a pack of lies the other day? What about your Hippocratic oath?"

"My dear young lady, I told you not a single lie! And the Hippocratic oath has nothing to do with such a case; it does not mention lies."

"You said you had never heard of my Great-aunt Fennel Culpepper! And you with one of her pictures in the boot of your car at that very moment—not to mention eight more in your parlour!"

"Ten, if we are to be precise. A very industrious lady, your great-aunt. Would you like to see the others?"

He led the way through an office into the sitting-room, which turned out to be L-shaped; on the wall that Lucy had been unable to see were two more of Aunt Fennel's pictures. Below them stood a modern upright piano with some manuscript music on it.

"So why did you tell me that you didn't know Aunt Fennel?"

"A—" he checked her with an upraised hand. "Let us be accurate. I said she was not my patient. Perfectly true. Naturally I had *heard* of her."

"Why? Why naturally?"

"Why, my dear girl, because as soon as I went to Appleby and saw some of those marvellous, those miraculous pictures hanging in people's houses I made it my business to find out who had done them. An old lady, I am told, who has recently moved away to Kirby. They seemed surprised that I find the pictures remarkable; just old Miss Culpepper's hobby, I am told."

"So why didn't you tell me this the other day?" demanded Lucy. "I'm her great-niece, after all!"

Dr. Adnan looked at her inscrutably with eyes as dark as mussel plums. "You took long enough to come and look for her," he said at last. "How am I to know whether your intentions are good or bad?"

"Why in heaven's name would they be bad?"

"How should I know? All I know is that something within the last year has given this old lady a bad scare and that she prefers to hide herself in Kirby where, perhaps, her loving relations cannot find her. I am certainly not going to be the one to give away her whereabouts."

"So you *did* know where she was!"

"I have not said so."

"Well, you needn't have any further scruples," said Lucy tartly, "because I know she's at Mrs. Tilney's in Reservoir Street; I suppose you've seen her there."

"Not as a patient; I visit one or two of the other old people in the house. She does not approve of doctors, you know. But she tolerates me because I like her pictures."

"So I notice!"

"But you have hardly looked at them yet; aren't they beautiful!" he said. In his enthusiasm he took her arm and piloted her round the room. "Which do you think is best? Sometimes I incline to Daniel in the lions' den, but that vision of St. John the Divine is really a masterpiece—it needs a bigger wall really, but that is the best I can do at present. Look at the detail! It is better than Breughel." He switched on some lights, muttering, "Light in this country is hopeless, hopeless, but when I take them back to Turkey, aha!"

"Aha!" said Lucy frostily. "Charming! So you leave the poor old girl to live in that den of squalor while you collect her pictures and take them back to Turkey. What do you think *she* would say?"

Dr. Adnan considered, frowning. A red velvet cap with a tassel lay on the piano; absently he picked it up and slid it to a comfortable position on his head.

"Do you know, I think she would not give a damn," he said. "My impression is that once she has finished a picture she does not care any more about it than if it were a—a dish of mashed potatoes. She has certainly given them away freely enough. And as for the den of squalor, she herself chose to live there—who am I to chase her about? You Anglo-Saxons are sadly predictable; benevolence with you always takes the form of organising people in ways which they probably do not enjoy at all."

"But that place is dangerous! Some old boy nearly broke his neck on the stairs the other day."

"So? The street is dangerous, but you would not prevent her going out, in spite of the fact that she might get knocked down by a car. (By the way they never did discover who knocked over that poor Clough)."

"Listen," said Lucy. There was a table behind her; absently she sat on it. Pushing aside her hair, she asked Adnan earnestly,

"Do you think she really *is* Great-aunt Fennel? Do you think she really *did* do those pictures? She doesn't seem to be doing any at the moment."

"Well, the circumstances are hardly conducive, are they? Also, I understand her eyesight has deteriorated in the last year. Besides, if she is not herself, who is she? You talk in paradoxes."

"She might be her friend—the one who fell into the stream. I mean, it might have been Great-aunt Fennel who fell in."

"What would be the point of the impersonation?" said the doctor slowly, sitting down on the piano stool.

"Well, my uncle's firm pays an annuity to Aunt Fennel. At her death it should stop."

He studied her thoughtfully. Lucy felt herself going pink. "This was my uncle's idea," she said defiantly.

"So he sent you to investigate?"

"Well? What if he did? It's his firm who are paying out the cash." Lucy felt she had slipped into a false position and returned to her original question. "The thing is—she seems so childish most of the time—"

"You think the person who did those pictures was not childish? But they are primitives, after all."

"Ye-es," Lucy agreed, "but when a person has created works of art on—on that scale, you'd think her character would give some indication of it?"

"And you consider Miss Culpepper's does not? Do you already know her so well?"

"I've spent the last few days with her, getting to know her."

"But perhaps she is cleverer than you! Perhaps she is pretending *not* to be Great-aunt Fennel!"

Lucy stared at him. "Why should she do that?"

"My dear Miss—what is your first name?"

"Lucy," she said mechanically.

"Thank you. In Turkey we prefer to use the first name. Lucy—aha! Very appropriate. Miss Lucy Snowe!" As usual he seemed to be enjoying some private joke at her expense. "How can I tell what your aunt's reasons might be for pretending not to be your aunt? You Anglo-Saxons are so often a great mystery."

"Just now you said we were sadly predictable."

"In the mass, yes; as individuals, no. Now with Turks it is just the other way round; you can tell what an individual Turk will do, but the nation, never!"

He spun round on the stool and suddenly sang, accompanying himself on the piano:

> Dial me on my Linguaphone
> I am cut off, I am all alone;
> Get your computer to call up mine,
> The number is neun, neuf, nono, nine;
> Oh, it will be a day for jubilation
> When nation can really speak to nation!

"Don't you think that is very good?" he said to Lucy.

"The tune is not bad. The words don't impress me." But in

fact she was quite impressed by his voice—a pleasant tenor—and by his nimble playing. Dr. Adnan grinned at her.

"Now, shall I give you a cup of coffee or seduce you?"

"You'll do neither," said Lucy coldly. "I came to get the name of a dentist for my aunt, who seems never to have been to one in her life."

"So we can't establish her identity by her bridgework. Well, Fawcett is about the best in Kirby. Mention my name, he'll see her sooner."

The surgery bell rang.

"What a pity," said Dr. Adnan. "I just began to feel we were getting to know one another. And it would have been the best cup of coffee you ever drank—Turkish, of course. Never mind—another time. You can go straight out by this door. I am so pleased to have met you again—good-bye."

"Just a minute," said Lucy. "What did you pay for those pictures—and who?"

He grinned his flashing grin again; it reminded her irresistibly of Mr. Jackson, in *The Tale of Mrs. Tittlemouse*.

"My dear girl, I am the doctor—people are mostly glad to give them to me in acknowledgment of my skill!"

Lucy walked crossly away, feeling that Dr. Adnan had learned a great deal more about her than she had about him.

She telephoned Fawcett, who had a cancellation at eleven and could see Miss Culpepper then; that gave her an hour. It was no use arriving too early; Mrs. Tilney, hobbling about with her hangover, stumblingly taking her elderly boarders their breakfasts in bed, could not abide people coming to her house before ten-thirty A.M.

Lucy went into an espresso bar and had a cup of coffee; not Turkish, but about a thousand per cent better than the brew offered to lodgers in Redcar Street. Someone had left an early edition of the *Kirby Evening Advertiser* on the seat next her; she picked it up, wondering if Aunt Fennel would enjoy being taken to the movies; but neither *Son of Dracula* nor *The Secret Life of Sexy Sandra* seemed suitable, particularly in view of the fact that Aunt Fennel had probably never set foot in a movie house in her life.

A familiar name caught her eye beneath the headline WIDOW

BATTERED WITH HAMMER: "Mrs. Geraldine Truslove, 44-year-old widow, of The Laurels, Tingwell Street, was admitted to hospital last night with shock and concussion after being attacked by a man. 'I had a difference of opinion with a neighbour about the name of his house,' she told our staff reporter. 'It has led to a lot of difficulties.' A man has been detained by the police . . ."

Oh dear, thought Lucy. Poor silly woman. Maybe if I hadn't tried to stop her she wouldn't have done it. I hope she's not badly hurt.

She read about a performance by the Kirby Thespians of *French Without Tears:* of how Clough, the Appleby gardener knocked down by a hit-and-run motorist had made a good recovery but the person responsible had never come forward; of how the Durham jail escapee was now thought to be in London.

"A stolen car was found by South London police in a thicket on Putney Heath; on the steering wheel were the fingerprints of Harbin, the escaped man, who was serving a 30-year sentence for his part in smuggling £30,000 worth of stolen gold out of the country; he still had ten years of his term to go. Harbin was apprehended with another member of the gang when the plane in which they planned to leave England crashed on take-off at Liverpool airport; Harbin lost a hand in the crash. Goetz, the second man, was released last year after serving the full term of his lighter sentence; both men had made several previous attempts to escape. The stolen gold was never recovered. The police had lost track of Goetz since his release . . ."

Before I was born, Lucy thought. She tried to imagine the emotions of somebody who had escaped from prison after twenty years. One would feel defenceless, at a loss, like an old person who has lost touch with progress; unhappy, probably, and antagonistic; one would have paranoid suspicions of everything and everybody—

That was why it was not possible to be utterly convinced by Aunt Fennel's fears; she appeared to entertain the same suspicion and terror towards her roommate who, she said, had stolen her warm winter vests, as towards the unknown hypothetical murderer of her friend Dill.

But old people really were defenceless; they had a right to their paranoid fears; whereas if you had come out of prison with

£30,000 waiting stowed away for you somewhere, you would presumably feel to some extent buttressed against the unknown.

Still, what a different world to come out into: space flights, kidney grafts, artificial fertilisation of human ova, pollution clogging the air and water; it would hardly seem the same place.

"The country doesn't seem to have changed much," Goetz said, looking out across the featureless expanse of moorland visible from Appleby Old Hall's third-floor bedroom. "Why did you want to buy a house in this God-forsaken place?"

"Property's cheap round here," Mrs. Marsham said shortly. "And it's quiet."

"By cripes it is."

"Well? Have you any complaints?"

"No, no," he said. "You've got the place very well fixed up, I don't deny."

"Yeah?" said Goetz. "It gives me the gooeys to see all those old nuts doddering around downstairs."

"Rinse, please," said Harold. Harbin, who was having his new dental plate adjusted, rinsed and spat. "Anyway," Harold went on, "Ma has a sentimental attachment to this part, haven't you, Ma? Can't say I share it; I'll be glad to get back to Brum, when I've got you fixed up."

"Sentimental attachment?" said Goetz. "Go on! I should think the only thing Linda would have a sentimental attachment to would be a humane destroyer."

Mrs. Marsham made no reply, but set her lips in a thin line; she was changing the dressing on Harbin's rebuilt nose with swift precision.

"You didn't come from these parts, though?" Harbin spoke with difficulty and cautiously moved his eyebrows up and down. "Merseyside born and bred, you were."

"Old flame of hers came from round here, though," said Harold, "or so she thinks. That's you done, then," he told Harbin. "Can't think why you wore your own for so long, they were in a terrible state. Wasn't there a decent dentist in stir?"

Goetz looked uneasy; Harold picked up a container of used dressings and left the room.

"Old flame?" Harbin had been peering at himself sideways in a shaving-glass; he glanced round sharply. "Who?"

Goetz reflected; after a pause he said, "You don't mean *Fred?*"

"Fred never let on where he came from," Harbin said. "Compared to Fred, oysters suffer from frantic verbal diarrhoea."

"Bet it was Fred though," Goetz said, studying Mrs. Marsham's inexpressive face. "Well, well! That *is* sentimental attachment for you."

"How did you find out?" said Harbin.

A bell rang on the stairs. "That's someone at the front door. I must go," Mrs. Marsham said.

"Oh, come on, Linda," said Goetz. "Don't be such a clam. After all, we're interested in Freddie too, don't forget. Whatsername will answer the door."

"It was only a guess, really," Mrs. Marsham said at last.

"You were always a pretty smart guesser, Linda, in those gay old days when you were queen of the B.I.C.A. air hostesses."

She was silent again. Then she said,

"There were just three little things he let fall at different times. The first time I ever met him he had a briefcase with the initials W.C. on it; you'd remember a thing like that, wouldn't you, and I did. Ever after that he was always Fred Smith. I asked him once about the briefcase and he said he'd borrowed it from a chap called Cooper; but the name didn't come out quite pat." Harbin nodded. "Then, another time, we happened to be talking about place names that are spelt one way and pronounced another, like Cirencester; he said, 'Oh yes, Appleby's another,' and then stopped short and looked annoyed at himself. Why should he think of such a tiny place if he hadn't got connections there?"

"Humph," said Harbin. "Pretty thin reasons for moving here, however. What was the third thing?"

"It was once when he'd had a bit to drink; Fred never drank much, he wasn't going to lose control of himself, ever. But it was in Hong Kong and we'd brought off a successful trip and he was feeling just a little more relaxed than usual. He said, 'I'm going to be a success in the world, Linda. I don't care what way. I just want my name to be remembered for more than because it's one of four on a village war memorial.'"

There was a silence while they thought about this. Then Harbin said, "I take it there are four names here?"

"A Holroyd, a Crabtree, and two Scarthwaites."

"Many surnames in the village beginning with C?"

"Quite a few. Crabtree, Crossley, Coxwold, Clough, Culpepper, there's a couple moved here recently called Carados—"

"Any of 'em with long-lost relations?"

"Nearly all," she said. "Appleby's a place most people move away from."

"Well—" Harbin shrugged. "It's a fairly remote chance he'd ever come back, don't you think? If he did come from here."

"Maybe. But Fred was greedy. If anyone died, and there was the question of a legacy, for instance—and as the situation suited in other ways—"

"Oh sure. I'm not complaining. This old folk's home is a bloody good idea. Be a little gold mine, I daresay."

The internal telephone buzzed. Mrs. Marsham picked up the receiver. Nora's voice came through.

"Oh, matron, there's a young lady here inquiring about accommodation for her aunt."

"Tell her we haven't got any—" Mrs. Marsham began irritably. "Or no—I'd better come down, I suppose. Say I'll be down in a moment, but I can't promise anything. What's her name?"

There was a pause; then Nora returned.

"She says her aunt used to live in the village here, that's why she's keen to come. You saw the young lady the other day. Her name's Culpepper."

VII

"Damn that girl!" exclaimed Wilbie vexedly, crackling the letter about and then throwing it down on the coffee table beside his untasted drink. "I tell her exactly what to do, I even pay her fare, and what happens?"

"What does happen?" Russ asked. He picked up Lucy's letter. He was a slow reader, and while his eyes made their deliberate way from side to side and down the blue sheet, Wilbie twitched and pressed his lips together and drummed on the arm of his chair with pink stubby fingers. The house was empty; Rose and Corale had gone off to a cocktail party; Wilbie was supposed to follow them when he had freshened up from his day's labours.

"Goddam little fool has found some old lady who's pulled the wool over her eyes properly. Now she's going to spend all the dough I gave her installing this old phoney in some de luxe residential home."

"Why are you so certain she hasn't got hold of the right old girl?" Russ asked lazily, dropping the letter back on the table and picking up his own drink.

"You can see she knows she's being bloody annoying," Wilbie went on angrily. "I ought to have had more sense, I suppose; ought to have seen she was the last person to do that errand; I know she hates my guts. But she can be smart when she wants, and she certainly was sold on those pictures—if it had worked it would have been—oh, well, to hell with it; there's no use relying on women, they always let you down."

"Reckon so?" said Russ. If Wilbie had been paying attention he would have noticed a certain irony in his assistant's voice, but he was irritably rereading Lucy's letter.

"And as for sending her to that Appleby place, what do they call it, Wildfell Hall, *that's* clean out of the question; I'll have to put my foot down."

"What's so specially wrong with that place—d'you know something about it?"

"What?—oh; no, but you can see a home like that is sure to cost a small fortune—just newly opened, all their initial outlay to cover," Wilbie said hastily. "There must be dozens of more suitable places. Though anyway I'm damned if Culpepper is going to shell out to keep some old fraud in luxury eating her head off in *any* of them."

"You'll get the bank to query the annuity payments?" Russ asked. "Cause a lot of stink—publicity—over such a flea-bite? After all, even if she is a phoney, you say the old lady's in her nineties? She can't last much longer."

"If she's not Aunt Fennel Culpepper, then it's money she's no right to," Wilbie said with the obstinacy of the mean man. "I don't care how much it is, it's the principle that counts."

"Well, it's your decision, of course. But you can bet your boots on one thing happening if you start a lot of legal investigations and proceedings—"

"What?" snapped Wilbie, taking an irritable gulp of his drink.

"Why, since young Lucy seems to have taken such a fancy to the old girl, soon as she finds out what's going on, she'll sell all the pictures she can lay hands on to raise cash to pay the old folk's home fees."

Wilbie turned a dark slate-red. His opaque eyes clouded and bulged.

"But that would be fraudulent!" he said sharply.

"Depends how she came by them."

"By God, if she did that, I'd—I'd—"

"You really do set store by those pictures, don't you?" said Russ coolly. "I know we reckoned they'd fetch something pretty handsome, properly handled, but are they really going to be worth maybe quite a lot of your time and energy when you ought to be keeping your mind on the Dinky Yank takeover—?"

Wilbie was paying no attention, however. With a set, fanatical expression he was staring out of the window, in a vaguely easterly direction.

"If I thought she'd do that," he muttered, "I'd damn well make the trip myself—*I* discovered those pictures and nobody else— certainly not that puny, ungrateful, two-timing little bag of bones —is going to get the credit. People are going to see that *I* know something about art—"

"Go to *England?*" Russ was astonished.

"I'm not going to have that cold-blooded, scheming little hypocrite pull a fast one on me."

"What would you do—go to this Appleby place and have a grand confrontation?"

Wilbie turned suddenly cautious.

"No, I guess there wouldn't be time for that," he said quickly. "But I could go to York—look in on Pugwash Pharmaceuticals while I was there and get that deal clinched, see—and I could tell Lucy to bring the old girl over to see me in York. *That'd* shake her fast enough—she'd soon climb down then, I bet."

"You're pretty certain it really is the wrong one claiming the money, then? What makes you so sure?"

"Oh—" Wilbie waved his pink, furry hand, "lots of little things. It all seems to add up."

"You'd better take *me* with you," Russ said. "If you're so sure. Then, while you're seeing Pugwash, I'll run over to Appleby and get things settled there."

"Don't be a fool," Wilbie said shortly. "How could you go? If I went—which I haven't decided—I'd need you to stay here and cover the Dinky Yank deal."

"You'd far better take me."

"I've just *told* you, Russ, I—"

"You see, when I was up in your attic that time I found out an interesting thing," Russ went on calmly.

Wilbie went cod-fillet white, under the healthy tan acquired from golfing, spear-fishing, skiing, duck-shooting, and client-watching.

"Found out—how d'you— What the hell are you thinking about?" he demanded.

"When I was dumping the pictures back upstairs for you that

day Lucy brought them down: the attic was all tidy and ship-shape, someone'd been straightening it up, I guess. I've always wanted to have a look round up there, it seemed a good chance. I found a bundle of envelopes marked Kernahan. So I stuck a couple of them in my pocket; Kernahan was my mother's maiden name, as you may recall."

Wilbie was silent, staring at Russ open-mouthed, as if a golf club in his hand had suddenly started transmitting messages from outer space.

"I always thought that tale Mom used to spin about my father having died in a freeway crash hadn't enough detail about it," Russ said meditatively. Then he grinned. "And I know now too why you got so mad at the idea of my marrying Corale—apart from the fact that it's got to be a Rockefeller, I mean. My marrying her would have a kind of classic touch, wouldn't it—the old Oedipus stuff, just about?"

Wilbie unclamped his rigid jaw and massaged his palate with a sticky tongue.

"Anyway, I'm not sorry about that," Russ went on easily. "Marrying Corale wouldn't have been an intellectual feast; if that girl ever had two ideas she probably tried rubbing them together to light a fire. The way things are suits me much better."

Wilbie had found his voice again.

"And do you mean to say"—he sounded really injured—"that you've been keeping all this under your hat ever since before Lucy went to England? Well, I am surprised at you, Russ—and sorry too! After all I've done for you! I wouldn't have expected *you* to be so ungrateful—"

"No doubt you'd planned to tell me all about it one day—in your own good time?"

"Sure—naturally I did! Didn't I fetch you in—haven't I been training you up for a key position in the firm?"

"Well, the day's come a bit sooner than you planned, that's all," Russ said kindly. "From now on I really am going to be your right-hand man, dear old Dad!"

"*Russ*—look here—for God's sake have a bit of discretion—"

Wilbie glanced agonizedly at the TV set, as if it might be listening to and recording their words.

"Oh, I'll be discreet," Russ said. "What did you send me to business college for, if not to learn how to manage the guy at the top? You play along with me, I'll be as discreet as the queen's chiropodist. And I'll come to England and handle this Auntie Fennel business for you. After all, she's my great-aunt too! And Lord knows little Miss Lucy Head-in-Air's snubbed me often enough —it'd be a pleasure to make her jump."

There was a longish pause. Then Wilbie nodded reflectively.

"Maybe there'd be something to it," he said. He seemed to have calmed down a good deal.

Russ, not usually analytical of people, was faintly surprised that Wilbie had taken the exposure with so little fuss. He seemed almost relieved—as if the revelation were not what he had expected, and, indeed, much less disastrous than it might have been.

Thoughtfully taking his leave, Russ determined to get back into the attic at the earliest possible opportunity.

Mrs. Marsham's office was small and tidy, furnished with desk, filing cabinet, and, as a minimal concession to visitors, two scrawny little fireside chairs by which the unfortunate sitter's knees were thrust up on a level with his breast-bone.

Mrs. Marsham entered the room warily, like the newcomer to the jungle, not certain yet if his role is that of hunter or prey. But a glance at the two pairs of eyes raised to hers gave reassurance. The girl she recognised as the same shabbily unimpressive, mousy, fair-haired, quiet-spoken little thing, who had called last week with some pointless inquiry about vacancies; tiresome, persistent creature, why had she come back when told plainly enough that there was no accommodation available at present? And the old lady with her must be the aunt, grandmother, great-aunt, or what-have-you; nothing out of the common about *her*, either, decided Mrs. Marsham, running an experienced eye over the shabby coat and hat, the various dangling scarves and bulging receptacles; old ladies of her sort are two a penny in every street. She would be the easy kind to keep in order if she were admitted, but of course there was no question of that.

"Yes?" she began briskly, shutting the door behind her. "I'm sorry you've wasted your time coming back here. I thought I made it quite plain when you came before that we had no vacancy, that it was quite impossible for us to accommodate anyone else at present."

She gave the girl a chill smile and her glance again brushed the old lady sitting so meekly with her knobbed feet in their medium black lace-ups pointing straight ahead, and the old-fashioned linen hat jammed down over her wispy bun.

"You didn't say you had no vacancy," Lucy replied, "you told me you had beds but were short-handed because one of your staff had just left."

"No beds, no staff, it comes to the same thing, doesn't it?" Mrs. Marsham's smile became more irritated. She glanced at her watch. "So in the circumstances I'm afraid there's no point in our discussing the matter any more. At some time in the·future, perhaps —but I can't hold out any promises. And now if you'll excuse me I'm really *very* busy—"

"So, as you seemed to be having such difficulties," pursued Lucy calmly, "I thought maybe you'd be interested in hiring me? In exchange for taking my aunt, as it were. I'm strong, I'm sensible, I did first aid and domestic economy at school—"

Mrs. Marsham's jaw dropped. For once she seemed completely nonplussed and gazed at Lucy blankly.

At this point the old lady, apparently perplexed by the silence, ventured to speak up for the first time.

"What is it, dearie?" she asked timidly. "Don't they have a vacancy? I couldn't quite catch. Can't they take me in?" She turned up the volume of her hearing aid until it rattled and whistled, glancing myopically meanwhile from Lucy to the matron and back.

"We aren't sure yet," Lucy answered slowly and clearly, giving her great-aunt a reassuring smile. "Maybe we'll be able to get something fixed up—don't you worry."

"Really, Miss—"

"Culpepper—"

"I don't think—"

"No, but *do* think!" Lucy urged her. "Think now. Think it over. I bet you've hired a lot worse help than me out in these backwoods; I cook okay, I've even worked as a stewardess. There's nothing you can tell me about taking basins to old ladies."

"Oh, this is ridiculous," Mrs. Marsham began. She was interrupted by a heavy knock at the door, which flew open. Everybody jumped, Mrs. Marsham not least.

The cook, Nora, surged in, wiping her hands on her damp, greasy apron.

"Mis' Marsham, I can't stop," she announced without preamble. "Nellie's just been in to say our Annie's terrible poorly with the measles. Raging fever she's got and can't hardly see out of her eyes. So I'm off home right away, I just come to tell you. Can't say when I'll be back."

"Off *home?* But you can't go off just like that!" Mrs. Marsham was outraged. "What about the lunch?"

"Very sorry," Nora said doggedly. "But my own flesh and blood gotta come first, hasn't it? Reckon you'll have to finish the lunch yourself. The taties is on, I'd done 'em when Nellie came. *She* feels queer, too, she said; shouldn't wonder if she'd took the measles too, she's all red-up and gummy-eyed. Meat's in the fridge. Here's the shopping-list what's wanted. I'll be getting along now then. I'll send a message when I can come back."

She left, pulling the door to behind her.

"Oh, good *heavens!*" exclaimed Mrs. Marsham furiously. "And that miserable child's been up here every day after school hanging about in the kitchen breathing germs everywhere—I wonder how many of the residents haven't had measles—"

She was speaking mainly to herself, staring out of the window at Nora's broad departing back, receding down the drive on an aged bicycle.

"You're in quite a spot, aren't you?" said Lucy calmly. "I heard them talking at the post office about measles in your cook's family; that was what gave me the idea of proposing myself for the job. Measles lasts a good two weeks. And I had it when I was fourteen, so you don't have to worry about me. What about you, Aunt Fen? Have you had measles? Measles?" she repeated, slightly louder; Aunt Fennel seemed to be afflicted by one of her extra-deaf spells today.

"Eh? Oh, yes, dear. Measles? Yes, long ago, when I was quite a child." Miss Culpepper looked bewildered.

"That's okay, then," said Lucy. "We'll go back to Kirby, pack up Aunt Fennel's things, give Mrs. Tilney a week's money in lieu, and come back tomorrow afternoon. Will you be able to manage till then? I'd make it today, but unfortunately Aunt Fennel has a dental appointment tomorrow at two and she oughtn't to skip it. Will that be all right?"

"Well—" Mrs. Marsham said slowly. She bit her lip, annoyed and indecisive.

"If that kid's been wafting germs about every day," Lucy went on, "such of your old folks as haven't had measles are due to come out in a rash any minute now. If I were you, I wouldn't look a gift horse in the mouth."

"Well, you must understand that this is a purely temporary measure. I can't offer anything permanent, either for you *or* your aunt—"

"Sure, sure. We can go into all that later. We mightn't suit each other—it cuts all ways. Anyhow I'm not looking for a permanent job—just thought if I offered to tide you over till you got somebody else in, it might persuade you to take Aunt Fennel! Now we'd better be off; you've got a lot on your hands."

Lucy grinned crookedly through her forelock at Mrs. Marsham as she helped Aunt Fennel up out of the awkward little chair.

When Mrs. Marsham opened the door, angry words could be heard from the hallway beyond.

"I'll tell matron on you."

"Just you dare, you two-faced bitch, I'll tell her about the time you pinched the cheese off the supper trolley—"

"Ill-treating a poor dumb beast—"

"Poor? That animal's better fed than you or I, and as for dumb—"

"Dumb, I wish some of you were dumb," exclaimed Mrs. Marsham irritably, brushing past Lucy and Miss Culpepper. "What's the matter now?"

"She kicked the cat!" breathlessly burst out one old woman, hanging on to the wall rail while she pointed accusingly at a second. "Kicked your poor puss-cat, matron, that never did her any harm!"

"I did not, then. Tripped over it, that's quite another matter. Can't be expected to see it pushing round my feet, can I, everybody knows how bad my eyes are. I've said plenty of times that it's dangerous to have an animal like that around in a house where there's elderly people. But as for going for to *kick* it—"

"And that's a lie! And haven't I heard you with my own ears saying you couldn't abide the scruffy overfed thing, that you wouldn't mind giving it a good clump—"

"Who's telling lies now? I never said any such thing!"

"You did, then!"

"Ladies, ladies, be quiet, please! What will the visitors think? What's all this about?" Mrs. Marsham said sharply. "What happened? Where is the cat?"

"He ran into the kitchen," said the accuser importantly. She was a small, beady-eyed woman, almost totally bald, clad in a long maroon-coloured knitted dress and bedroom slippers; she gestured vehemently with one hand while continuing to cling to the rail with the other. "Mrs. Crabtree was coming down the stairs and the cat ran past as she got to the bottom so she gave it a great kick, poor thing! And she went for to hit it with her stick too, but she nearly toppled herself over and it ran off before she could get her balance."

"There isn't a word of truth in what Emma Chiddock says from beginning to end! Got a spite against me, she has, because I saw her at the cheese. Anyway," said Mrs. Crabtree, fatally weakening her case, "the cat was going upstairs, and that's not allowed."

Mrs. Crabtree was a stocky woman with the high colour that denotes temper, thick-lensed pebble glasses, a shock of untidy white hair, and a white stick. She peered defensively in the matron's direction. "But I never *went* for to kick it," she repeated.

"Mrs. Crabtree, you're getting over-excited, it looks to me as if you might have a temperature," the matron said. "I think you'd better go and lie down on your bed and take out your dentures. Remember what the doctor said, you'll have to go back on the pills again if you get worked up."

These words were calmly spoken, but they had a quelling effect on Mrs. Crabtree, who turned without any reply and hobbled off upstairs at top speed.

"She did kick your cat, you know, matron," Emma Chiddock said importantly as soon as her opponent was out of earshot. "Right in the stomach too!"

"All right, all right, I don't suppose she hurt him, he can look out for himself," Mrs. Marsham said irritably. "Now for goodness' sake don't worry me with any more tales; you can go and set the tables in the dining-room if you want to make yourself useful. Let yourselves out, will you?" she said to Lucy and Miss Culpepper. "I'll expect you back about tea-time tomorrow, then. Now I must see to the lunches." And she hurried off in the direction of the kitchen.

"Gone to see how her precious cat is, more likely," said Emma Chiddock with considerable malice. "She worships every whisker on that fat thing. Bet she *does* make Alice Crabtree take the pills. Alice don't like pills—give her bad dreams, she says."

Chuckling a little, she turned and groped her way along the wall to the dining-room.

Lucy was somewhat dismayed.

"Are you sure you want to come here, Aunt Fen?" she said, piloting Aunt Fennel out to the car. "They seem rather a quarrelsome lot."

"Oh, old people always quarrel, dearie," Aunt Fennel replied placidly. "It's the same in any home, however it's run. Quarrelling's what keeps them alive, you know."

Lucy was impressed, as so often, by the old woman's sudden flashes of insight.

Just the same, something troubled her about the atmosphere of Wildfell Hall; something intangible and hard to pin down. It was not the feud between the old ladies; not their attitude, half defensive, half propitiating, towards the matron; it was not the faint threat implicit in Mrs. Marsham's disciplinary suggestion, but a combination of all three things and something else besides which seemed to give the place a faint sour flavour, like the anonymous, chemical, vaguely disquieting smell of a laboratory. I'm probably imagining it, decided Lucy. Old people's homes are always full of ornery old cusses missing the families they used to boss about. It would take a saint not to get mad at them at times, and plainly Mrs. Marsham's no saint. Still, she seems sensible enough. Anyway, if I'm there for a week or so there'll be time to get the feel of the place, and then if it really doesn't seem right I can easily whistle Aunt Fen out of it, take her down south maybe, and find something near where I'm studying with Max.

But Aunt Fennel certainly seems quite pleased with Wildfell Hall.

"Alice Crabtree," Aunt Fennel said meditatively. "She always was headstrong and wilful, even as a girl. I remember the time Lenny Thorpe—no, what am I thinking of, it'll have been Lenny Thorpe's father, of course, Sam Thorpe—he dared her to go in to

Galloway's field where the bull was kept. How they ever got her out alive! It took five men to keep that bull at bay and one of them had his leg broke—"

"You *know* Mrs. Crabtree, then?"

"Oh yes, dearie, she always lived at Appleby. She and I were never close friends, of course, but still I shan't object to a chat with her now and then."

Aha, thought Lucy, here's a first-hand witness coming up; someone who actually knows Aunt Fennel. What a piece of luck. Patience, patience, and all will be neatly unravelled. Dear Max, I'll be just a little longer than I expected, on account of the measles and this job, but it's very temporary—something tells me strongly that Mrs. Marsham doesn't want me sculling around in her one-woman kingdom longer than strictly necessary—so the end is in sight.

She glanced up at the rise of moorland which they were skirting. A sky of plum-grey cumulus had assembled, through which the sun ducked palely; scurrying cloud shadows over the convex land were exactly the same colour as the sky above but in a darker tone. Far away, on a humped bloomy shoulder of hill three immense silvery globes were aligned across the slope like beached moons.

"What are those things, Aunt Fennel?"

"What things, dearie?"

"Over there."

"Too far for my poor old eyes. What are they like?"

"Round and silver, like balloons, only bigger."

"Oh, *those.* Something to do with the Russians, dear. When the Russians are coming I believe they ring a bell."

"Kind of bicycle bells. I see," Lucy said cheerfully. Aunt Fennel always came out the winner in these little contests, but Lucy bore no ill-feeling on that account. She was becoming daily fonder of the old lady.

"Lot of nonsense, if you ask me," Aunt Fennel went on. "If the Russians *did* come, I daresay they'd turn out to be like anybody else. Very fond of cucumbers, I believe, and jam in their tea. Nothing wrong with that, if it's home-made jam."

Lucy drove slowly, her eyes on the racing purple-black shadows.

"Don't you sometimes feel like doing another picture, Aunt Fennel?" she said.

She put the question, expecting another fobbing-off answer about weak eyesight, but Aunt Fennel surprised her by saying,

"Yes, dearie, sometimes I do. Well—you never know, if there's some old garden-room or store-room at the Hall where I could have my bits and pieces and paints—I don't deny it *would* be rather nice."

Lucy almost held her breath. Aunt Fennel was smiling to herself, a sweet, secretive smile, like that of a frail, ancient mouse who has just discovered a whole Stilton cheese. "If my eyes are up to it, of course. But we shall have to see. That matron probably wouldn't allow me," she ended tranquilly. "Fond of her own way you can see *that* one is."

"Where are all your picture materials, Aunt Fennel?"

"Why, at the cottage, dearie. At High Beck."

"Wouldn't you like to go and have a look over the place—see your things aren't getting mildewy or eaten by moths?"

The old lady considered.

"Well—I don't know—" she said doubtfully.

"Do you have the key on you?"

"Oh yes, dear, of course; I always carry it." Aunt Fennel laid a hand protectively over her diaphragm.

"Well then—?"

"But suppose That Other One was still lurking around, waiting for me to come back?"

"Aunt Fennel."

"Yes, dearie?"

"Who *is* That Other One?"

"Oh, dearie, I couldn't tell *you!*" The old lady sounded appalled at such a suggestion. She pulled out a handkerchief from a little black velvet bag and pressed it against her forehead. Her lips trembled. A violent green flavour of tansy drifted about the car.

"But why not?"

"If he knew that *you* knew, he'd be after you too, as like as not."

Lucy knit her brow over this tangle.

"But, Aunt Fen—"

"Well, dearie?"

"How do you know that I *don't* know?"

"Well, you just asked me, didn't you? Where'd be the sense in asking if you knew?"

"Oh gosh," Lucy said, "we're going round and round. But what made you certain that I wasn't something to do with That Other One? Suppose he really sent me to clobber you?"

"Well, dearie, I *was* a little doubtful at first—" *Doubtful*, thought Lucy, remembering that agonising pursuit over the shingle. "—But when I came to know your character, of course I very soon saw you couldn't have had anything to do with That Other One. She's a *good* little thing, I thought, as soon as I knew your character."

A thin, birdlike claw came out and patted Lucy's hand on the steering-wheel; Lucy gave the claw a squeeze, replaced it gently in the owner's lap, and drove on, feeling unusually humble.

"Dearie—"

"Yes, Aunt Fen?"

"You *are* looking out for that tractor, aren't you?"

"Oops, thank you—not quite my usual care and attention!"

With a slight grin, Lucy deflected her course. The danger had not been imminent; the tractor, on which was mounted a telescopic crane attachment with a rake and saw-blade combined, was chugging slowly along on the other side of the lane, demolishing the hedge to half its height. The driver's attention was concentrated on keeping his chopping attachment tilted at the right angle; he had little to spare for other traffic.

"None of that sort of thing when I was young," Aunt Fennel said disapprovingly. "People cut hedges properly with bill-hooks in those days, instead of leaving them a nasty haggled mess. And as for those roadside sprays—they just ruin the wild flowers."

"But what about That Other One if you come to live at Wildfell Hall?" Lucy said, harking back to their previous topic. "Shan't you be worried about him there?"

"There'll always be company—he wouldn't dare come into a big, well-run place like that. Besides, he wouldn't expect me to come back there, you see."

This sounded rational, and was certainly unarguable.

"Did you know that man driving the tractor?" Lucy said irrelevantly.

"Good gracious, dearie, I couldn't see as far as that—not to recognise a face!"

Thirty all, thought Lucy. She said mildly, glancing sideways, "Your hearing aid is switched off, did you know?"

"I can always hear much better in the car," Aunt Fennel explained serenely. "It's the vibrations, I daresay."

Forty-thirty.

"Anybody you'd like to call on in Appleby as we pass through?"

"I don't think so, love, thank you all the same. Dill and I had got so old, we didn't bother with seeing neighbours much. Most of our own friends had died long ago, young folks don't want to be bothered visiting two queer old ladies—daresay they hardly knew which of us was which."

Game and set to Aunt Fennel, Lucy thought.

"—But I *would* rather like to go and just look at High Beck," Aunt Fennel ended. "Do you think you can get your car up the lane?"

"I'll have a darn good try. But what about That Other One?"

"Well, I was thinking—you can lock up the car, can't you? You always lock it when you go off and leave it in that underground car park place?"

"Sure."

"So you could lock me inside the car, couldn't you, while you went to the cottage? And then even if That Other One was about, he couldn't get me, could he?"

As so often with Aunt Fennel, Lucy hardly knew whether to laugh, cry, or curse; the old lady's mixture of fantasy and common sense filled her with admiration and despair. Never having lived at close quarters with a car before, Aunt Fennel had taken a huge fancy to little PHO; she was never so happy as when being driven about, no matter where, and now seemed to have endowed the little Austin with magical protective qualities as well.

"Sure I could lock you in. That's a fine plan," Lucy said gently. "What do you want me to do at the cottage?"

"Well—you could have a little look round, make sure things aren't getting too damp. And—yes, you could bring out one or two things—canvases and tubes of paint, and my embroidery bits, if any of them are worth saving."

"Right, then, here we go." Lucy braked to a crawl and turned left up a cart-track which parallelled the stream on the opposite bank from the haunted public lavatory.

"There's a footbridge by the cottage, isn't there?"

"That's right, dearie. There's room to leave the car just this side of the footbridge. Sometimes in really bad weather, when there's been a lot of rain or snow up on the moor, the beck floods right up over the footbridge and then the cottage is quite cut off; you can't climb the cliff at the back, you see, or we couldn't anyway; once we were cut off for three weeks."

"That must have been fun," Lucy remarked, cautiously manoeuvring little PHO on up the steep stony track, with the stream in its gully below on her left.

"Oh it *was*, dearie." Aunt Fennel's tone was full of reminiscent pleasure. "Of course we always had plenty of stores and our own eggs and vegetables—Dill made the bread, and we had parsnip wine and elderberry jam."

"What about mail . . . fuel?"

"Plenty of wood. And no one ever wrote—except once your Aunt Rose, to thank me for the pictures. Delighted with them, she said they were."

Lucy felt a pang, remembering Aunt Rose: "Wilbie told me to write a letter of thanks and put them up in the attic. She'd never know."

She said warmly, "They were *marvellous* pictures, Aunt Fen. I specially liked the Infant Samuel. Are there any left in the cottage?"

"I daresay, dearie. I really can't remember," the old lady said vaguely. "I gave away most of my things when I made up my mind to leave. Old Colonel Linton said he'd take them round to people for me. Very kind, he was; when Dill was alive he often used to come in and have a glass of our home-made wine."

"Colonel Linton. Would he be the old boy who lives at the vicarage? White hair and rather deaf and short-tempered?"

"He's had a lot of troubles, dearie." Aunt Fennel's tone was reproving. "He used to own the Hall and all the land round here, you know, but he lost all his money at the races and had to sell up. Very sad that was; his people had been here since goodness knows when."

Another first-hand witness; good, thought Lucy, edging little

PHO away from the precipitous bank of the stream and into a kind of niche in the steep bank on her right. I must go back and have another try at Colonel Linton.

She parked and got out by the footbridge. Aunt Fennel began a lengthy rummage among her garments; first she removed several scarves, then unbuttoned the front of her woollen dress and liberty bodice. Some hooks about midway down the front of her corset were then unfastened with considerable difficulty.

"Can I help?" asked Lucy.

"No thank you, dearie, I can manage; ha, here we are." She hauled on a sort of fishing-line attached to a safety-pin and up came a little chamois-leather bag, warm and creased. "This is where I keep the wealth, you see," and once again her face broke into its triumphant smile. Incredulous, Lucy had a momentary glimpse of a thickish wad of currency notes before Aunt Fennel extracted a door-key from the middle of the wad, which she replaced in the bag. She then began the complicated process of restowing and rebuttoning.

"Aunt Fennel—"

"Yes, dearie?"

"Do you think it's sensible to carry all that about with you?"

"Where else would I carry it, dearie?"

This seemed unanswerable.

"But if you've got such a lot of ready cash, why go to all that trouble to change a cheque at the drugstore?"

Aunt Fennel was scandalised. "This is only for *emergencies.*"

"Oh, I see . . ."

Rather shaken, Lucy got out of the car and carefully locked Aunt Fennel inside it.

"Shan't be long!" she called loudly, emphasising lip movements, and made her way down to the footbridge. It was a slender affair, made of transverse wooden slats which were slung on two strands of heavy fence wire, triple-twisted; it jiggled and swung as Lucy crossed it, and she had to hold on to the wire guard-rail on both sides. Below her the cider-coloured beck dashed between mossy stones. Down three wooden steps from the bridge—what a structure for two old ladies to cross every time they went to the village! —and then up a stairway of irregular stone slabs to where High Beck cottage perched, halfway up the bank-side. Terraced flower-beds in front of the cottage had reverted to wild but still showed a few marigolds and nasturtiums among the tangle of rank growth. Two granite pig-troughs on either side of the front door were full of buttercups.

The key turned rustily and Lucy stepped inside.

A smell of dank and cold met her; damp stone primarily, and behind that a whiff of soot and mouldering wood. A flight of narrow stairs faced the porch; doors lay on either side; Lucy chose the left and found herself in a large kitchen with a red-flagged floor, a dresser, a grandfather clock stopped at twenty to five, a table, and two wooden stools. In one wall was set a primitive cooking-range with oven; a door at the back led to a scullery, and there were seats inset under the two windows, which had heavy wooden shutters pushed back. No pictures on the papered walls. Lucy tried the other little front room, which had evidently been used as a parlour and had a trellised wallpaper with roses and blue-birds, very damp and peeling. No pictures here either, but in a fireside cupboard she unearthed a box full of embroidery silks and scraps of material, too sodden and mildewed to be any use. Up-stairs in one of the two little bedrooms stood a stack of old frames and pictures, the kind found in farmhouses, Victorian engravings and water-colours. One or two of them had been painted over with a matte colour, or had a bit of linen stretched across them; evi-dently Aunt Fennel had thriftily used these as the base for her own works. Lucy also found some tubes of oil paint, hardened and useless. No pictures; evidently Colonel Linton had made a clean sweep, or somebody else had; it would, of course, be easy for anybody to enter the cottage with its broken windows.

She turned and looked out of the casement at the tree-filled glen and slender, spidery bridge. Down below, out of sight from here, the beck could be heard chattering among its rocks. On the other side little PHO and Aunt Fennel waited patiently.

Lucy turned back to her investigation of the house. She did not know what she had expected to find; only that she was not finding it. Photographs? Evidence of identity? There was nothing of that kind. But what met and engulfed her, stronger than the smell of damp soot, was an almost unbearable sadness, a feeling of betrayal.

"You abandoned me! You left me alone to die!"

"I couldn't help it." Lucy muttered—to whom? To the house?

"It wasn't my fault! I wasn't even here." But the reproach went on assailing her, until she wanted to press her fingers into her ears, into her heart. It was like a continuous cry of pain. Thank God I didn't bring Aunt Fennel up here, she thought. If *I* feel it so, how could she have borne it? No wonder she left. It's as if there were a curse on the place.

Her head had started to throb violently. She picked up an armful of the canvases at random and made her way awkwardly down the narrow stairs with them. Pausing in the kitchen to rearrange the load she was overtaken by a giddy spell and had to wait, leaning against the doorpost, till her sight cleared. For a moment she had the mad impression that she could see two images, one superimposed on the other, like a three-colour picture out of register. She saw the kitchen furnished, sunlit, fire in the range, cat asleep on a rag hearthrug, wallflowers in a brass pot on the table, a grey-haired figure in a print overall busy chopping something on a pastryboard . . . The picture faded.

"Hell's bells," Lucy muttered. "Seeing spooks, yet! I'm getting out of here."

"Come back!" the little house entreated as she dumped her load of canvases and turned to lock the door. "Please, please come back!" Then, ominously, "You will come back, you'll have to come back."

"Oh yeah? You have got a hope!" She stuck the key in her pocket and hitched up the canvases once more. A tabby cat, the one she had seen on her former visit, wrinkled its nose at her in a silent hiss and fled round a waterbutt. Lucy picked her way cautiously down the stone steps. She felt drained and sick; her head still throbbed. Negotiating the unsteady swing bridge with the canvases took all her concentration. She made her way slowly back along the track to little PHO. Aunt Fennel appeared to be dozing, chin on chest, and started violently when Lucy unlocked the car door.

"I got some canvases, Aunt Fennel, but the embroidery things weren't worth bringing. Too damp—all rotten. I'll put these in the trunk."

She did so, then sank into the driver's seat.

"How did the house seem, dearie?"

How to explain, or how to conceal, that frightening miasma of grief and reproach?

"Oh well—it was rather dusty and damp," she said.

"You have to expect that when a house is left empty," Aunt Fennel said placidly. "Otherwise everything all right? You look a bit pale dearie—you didn't see anybody? No one about? Not —not That Other One?" She sank her voice to a whisper.

"No—nobody. It's just that one of my headaches has hit me. It'll be better in a minute."

"Oh *well* now, we know what's good for that, don't we—comfrey tablets. And a sniff of my rosemary essence—such a good thing Mrs. Tilney let me use her kitchen to make some."

"I can't swallow a tablet just now, Aunt Fennel, bless you, but the rosemary's lovely—a big help. Let's get out of here, shall we?"

The whole glen, for Lucy, now seemed filled with the cottage's aura; she could not wait to leave. Craning her head out of the window she backed dangerously fast down the rough track until there was room to turn and rejoin the main village road. Her call on Colonel Linton at the vicarage would have to wait; she did not feel she had the stamina to deal with him at present.

But halfway along the village she braked.

"Aunt Fennel I think I will try to take a couple of your pills— and I'm dying for a drink of water. There's a girl living in that cottage who'd give me one, I daresay—could you bear to wait another couple of minutes? Or will you come in too?"

"Oh, I'll wait, dearie, thank you. You can lock me in again. Baker's Cottage—let's see, that was empty when I left. Wonder who's in it now?"

"People called Carados—strangers to the village," Lucy supplied obligingly, as she relocked the car.

The name appeared to mean nothing to Aunt Fennel, who settled herself placidly.

"—Yes?" said Fiona Carados, opening the door. "Oh, it's you again, what d'you want?"

"I wondered if you'd be kind enough—oh," said Lucy, "you've had your baby then!"

"It does happen; old Dame Nature's way," Mrs. Carados rejoined coolly. "That wasn't what you came to tell me, however?"

"No; sorry; could you be very kind and let me have a glass of water to take a couple of pills with, do you think? I've got a splitting headache."

"You do look rotten." A trace of sympathy became apparent in Mrs. Carados' well-bred voice. "Come into the kitchen and sit down. Sure you wouldn't rather have a whisky?"

She seemed a great deal more relaxed than on Lucy's previous visit.

"No, just water's all I want, thanks."

The kitchen, this time, was in a slightly less baleful condition of clutter; faintly here and there signs of tidying-up were apparent. A very minute infant slept in a Moses-basket on the floor.

"That's my bub; isn't he a funny," said Fiona, handing Lucy a thick white mug of very cold water.

"You can't have had him long; isn't it rather soon for you to be home from hospital?"

"I never got there; by the time I began to feel a bit queer it was too late. Even the old sawbones didn't arrive till it was all over."

"Good heavens." Lucy swallowed the tablets and eyed her hostess with respect. "Must have been scarey for your husband."

"Oh, *he* wasn't here either; I'd slung him out. Horrid little tick. Anyway he wasn't my husband," explained Fiona, in whom childbirth seemed to have worked a liberating change.

Lucy found it hard to think of an appropriate comment.

"I see," she said, and took another swig of water.

"It's *marvellous* not to have Robin skulking furtively around being ashamed of my non-marital status," Fiona confided. "Only thing, I'll have to find a way of earning some cash. How's the head?"

"Improving, thanks. What did you do before?"

"Ran a boutique in the King's Road. Sure you're okay?"

"Yes, much better. I ought to get back to my aunt, and thanks a lot."

"You're welcome. Something tells me," Fiona said, glancing through the window at the desolate main street of Appleby-under-Scar, "that there wouldn't be much demand for a boutique hereabouts."

"I guess not."

"I suppose you couldn't lend me a fiver?" Fiona remarked suddenly and casually. "Bloody little Robin, you see, doesn't send me anything at all now, though the baby's his. But the rent here's paid up till December, so I'm damn well not shifting till then."

"Well—" Lucy was not particularly keen to part with her own scanty cash. She hesitated.

"Or we could make it a sale if you don't like loans," Fiona went on. "Buy something—anything you fancy—how about my old bit of rabbit?" She gestured towards a shaggy bundle—could it be sable?—slung carelessly over the handlebar of the pram.

"Thanks, but you'll be wanting it yourself here, come winter. Anyway I'm not crazy about fur." Suddenly Lucy was visited by a brilliant idea. "Tell you what though—the picture you had over the sitting-room mantelpiece—is it still there? Could I have that?"

"Good God, yes. Can't think why you want it, but have it, by all means."

"Your landlord won't object?"

"If he does I'll tell him the baby was sick on it. Shouldn't think he'd notice actually—for one thing he hardly ever comes to the house. Doesn't care for the set-up," Fiona said dispassionately. "Here, I'll reach it down for you—thanks"—as Lucy dug out five pound notes—"that'll keep us in Cow-and-Gate and Scotch for a week or so."

"That's good." Covetously hugging Adam and Eve and the Serpent, Lucy made her way towards the door.

"By the way," Fiona said casually, "weren't you looking for some old girl with a funny name last time you came this way? Culpepper, Fenella Culpepper, something like that?"

"Yes I was." Lucy paused with her hand on the door-handle. "Why?"

"I just wondered if you'd found her, that was all."

"To be honest," said Lucy, "I really couldn't tell you."

VIII

The large white metal basket containing Lucy and Dr. Adnan revolved round and then, without ceasing its horizontal spin, turned right over vertically, describing at the same time a complicated figure-eight jiggle.

"Holy cow!" exclaimed Lucy. They were securely strapped in, but she made a grab for the rail.

"Pray do not be discomposed, my dear Miss Lucy Snowe. No harm will come to you, I promise." Dr. Adnan was laughing at her, a large expanse of impeccable teeth in his pink face. Through the pale strands of her tossed hair, Lucy grinned back.

"I'm not scared, thanks; it's just that I hadn't expected it. But I'm glad I didn't have any lunch!"

"No lunch?" He looked disapproving. "You young ladies have no notion at all of looking after yourselves. Had I known this when we met outside the dentist's surgery I would have given you some beer and sausages first—"

"Couldn't possibly have eaten them," Lucy told him. "I had a headache."

"A headache?" For the first time his total satisfaction with himself and the occasion seemed shaken. "Had I known *that* I would never have suggested coming to this noisy place."

"It's all right; I thought this might do it good. Kill or cure." From their loftily revolving perch Lucy looked down at Kirby fun fair spread out below. "And it has; I feel much better. All the fresh air!" She laughed at him as she vainly tried to control her blowing hair; the basket spun over once more.

"What brought on this headache?" Dr. Adnan inquired professionally.

"Oh, my headaches are a bit odd; they often seem to come on for no reason. And then sometimes they go just as quickly. This one did that; I'd had it since yesterday afternoon. It's gone now." Lucy avoided mention of High Beck; she still did not want to dwell upon exactly what had happened there—if anything had—and she felt certain that Dr. Adnan would have a strongly sceptical attitude towards any such phenomena.

"Well, let us now go and have a coffee to complete the cure." Their basket glided down to ground level, and the door automatically opened. An attendant came round, undoing safety-belts. The passengers climbed out unsteadily, giving one another sheepish smiles.

Adnan led Lucy to an open-air lunch bar under a plastic palm, where he bought her a paper cup of coffee and a large rectangle of something that resembled sandstone.

"Parkin," he explained gravely. "A local delicacy. Oh, but I was forgetting that your forebears came from these parts. And this, I am afraid, is not quite the best cup of coffee you ever drank. No matter; another time we will do better."

"It's okay. It's hot." Lucy drank the coffee gratefully and then glanced at her watch.

"Pray do not keep doing that. It gives me a feeling of impermanence when I wish to enjoy myself in your company. Your old lady is safe with Fawcett for a good two hours—he told me he had a lot of complicated bridgework to perform. And he has a very nice little receptionist-nurse who will keep an eye on her should he finish before you return. So relax and have fun!"

"I'm not used to doing that."

"So I can see. I shall have to teach you."

Dr. Adnan was plainly an adept at having fun. Today he wore a dark-green suede waisted jacket, a white frilled shirt, buckled shoes, and a lot of rings. Stocky, dapper, and cheerful, he set about the business of their entertainment with immense firmness of purpose.

"Another slab of parkin?" he said, taking one himself. "No? You should get your weight up, you know. In Turkey young ladies as thin as you are not considered sexually attractive."

"Too bad. Anyway," said Lucy, "we are not in Turkey now. Dr. Adnan I want to talk to you about my aunt's paintings. I really want to get hold—"

"A—" He raised a reproachful hand. "Later, later. Let us not mix business with pleasure! I brought you here to give you a good time. Let us continue to do so within the limits provided. What would you like to do next? Bingo?"

"Good grief, no. One of those stalls, perhaps?"

The fun-fair ground was dotted about with circular booths offering prizes for feats of skill: darts, hoop-la, air-pistol gallery, and more esoteric games involving goldfish bowls, ping-pong balls, miniature shrimping nets, and magnetic fishing rods. The prizes were large, shiny, and hideous; the booths ill-patronised; Dr. Adnan looked at them disparagingly.

"I consider those sideshows a gross waste of money, not worth it."

"Rather stingy with your cash, aren't you? I thought you proposed to give me a good time?"

"Come, come, my dear Miss Lucy Snowe, a girl of your sense would not wish to fritter money and energy on such stupidities; for one thing the odds against winnning any of those ugly objects are weighted at about a hundred to one."

Lucy knew this was true; however, she gave Dr. Adnan a malicious crossed-tooth grin and said that she wanted to win a goldfish.

"It will be company for me and Aunt Fennel at Wildfell Hall."

"I doubt if Mrs. Marsham allows pets. I do not at all approve of your dragging this poor old lady up to that place."

"Oh, and why not?" asked Lucy, receiving eight ping-pong balls in exchange for half a crown, and tossing one of them on to a glittering tableful of goldfish bowls with narrow necks; it bounced into a bowl, bounced out again, and was fielded by a world-weary lad with a shrimp-net.

"Bad luck. It is too solitary, that village. In Kirby, at least there is company and the amenities of civilisation. Up there, who knows what may go on?"

"She likes it up there. It's her native heath." Two more of Lucy's balls went astray.

"Hard luck. Well, we shall see. Myself, I think Mrs. Marsham will change her mind. You will arrive there this evening to find yourself not welcome. Then what?"

"Back to Mrs. Tilney, I suppose." Three more balls bounced off the table.

"Hard lines. Ah well, I suppose, if the worst comes to the worst, my housekeeper could accommodate you."

"Oh, so you have a housekeeper, do you?" The last ball shot on to the grass.

"Tough cheese. Naturally I have a housekeeper, a most capable one. She has a genius for cookery (an accomplishment I doubt that you possess, Lucy Snowe); she is also kind-hearted, unmalicious, and intelligent."

"A perfect paragon," said Lucy coldly. "As a matter of fact I cook quite well."

"I rejoice to hear it. Shall we try this roundabout?"

"Yes, let's. Isn't it pretty?"

"Remarkably so. It quite puts me in mind of your aunt's art."

"Yes, it does, doesn't it. Talking of which—"

"A—a! Pleasure first. Allow me to help you up."

The main roundabout was indeed charming. The seats—gaily painted horses—hung on ropes in rows of three round a central steam-organ whose silvered pipes rose up to a cluster of baroque decoration embodying enormous sequins and fluted glass in gaudy red, green, yellow, and sugar-pink. Dr. Adnan swung Lucy expertly on to a central horse and took a seat beside her on the outer one, nodding significantly as he did so to the man in charge.

"One of your patients?" inquired Lucy.

"Just so. How small you look perched on that fiery steed. Ah well, we have a proverb in Turkey: all excellent things are found in little packets."

"We have it too; but I thought you said young ladies as thin as I were not considered—"

"Hold tight, we are off!"

Lucy could not help suspecting that Dr. Adnan had bribed his ex-patient to run the roundabout at twice the normal pace, for they soon accelerated to a frenzied, a demonic speed; the fair ground about them blurred into a series of vague stripes, and the centrifugal pull swung their horses out until the cables were nearly horizontal; Adnan must have been a habitué, for he rode nonchalantly, with one elbow crooked round his rope and the other arm gallantly supporting Lucy, who found she had to use all her energy to stay sitting on her horse and to keep breathing; as soon as she snatched in a gulp of air it seemed to be sucked away out of her backwards until she felt like a balloon that has been untied and left to whirl about until it expends itself.

"How you can sit there so calmly—" she gasped, when the mad circuit began to slow down and gravity reasserted its pull.

Dr. Adnan smiled imperturbably.

"It is all those days of youth spent riding a mettlesome camel in the desert."

"Are there camels in Turkey?" Lucy asked with suspicion.

"If there were not, how could I have ridden them? Allow me!" He lifted her down and supported her solicitously while her endolymph continued to revolve.

"Now, how about a turn on the Dodgems?"

"Good God, no!"

"You may come in a car with me and I shall drive; all you need do is relax."

"Thanks, but I would definitely prefer not!"

Lucy had already had experience of Dr. Adnan's driving; after their encounter on the dentist's doorstep he had swept her down to the fun fair in his Alfa with an insouciant disregard for steep hills, blind turns, and traffic lights; she felt sure that his technique on the Dodgems would be still more uninhibited.

"I'd like a hamburger now," she said firmly. "All that release of adrenalin has made me hungry. And then I must go back to my aunt."

"Devoted girl! Very well, if you insist."

Taking her arm, he piloted her to the hamburger bar where he bought her a Giant Log Cabin Planter's Punchburger and a Super Kreemy Dairy Nut Maple Butter Swiss Surprise.

"Now tell me about yourself. You interest me greatly, dear Miss Lucy Snowe," he said, taking an enormous bite of his own Kingsize Yorkshire Bangerburger. "For instance, what is your pro-

fession? Something tells me you do not intend to spend your life
washing up dishes for old ladies."

"I'm a pianist; going to be a pianist."

"Aha! With whom do you study?"

"I'm going to learn with Max Benovek."

He looked up sharply; studied her attentively.

"So? It is to be hoped that you will prove a speedy and pro-
ficient pupil."

"I shall," Lucy said with calm certainty.

"And how shall you afford his fees? Players of a reputation such
as his, in a state of health such as his, do not teach for chicken-
feed."

"He said I was not to worry about his fees. So I'm not worrying.
But of course I shall pay him back if I get the chance. In the
meantime I've sent him one of Aunt Fennel's pictures; it was
the best present I could think of."

"Good God, my dear girl, what a singularly reckless thing to
do!" Adnan appeared startled and not best pleased; he set his
coffee mug down with a splashing jolt.

"Why?" It was Lucy's turn to scrutinise him intently; she pushed
aside her fringe.

"Why? Are you not aware that Benovek is a friend of Picasso,
of Britten, Kermansky, Writtstein? If he likes this picture—as no
doubt he will—in no time there will be a horde of experts and
collectors descending like lemmings, like locusts, hunting for every
scrap of material that your aunt ever pinned together."

"So what? That's what I hope. They'll pay handsomely, and
the old girl will end her days in comfort."

"Lucy, Lucy, you are a simple, naïve, trusting girl! (That is why
I have taken such a fancy to you)," Dr. Adnan said in parenthesis.
"But I think it unlikely that matters will work out as you expect,
I think it very unlikely. For one thing there is the small but important question of present ownership. All those dear souls in the
village who still have pictures; do you think they are likely to
endow your aunt with the proceeds if art dealers come offering
them hundreds of pounds?"

"Of course they will," Lucy said stoutly, but she did suffer a
slight qualm. Ought she to write a warning to Max Benovek? No,

the thing was simply to get on with collecting pictures as fast as possible. Living up at Appleby would facilitate this.

"Then what about the uncle who employs you to hunt down the old lady's works? If they become international art treasure it will complicate his affairs. Did you know that an export licence is needful if you ship out of the U.K. a picture or bit of sculpture worth more than two thousand pounds? The worthy British are not averse to selling their best art abroad; they just want to be sure they make plenty of cash out of it."

"I somehow doubt if Aunt Fennel's pictures would be valued at sums like that. Who decides, anyway?" Lucy took another bite of Planter's Punchburger.

"There is a Reviewing Committee for the Export of Works of Art."

"You seem to know a lot about it?" She glanced at him narrowly.

"To be sure. I take an interest in all such matters. So you see it is to be hoped that Benovek acts with discretion."

"Oh, he will," Lucy said with confidence.

"You are in love with this Benovek," Dr. Adnan said crossly. "It is a great piece of folly on top of all your other follies. How could you have embarked on such a short-term venture—"

Lucy's mouth dropped open; her face slowly went pink.

"What utter nonsense!" she said.

"Nonsense? Every time you speak of him your face, your voice, your whole personality changes. For the better, one can't deny, love is a very humanising influence which there is no doubt you need, but what a waste! It makes one impatient."

"How can you be so silly? I only met him once for fifteen minutes. Anyway, I don't see what concern it is of yours if I am in love with the whole Vienna Philharmonic Orchestra," Lucy said with spirit. "And now I should like to go back to my aunt if you'll be so kind as to drive me; Fawcett must have finished with her, or just about."

Adnan looked at his watch.

"I doubt it; but very well. I was going to offer to take you back to my house and give you a choice of one of the aunt's pictures that I have there," he said. "Mind, it was against my own inclinations, but one must occasionally perform a disinterested action;

and a single picture I think I might be able to part with. Two? No, I think not. One, however, you may have! In token of my friendly regard for you."

"That's big of you; I appreciate it," Lucy said drily. She glanced at him, half touched, half suspicious. "I'll take you up on that, but not right now." She looked at her own watch. "I really am anxious to get back to Fawcett's surgery."

"If you must! What a stickler for punctuality. But how will you ever have a chance to come and select your picture when you are washing dishes at Wildfell Hall?"

"I guess Mrs. Marsham will give me an evening off now and then in between the measles."

He paid the bill, and they crossed the promenade and descended the steps of the subterranean car park.

"The Borough Surveyor," Adnan told Lucy, leisurely selecting a key and opening the passenger door of his Alfa, "informs me that this place is highly dangerous. Never use it in stormy weather unless drowning is your preferred death."

"Oh really? Why?" asked Lucy, wishing he would hurry.

"Inadequate drainage. If the sea were to break over the promenade—as occasionally happens in a northeast gale—in sufficient quantity to cover the cars—to prevent people driving them away—"

"Yes; I see—" She gave a slight shudder, scanning the dark, cavernous place. "Nasty, wouldn't it be? I don't so much mind the thought of drowning, but to drown in a trap—"

"Just so." He started his engine, and paused at the barrier to pay. "So in stormy weather it is better to risk the chance of a parking ticket."

"Speaking of which," Lucy said, "I do hope you were right when you said it was okay to leave little PHO outside Fawcett's. I didn't like the look of those double lines."

"Oh, the police never come up so far. I have left my car there for hours when playing chess with Bill Fawcett."

"Yes, but you and Bill Fawcett are probably on very pally terms with the local fuzz—he extracts their molars, you deliver their babies—"

"No, no, there is no such corruption in this town I assure you!"

"Except for inadequate draining in the car park and the indiscretions of the Borough Surveyor."

"As to that," said Adnan cheerfully, whirling his steering wheel and turning up a steep incline off the promenade, "he has told me far worse things about the state of the reservoir on Appleby High Moor. The contractor (a brother-in-law of the mayor) cheated on the quantity of concrete required, skimped on the quality, the whole two thousand tons of water might break loose at any moment—"

"Oh, charming! And you still say I did wrong to take Aunt Fennel out of Reservoir Street, down which I presume the whole two hundred thousand tons would come cascading?"

"Oh, I daresay it is quite a remote contingency, after all. And now if you will excuse me—" He pulled up outside Fawcett's and glanced at his watch. "I really am rather late for my family planning and cervical smear clinic; the charm of your company has seduced me, but duty calls—"

He reached across and opened Lucy's door, collected her hand neatly on the way back, pressed a rapid kiss on it, and levered her out of the car, all in one smooth sequence of movement. Then the door slammed and the Alfa spurted away.

"Well!" said Lucy gazing after him in astonishment. "If that's oriental politeness! *He's* late—the rude rat!"

She ran indignantly up Fawcett's three immaculately white front steps and pressed the brass bell.

"Miss Culpepper? The very old lady?" Fawcett's nice little receptionist-nurse—a velvet-skinned, kittenish child of surely no more than sixteen—was nevertheless at least five months pregnant; ought to have attended Adnan's family planning clinic, Lucy thought uncharitably. "The old lady in the white hat? Oh, yais, she left *ages* ago."

"She left? But I thought Mr. Fawcett said he was going to be at least two hours with her?"

"Oh yais, he got through *ever* so much quicker than he thought he would."

"But I told her to wait here till I came to pick her up!"

"Did you?" The receptionist was not really interested. "Yais, she went off; remembered some shopping she wanted to do, I expect. Yais, *ever* such a long time ago, that would be."

She had an extraordinary accent; a hopeful attempt at cockney overlying her native Yorkshire.

"You didn't notice which way she went?"

"Aoh, naoh!"

I suppose she might have gone back to Mrs. Tilney's to finish her packing, Lucy thought with a pang of guilt. She herself had meant to go and do a final tidy-up while the dentistry was in process, if she had not been beguiled away by Dr. Adnan's offer of coffee and entertainment.

"Well, okay; thanks," she said crossly, and turned uphill to where she had left little PHO parked. But little PHO was there no longer; it seemed that Lucy had lost both her aunt and her car.

"Your Lucy's sent you a parcel now," sniffed Dee Lawrence, stomping in with the large corrugated-and-paper-wrapped square. "Want me to undo it?"

She set it down on the piano with an off-hand thump.

Max Benovek raised his eyes from the *Guardian* foreign news page. His face today had the bluish pallor of a lightless bulb; his movements were heavy and slow as if he had to plan each one beforehand in kinesiological terms of direction and muscle-power; this inertia was not relaxation but the wary avoidance of pain. Just the same, when Dee laid down the parcel a light came on in his eyes. He half lifted a hand and then let it fall.

"Not just at the moment, thanks, Dee," he said mildly. "Rees-Evans is due round quite soon; no need to have a lot of string and clutter lying round when he arrives."

"He won't be along for *hours* yet," sniffed Dee. "I noticed him having coffee with the matron as I came by; she was training all her magnetism on him; bet she'd do it with him in a wheelbarrow if only he'd drop the handkerchief."

"Really, Dee!" His tone was weary, not affronted; her flights of malice were more than he could be bothered to follow.

"Oh, sorry, sorry!" Dee was edgy these days; her large, hearty personality had become a focus of tension. She looked at the parcel with exasperation, longing to get it unpacked, disposed of, and tidied away, yet she could not help being secretly pleased that Max seemed in no hurry to undo it.

"Oh well, if you don't want to look at it I'll wrap up those tapes for the B.B.C. and take them down for the messenger. Had your pills? Drink of lemon barley? Right, I'll be back in half an hour or so."

As soon as her firm tread had died completely away down the corridor Max, who had listened with care, got up out of his armchair and moved slowly over to the piano. He had become weaker since Lucy's visit, and also thinner; his shoulder-blades, elbow-knobs, and hip-bones protruded angularly from the dark silk robe he wore. But his expression was calm, intent, and purposeful.

The knots in the string defeated him, however. After two or three minutes' struggle he gave up, sweating, and looked round. A pair of nail-scissors lay on the dressing-table; he made his way across the room and then carefully back with them; he haggled through the tough string. The parcel was secured as well with lavish quantities of gummed brown-paper tape, one layer on top of another. This had stiffened to the solidity of wood; Benovek scratched and stabbed at it unavailingly with the puny scissors.

"Hellish stuff!" He was breathless, half with effort, half with rage at his own inadequacy. "If that gnat-like creature could do it up, I ought to be able to undo it. She certainly is an efficient girl, blast her." He looked with a curious sense of comfort at the address, written large and black in felt-tip: MAX BENOVEK, Queen Alexandra Sanatorium, Coulsham, Surrey, and the return address, equally firm: LUCY CULPEPPER, Poste Restante, Kirby. "I must get her playing Beethoven; why didn't I make her while she was here?"

"Hey!" Rees-Evans had come in behind him. "What goes on here? Undoing parcels? Where's your guard-dog? She ought to be doing that."

"Oh, she's away on some errand or other."

"Well, let me do it. You sit down."

"Thanks, Hugh."

"What is it, a framed certificate to say you passed your R.C.M. Intermediate? Oh no, Kirby, I see; your north-country admirer. It'll be Yorkshire pudding, a frozen slab; all you do is heat and serve."

"I've never yet had genuine Yorkshire pudding," Max remarked absently. "Every time this delicacy has appeared in whatever form —and they have been numerous—somebody at the table has said,

'Ah, this isn't Yorkshire pudding as it should be,' but none of the descriptions as to what it should be have ever tallied." His tone was vague, but his eyes never moved from the lengths of paper tape that Rees-Evans was stripping, with casual strength, from the parcel.

"Yorkshire pudding ought to crunch, like toast. What shall I do with this garbage?" Rees-Evans dropped a handful on the floor and stepped on it.

"Leave it there. Dee can tidy it when she comes back," Max said indifferently. "Can you undo the corrugated stuff?"

"Easily." He tore it apart with one rending tug. "There you are, then; something to hang over your bed, would it be?" He removed a last layer of *Kirby Advertiser*.

"Good heavens."

"Good heavens, as you say." Rees-Evans stared blankly at the canvas he had unwrapped, and then crossed the room and stood it upright on the piano, leaning against the wall. "A Yorkshire primitive," he said with awe. "Eden as seen by a Rochdale Pioneer."

Max Benovek said nothing but, as he sat looking at the picture, he began to smile. It was a smile of such pleasure that Rees-Evans, turning to glance at him, was visited by the insane thought:

"He could recover. There *have* been cases of spontaneous remission. Even now, even in his condition, I believe he could recover! I've never seen him look like that before. I don't think I've ever even seen him *smile* before."

"Adam and Eve and the serpent," Max said dreamily, "I never saw a longer serpent, did you, Hugh? 'Some flow'rets of Eden ye still inherit, But the trail of the serpent is over them all.' She's got the greenness of Eden, hasn't she? That's the thing we've lost. Green never lasts at its greenest. But in Eden it did."

"Lot of character about the participants, too," Rees-Evans said, grinning. "You can see Adam's an indecisive dreamer and Eve obstinate as they come."

"And the serpent is a species of Hamlet, blaming them both for the rôle he has to play; he has tied a knot in his tail from sheer tension."

"I always did have a soft spot for the serpent. After all, it wasn't even as if he wanted the apple for himself; it was a rotten part to be assigned."

"Nobody is ever assigned the part they would have chosen for themselves." Benovek looked down at his hands, thin and transparent as bunches of quills.

"And that's the truth! Oh well, let's have a look at you, shall we?"

While the examination was proceeding, Dee bounced back into the room.

"Well!" she said. "Whatever has been going on here? I never in all my born days saw such a mess. Didn't want the room untidied for Dr. Rees-Evans, huh!"

"Tidy it up, will you, Dee, there's a good girl," Max said calmly. She did so, lips pressed together, with ostentatious thoroughness. A sheet of writing-paper drifted out from the wrappings, and she picked it up.

"Here, don't you want to read your billet-doux? This is becoming a real Daddy-Long-Legs affair," she said to Rees-Evans, who smiled politely and said nothing.

Max took the paper without comment and held it while Rees-Evans completed his check. Then he read the first line.

Dear Max, I wish I could be there when you opened this. I do wish I could have seen your face when you first looked at it.

"Good Lord," said Dee, for the first time deigning to notice the canvas on the piano. "Is that what Lucy Culpepper sent? What a weird production. Looks more like the effort of a six-year-old to me. Is that how this famous great-aunt spends her time?"

"Miss Lawrence," said Rees-Evans, glancing at his watch, "I wonder if you could spare a moment to come down to my office with me and collect a couple of books I promised to lend Mr. Benovek? You will? That's so kind of you—I must really get on, I'm an hour behind schedule as it is."

Pausing after he had ushered Dee out of the door, he said, "Didn't you tell me that Writtstein was coming to see you one day this week?"

"Wednesday." Max raised his eyes briefly from the letter.

"I wonder what he'll make of the Rochdale Eden," Rees-Evans said, and gently closed the door behind him.

I do wish I could have seen your face when you first looked at it.

Max raised his eyes to the blank wall opposite.

He had no need to make such a wish. He saw her face continually: pale, freckled, alert, looking up through a fine spray of hair like some friendly sea-urchin. He knew its contours by heart; he enveloped her with thought all day long, quarrying out her outline from the cliff of his ignorance, brooding, speculating, probing, discarding. Each letter from her directed his exploration to a new quarter.

No, but Max, don't you think it is a beautiful picture? And it is just like Aunt Fennel herself. When you meet her (you must meet her, Max, you'll love her) you feel that she is completely innocent and good, and also slightly mad, or at least off-centre; her values are quite individual, not formed at all from anybody else's. Do you suppose this is genius? Or a kind of genius, anyway? You have genius too, I know, but I didn't get this feeling about you, that you hardly realised the rest of the world existed —on the contrary, your separation from the world seemed to cause you distress. (I hope I don't distress you more by saying this?) I'd like to think that Aunt Fennel's picture will give you back a little bit of the world.

I must stop now—I bought some paper and string at a stationer's and I'm parcelling up the picture at Kirby post office. Tomorrow, after the dentist, I take Aunt Fennel up to Wildfell Hall, where I'm going to help look after her and all the old things with measles for a couple of weeks. I hate to waste even this much time from our lessons, Max. But I do feel an extraordinary bond with Aunt Fennel—I simply *can't* leave her till I'm sure she's okay. And it's good to feel useful and needed. I'm sure you'll understand —I feel this bond with you, too! But the minute I have Aunt F. comfortably settled I'm coming south. Love from Lucy.

P.S. Remember the Carados girl I mentioned in an earlier let-

ter? I found out a funny thing. Tell you in my next. But I may
not be able to write for a while—bother this postal strike!

"Useful and needed!" Max said bitterly.

"Who's useful and needed?" Rees-Evans had come back. "Left
my stethoscope behind," he explained blandly, strolling over to
take another look at Aunt Fennel's green Eden.

"I thought you were an hour behind schedule? What have you
done with Dee?"

"Set her to arranging my books; I thought she seemed to be
getting you down a bit. Who's useful and needed?"

"I don't seem to be, for one. That girl's becoming more and
more involved with getting the great-aunt settled—I'm beginning
to have a premonition about her lessons."

"What sort of premonition?" Rees-Evans asked uneasily.

"Oh, I suppose, that too many things will conspire to delay her
and that she'll come south just too late. That I'll never teach
her."

When you have lost both a car and an aunt, which do you seek
first? And how do you set about your search?

Lucy stood on the pavement in a state, for once, of total indeci-
sion, empty-handed, empty-minded, bereft. She could not even, as
yet, feel rage at the receptionist for her stupidity, at Adnan for
his delaying tactics, at herself for letting Adnan delay her. Rage
would come later. All she experienced at present was shock and
loss.

A sea-mist had descended, with the unpredictable suddenness
of coastal weather. Kirby, in its cuplike hollow, was muffled and
ghostly; the little pantiled houses climbed the hill into obscurity,
the masts in the harbour dwindled away, insubstantial as pencil
scribbles against a white blankness. Traffic seemed to have come
to a halt; the only sound was the regular, melancholy cry of the
lighthouse, warning ships to beware of the narrow tricky harbour
approach and the flanking merciless cliffs.

It was pointless, of course, to stand waiting in the empty street,
hoping for a miracle; Lucy set off walking at a rapid pace. Mrs.
Tilney's first: perhaps Aunt Fennel was there, perhaps she was
safe; perhaps. All the unformulated doubts, the half-beliefs that

Lucy had entertained regarding Aunt Fennel's fears now returned, nagging and pricking; the old lady's dread projected itself on to Lucy and assumed in the grey dimness, a sudden reality, all the more threatening because of its unknown nature. The existence of That Other One, which hitherto Lucy had treated with scepticism, now all at once became possible, probable, *certain*; she caught herself listening for the echo of footfalls behind her on the cobbled hill, and shook her head impatiently.

Dear Max, here we are caught up in a proper old horror-comic. All we need now is an eerie shriek and some vampire talons reaching out of the brume. Oh Max, why the devil did I let myself go off junketing with that smooth-tongued Turk? I thought I could find out some more about Aunt Fennel's pictures and who had them; no, but that's not the whole truth, I thought it would be fun, he seemed genuinely friendly.

And it *had* been fun too, she thought angrily, reaching Mrs. Tilney's gate at a half run, only now all the pleasure, in retrospect, had turned sour and seemed a heartless piece of irresponsibility while the old lady might be lost and wandering.

But perhaps she was safe all the time at Mrs. Tilney's.

Suddenly very tired, Lucy leaned against the door-jamb, pressing the rusty bell. For a long time there was no answer. But surely somebody must be in the house, all the aged infirm residents could not simultaneously have decided to go out in such murky and inclement weather? Probably they were too deaf to hear the bell. But what about Mrs. Tilney herself?

At last the door was opened by a frail man whom Lucy remembered to have been among the other motionless gargoyles ranged in front of the TV set; he peered suspiciously round the edge of the door, ostentatiously pulling a fawn plaid muffler up to his ears against the wreaths of fog that instantly began drifting in among the umbrella-stands and bicycles in the crowded hallway.

"Is Miss Culpepper here?" Lucy asked. His face remained quite blank; he seemed either deaf or withdrawn into some unapproachable region of himself; having let Lucy in he evidently felt that his responsibility was ended and limped back into the parlour. Lucy, following, scanned the group who were now seated patiently, like old dogs round a fireless hearth, watching the blank

TV; apparently it was not yet time for the evening's programmes to begin.

Aunt Fennel was not among them.

"Is Miss Culpepper upstairs?" Lucy asked loudly. One or two heads slowly shook, either in non-comprehension or denial. "Well, can you tell me where Mrs. Tilney is?"

"Isn't she in the kitchen?" an elderly voice presently volunteered doubtfully. "The kitchen's where she mostly is, afternoons."

If so, why not answer the bell, Lucy thought, but she thanked the speaker and retreated, picking a cautious way between thin old legs and out-thrust white sticks.

The kitchen, filled with the usual miasma of stale frying and unclean, aged animals, also contained the solution to why Mrs. Tilney did not answer the bell. She slept in a basket-chair among her pets, her head nodding forward at an uncomfortable angle, a half-empty bottle of Gordon's on the floor beside her. From time to time she let out a rattling snore. The room was in its accustomed state of filth; a large washbasin full of potatoes stood on the table waiting to be peeled, for supper presumably.

Looking at the empty sleeping face with its open mouth, slack and dribbling, its broken purple veins, crumpled cheeks, and air of total surrender, Lucy experienced a disconcerting reversal of feeling; instead of a drunken harpy who made a living by exploiting poor old people in worse case than herself, Mrs. Tilney suddenly appeared ill, exhausted, pitiable. Lucy looked with a kind of anguish at her gnarled swollen hands, shiny with grease from washing dishes. There seemed no sense in rousing her from a sleep of such exhaustion; besides, from the moment of entering the house, Lucy had felt in her bones that Aunt Fennel was not there. However she climbed the stairs to make sure, negotiated the guardian Venus on the upper floor, and looked into the room where Aunt Fennel slept with the two other old ladies. Nobody there. A handkerchief and spare tin of raspberry leaf pastilles lay on a chair where they had been discarded that morning. The room smelt of fusty old ladies. Standing by the bed, wondering what to do next, Lucy had an unexpected burning stab of pain in her side; she could not decide whether its origin was mental or physical; it felt like the clench of grief on her heart. Not only grief:

shame. I have lost my family, she thought, and it was due to my own stupidity and carelessness.

Two hot difficult tears found their way down her cheeks.

Impatiently she shook herself and hurried downstairs. Mrs. Tilney still slept; the old gargoyles still waited trustfully in front of the blank screen; Lucy let herself out into the fog.

Her obvious next step was to call the police; she started hurrying down the steeply tilted little terraced streets hunting for telephone booths, which seemed scarcer here than red herrings that grow in the wood. Better make for the harbour and shopping district. She wished she had not left her duffel coat in little PHO when she went off with Adnan to the fun fair; the sea-mist struck dank and chill through her cotton shirt and jeans.

Where could Aunt Fennel *be?* What could she be doing? In the last few days the old lady had become so completely, trustingly geared to Lucy's directing force that it seemed almost impossible to imagine her suddenly taking independent action, going off into the fog on some ploy of her own. Down to the drugstore for powdered elm bark or lettuce soap? No, because all the stores were shut, early closing day, and Aunt Fennel knew that perfectly well, for she had reminded Lucy to buy writing paper and shampoo before lunch.

Unexpectedly a tall black shape like a ninepin loomed up out of the dimness; with immense relief Lucy realised that it was a policeman crunching ponderously along, pausing to peer into foggy alleys and through the windows of parked cars.

She hailed him hopefully.

"Can you help me, please? I've lost an old lady and a car."

"An old lady and a car?" He scrutinised her with not unreasonable doubt. "What kind of a car, then?"

"A plum-coloured Austin A.30." And what kind of an old lady, Lucy thought. You might well ask. A unique old lady, an ambiguous old lady, an irreplaceable old lady.

"Was the old lady *driving* the car?" the policeman asked.

Even in her distress Lucy found it hard not to chuckle at the thought of Aunt Fennel, green eyeshade in place, white linen hat pulled well down, careering off through Kirby at the wheel of little PHO.

"No, that's what's so mysterious, you see; the two mishaps seem to have been quite separate."

"Where had you left the vehicle?"

"In Market Street, outside Fawcett the dentist's. And the old lady was *inside* the dentist's."

"Oh well, if you left the vehicle in Market Street, it will probably have been towed away by the police." The constable sounded reproving; he put away his notebook. "That's a no-parking zone, didn't you know? Didn't you see the double lines? Your best plan is to go down to the station and make inquiries there."

"The station?"

"The police station. Round the other side of the harbour. That's what you ought to do."

Lucy felt an easing of her heart. This seemed such a rational explanation that she wondered why it had not occurred to her already.

"And the old lady? Do you think they towed her away too?"

His face remained blank and unresponsive.

"Is this old lady subject to fainting fits or blackouts?"

"Not so far as I know. She's my aunt, Miss Culpepper."

Out came the notebook again.

"How do you spell that?"

Lucy spelt it for him, slowly, twice, but noticed with irritation that he still got it wrong as he laboriously wrote it down. "Well, you'd better ask at the station about her too, that's all I can advise," he said then, unhelpfully. "If there's been any report of an accident they'll be able to tell you there."

"Well, thanks," Lucy said without joy. "What's the quickest way to the police station?"

He gave her directions, but seemed quite surprised when she followed them, as if he suspected her of perpetrating some dubious teen-age joke.

Kirby police station was solidly built of granite in a rococo style; it looked like a setting for the kind of grim fairytale in which people are shovelled into ovens or rolled downhill in barrels of nails.

But the middle-aged sergeant who interviewed Lucy seemed not unfriendly.

"You lost a car, miss? A pink Austin, registration PHO 898A? Can I see your licence, please?"

Lucy handed over her papers and waited, with the usual feelings of anxiety and guilt, while he studied them for a long time in silence. How stupid it is, she thought irrelevantly, that society always makes one feel guilty for the wrong thing. I am to blame for losing Aunt Fennel, but if they punish me it will be for doing something that I didn't even know was forbidden. Wilbie's always saying that the tax authorities ignore his legitimate expenses and oblige him to invent a lot of false ones. Though that's not a very good analogy; whatever society did to him, I bet Wilbie would be as crooked as a pair of dividers. Why did I think of him?

Having entered her mind, the thought of Wilbie would not leave, but stuck there like a burr; she imagined how angry, how disinclined to help he would be if he knew of her present predicament.

"You got yourself into the jam, Princess, you get yourself out again! Of all the goddam stupid things to do, getting into parking trouble abroad! If there's one thing I cannot abide, it's stupidity. No, I will *not* pay your fine."

She wondered how much the fine would be, if there were a choice of fine or prison. The question seemed trivial compared with her worry about Aunt Fennel. Except that if she had to go to prison, who would look for the old lady? She was on the point of bursting out with this when the sergeant handed back her documents and turning shouted over his shoulder,

"Harold!"

A distant voice answered indistinguishably.

"Pink A.30, registration PHO 898A, left in Market Street 2 p.m.? We got the owner here." Then turning back to Lucy he said, "Well, we won't be hard on you this time, as you haven't been in this country long. But don't do it again, mind!"

"You're not going to send me to prison?" She could hardly believe her ears.

The sergeant grinned. "Not this time."

"And you've really got the car?"

"It's down in the yard at the rear."

"What about my aunt? Is there any hope you've got her up your sleeve too?"

The return of little PHO had given Lucy new heart; she felt like a snail that has had its shell restored.

"Ah, now, I'm afraid we can't work miracles, young lady! We'll keep a look-out for your aunt, that's all we can promise. Can you give me a description of her?"

Lucy did so, but the sergeant shook his head.

"Kirby's full of old ladies like that."

"You're telling me. But where could she have *got* to?" Lucy cried in despair. "She's nearly deaf, she's almost blind, she walks so slowly—"

Are those things the truth, she suddenly wondered. Have I a totally false conception of Aunt Fennel? Has she been skilfully deceiving me all this time?

"Probably gone into Joe Lyons for a cup of tea," the sergeant suggested bracingly, shepherding Lucy to the door. It was plain that, while sympathetic, he thought she was making a great pother over a trifle, for which some perfectly reasonable explanation would soon present itself.

"Now, you just step round to the back, miss, and pick up your car—sign this and give it to the constable on duty there—and then if I were you I'd go up to the old lady's lodgings again; ten to one she's found her way home by now. But keep in touch with us, and I'll put out a call for her. Oh, and miss—"

"Yes?"

"If you find she has turned up at home, you won't forget to let us know, will you? We don't want to go wasting time and man-power looking for someone that isn't lost, do we?" He smiled at Lucy benevolently. "Now, don't you worry; if she's been in any accident we'll hear soon enough."

And what good will that do, thought Lucy glumly, going down some back steps to a dusky, mist-filled yard where little PHO stood humbly among a lot of police Jaguars. A traffic policeman was waiting impatiently to oversee the removal, so Lucy did not wait to put on her coat, which was bundled on the floor at the back with the blanket and sleeping-bag, but switched on lights and heater and hurriedly drove away.

I'll go back to Mrs. Tilney's first, she thought, that was good advice. But if Aunt Fennel still isn't there, *then* what shall I do?

By the time she reached Reservoir Street true dark had descended, thickened by the fog. She drew up outside Mrs. Tilney's (the massive pile of junk in the front yard was visible by the dim diffused light of a street lamp ten yards off) and reached into the back for her duffel coat.

Her hand encountered something warm, which moved.

Lucy had had a long, tiring, and anxious day; her nerves were not in a good state. She let out a yelp of pure fright and snatched her hand back.

A timid, quavering voice said, "Is that Lucy?"

"*Aunt Fennel!* My goodness, is that you?"

Hardly able to believe it, Lucy tipped forward the passenger seat and scrambled into the rear.

Feeling around among the tangle of coat, blanket, and kapok-lined bag, she found a hand, an arm, a bony shoulder; the old lady was tightly jammed in the small gap between the front and rear seats, with the duffel coat pulled over her head. Gingerly, carefully, Lucy helped extract her from this awkward slot and eased her on to the back seat. Even now she could hardly believe that Aunt Fennel was really there; she hugged the old lady, felt her up and down, hugged her again.

"But, Aunt Fennel, what were you doing there? Did you go to sleep and slip down? What *happened*? I've been worried to death about you—I thought somebody must have abducted you! Didn't you wake when the police towed the car away?"

Two frail old arms came out and went round her neck; a claw-like finger was laid across her lips.

"*Hush*, dearie! Where are we?"

Aunt Fennel was whispering; Lucy suddenly realised that she was trembling, and tense as a bow-string. Something had frightened her badly—was frightening her still.

"We're outside Mrs. Tilney's. D'you want to go in? Pack up your things?"

"Is there anybody in the street, dearie?"

Lucy scanned the short, dimly lit terrace.

"Not a soul."

"Let's wait a little while, just the same. In—just in case." Aunt Fennel was silent a moment; Lucy could feel the pounding and fluttering of her heart, even through velour coat, cable-stitch cardigan, serviceable jersey dress, corset, vest, and liberty-bodice.

Or was it Lucy's own heart, thumping in a sudden acceleration of fear?

"You see, dearie," Aunt Fennel was whispering. "I *saw* him."

"Who? Who did you see?"

"That Other One. I'd come out of the dentist's, and you weren't there." There was no reproach in the mild voice.

"I'm *sorry*, Aunt Fen. I was a pig, not to get back in time."

"It didn't matter, dearie. You'd left the car unlocked, so I got in and sat in it."

"*That* was sensible." Lucy hugged the old lady again. Finding the car taken she had cursed herself for her negligence in leaving it unlocked; what a stroke of good fortune this had turned out to be.

"Was that when you saw That Other One?"

"Yes, dearie. I was sitting in the car when he came along; he went into the dentist's. But he didn't stop; he came out and stood looking up and down the street. He didn't see me though; well, of course, he wouldn't expect me to be sitting in a car, you see. Didn't look."

"How far away from you was he?"

"Just along the pavement."

"You were able to recognise him?"

"Oh yes, dearie. He has a special way of walking; bouncy; I'd know it if I met him in China. And those things he smokes too; I smelt them. I'd know him anywhere."

Professional observation, Lucy thought; the artist's eye. After her own recent agony of anxiety she was more inclined to take Aunt Fennel's story seriously; this sounded like genuine evidence.

"What happened then?"

"He went off along the street. And I hid down behind the car seat, in case he came back again looking for me."

"But, Aunt Fennel—why are you so positive he'd be looking for *you*?"

"Why else would he be in Kirby, dear?"

"I don't know. Doesn't he live here?"

"Oh no, dear. Goodness only knows where he lives."

"What does he do? What's his profession?"

"I don't know, dear. And if I did I wouldn't tell you."

The blank end again; there was no getting past it. "But Aunt

Fennel—what did you think when the police came and moved the car—did you think it was him taking it—or what?"

"No, dear, I heard their voices. I was worried of course," the old lady said simply, "but I knew you'd come and find me in the end."

Sometimes Lucy felt unequal to Aunt Fennel. This was one of the times. She swallowed, drew in a deep breath, squeezed the old lady's hand and, after a moment, said, "Well, I'd better finish those bits of packing and we'll be off. Do you want to stay in the car? I can lock you in."

"I think that would be best, dear."

"Shall I say good-bye to Mrs. Tilney and the others for you?"

Occasionally Aunt Fennel showed an unexpected vein of calm unsentimentality.

"No, dearie. They didn't mean anything to me and we shan't miss each other. Just you bring my things out."

On the long, dark drive up to Appleby, Lucy, partly to break the silence of undischarged question and emotional fatigue that had fallen between them, risked a topic that had been in her mind for days.

"Aunt Fennel?"

The old lady came out of a fit of abstraction.

"Yes, lovey?"

"You knew my father quite well when he was young, before he was married?"

There was another considerable pause. Then Aunt Fennel said, "Yes, I did, dear. Quite well. Both those boys. Their father and mother died when they were in their teens, you see, so I was their only relative."

There was some qualification in her tone; Lucy could not analyse it. She went on, "I'd like it very much if you'd tell me a bit about my father. Nobody ever has, you see—except Uncle Wilbie, and everything he says sounds like a great big jealous lie."

Aunt Fennel was silent for another long time.

"There's not really much to tell, dearie."

"There must be something," Lucy persisted.

"Well, dearie, I'll think, and tell you some day," Aunt Fennel said, with that same light, unexpected decisiveness. "But not just now. Not this evening. After all that fright, I'm a little bit tired."

Feeling justly rebuked, Lucy drove on over the dark moorland.
Guessing that the old people retired early, she had expected
Wildfell Hall to be cloaked in repose and obscurity. But this was
far from the case. Windows on several floors were lit and uncur-
tained; a considerable bustle prevailed.

"There you are!" Mrs. Marsham exclaimed, coming into the
portico as Lucy helped Aunt Fennel out of the car. "I thought
you said you'd be here at tea-time."

"We were held up; sorry." Lucy had no intention of going into
explanations; Mrs. Marsham did not wait for them.

"Well, now you've come, you can make yourself useful. I've put
your aunt in a small bedroom with one other old lady on the first
floor; she'd better go straight to bed."

"She hasn't had any supper," Lucy said coldly.

"Well, you can take up a tray to her room."

Lucy was ready to rebel against this high-handed treatment, but
Aunt Fennel interposed mildly, "I'd like that, dearie. I really am
rather tired."

Swallowing her resentment, Lucy helped Aunt Fennel upstairs
to a small, pleasant room, probably once a dressing room, which
looked out on to the front sweep. One of the two beds was already occupied. As soon as Mrs. Marsham had left them with their
luggage, instructing Lucy to come to the kitchen as soon as she
had settled her aunt, the inmate of the second bed shot upright.
Lucy recognised one of the two old ladies they had seen quarrelling about the ginger cat. The small, beady-eyed bald one; Chiddock, that was the name.

"Had measles?" she inquired importantly.

"Yes, both of us. Why, has anyone come down with it?" Lucy
rapidly extracted and disposed Aunt Fennel's immediate neces-
saries, pulled her cubicle curtain, and turned back the gay
knitted-patchwork bedcover. "Here's your nightie, Aunt Fennel;
I'll run and get you a hot-water bottle in a moment."

"My goodness, yes! Four or five of 'em have temperatures and
two has rashes—matron's in a rare old taking," Mrs. Chiddock
said with satisfaction at being able to convey such dramatic tid-
ings. "She hardly knows where to put 'em all for quarantine. And
that Mrs. Crabtree's very bad—got pneumonia with it. She ought

to go to hospital really, I heard the doctor say, but she's too ill to be moved."

Lucy felt more sympathy with the hard-pressed Mrs. Marsham and accelerated Aunt Fennel's slow progress into bed.

"There you are, Aunt Fen—hot bottle, rosemary, raspberry tablets—you know where the bathroom is, one door along—now I'll just nip down and get your supper-tray. Have you had yours?" she asked Mrs. Chiddock.

"Yes, dear, thank you. The rooms across the landing are the quarantines. Mind you don't go up to the next floor, that's matron's private quarters, she won't allow anyone up there. Where were you living before you came here, dear?" inquired Mrs. Chiddock of Aunt Fennel, obviously hoping for a good gossip. But Aunt Fennel took off her hearing aid and hung it with ostentatious care over the end of her bed.

"I'm afraid I'm nearly stone-deaf," she said loudly and slowly. "I shan't be able to hear you right across the room."

Mrs. Chiddock sank back, disappointed, to her transistor radio, as Lucy left the room.

In the kitchen Mrs. Marsham was darting efficiently about, boiling, sterilising, preparing hot drinks. "Help yourself to whatever you please out of the larder for your aunt," she told Lucy. "Do you mind waiting a bit for your own meal? I'm all behind with the bed patients and I'm expecting the doctor back for Mrs. Crabtree."

Hah, Lucy thought sourly; I bet he won't like having to come all the way up here at this time of night. Him and his family planning clinics.

She prepared a tray and a hot drink for Aunt Fennel and, having seen her supplied, was kept on the run by Mrs. Marsham for a couple of hours, taking aspirin and drinks to feverish patients, remaking beds, escorting tottering old inmates to the bathroom and emptying the slops of others who were too feeble to get up.

Real F. Nightingale stuff, she said to herself. Well, you asked for it and you got it. Dear Max, maybe you wouldn't approve of this, but really it's as well *someone* should be doing the job, there don't seem many other candidates. Apart from herself the help seemed to consist of a sulky girl from Kirby who grumbled that it was really her evening off and she didn't know what mum would say she was sure. Lucy was impressed, nonetheless, at how immaculate Mrs. Marsham succeeded in keeping Wildfell Hall despite the present crisis, despite the evidently impermanent and unreliable nature of her hired help. Every room she entered was spotless and tidy, floors shone with polish, the old people were plainly well fed and well cared for; what a contrast to Mrs. Tilney's ramshackle establishment. And yet, were the inmates really happy? There seemed an air of tension and anxiety about the place; but that could easily be attributable, Lucy conceded, to the epidemic. Or perhaps it was purely her own subjective reaction; it had been a long hard day. And was not over yet. At half-past ten the front-door bell rang. Lucy and Mrs. Marsham were trying to shepherd back to his own bed a slightly delirious old man who had been found wandering down the hallway under the impression that he must hurry or he would miss the night train to Euston.

"You answer it," panted Mrs. Marsham. "I've got him now. *Come* on, Mr. Cordwainer; I've booked a sleeper and they're keeping it for you, but they won't hold the train forever! I just hope Adnan's brought plenty of sedation; it's going to take a king-size dose to keep this one down."

Grinning, Lucy ran downstairs and opened the front door to Adnan. At sight of him, standing between the pillars of the portico, her amusement faded; she remembered too vividly the heart-wrenching anxiety of that afternoon.

"Ah, so you are all safely installed, dear Lucy Snowe!" he greeted her. "How delightful that is; it quite reconciles me to the need for this uncongenial visit. And the aunt—she is snugly bedded down I trust?"

"No thanks to *you*," Lucy said icily.

His black brows shot up. They were thick, like furry caterpillars. Tonight he wore a sheepskin car coat, with exotic embroidery, over a black whipcord boiler suit and Beau Brummel white stock. Despite her anger with him, Lucy could not resist looking to see if there were spurs on his black boots; there were not, but only just not; she felt he might have left them in the car.

"No thanks to me?" he said, but Mrs. Marsham leaned over the banisters and called in a low voice,

"Come up, Doctor, will you? I'd like you to look at Mrs. Crab-tree right away."

There was a long conference over Mrs. Crabtree, whose state, apparently, was causing grave anxiety. While this went on, Lucy, who had not been allowed into Mrs. Crabtree's sickroom, carried drinks to two other feverish patients and hot-water bottles to a whole series of unmeasled inmates who had been roused by all the disturbance and were fretfully complaining of cold, for the moorland night had turned sharp; she found a store of extra blankets and dealt them round. She also settled Aunt Fennel for the night.

"I *am* glad you brought me here, dearie," the old lady said drowsily. "This seems to be a very well-run place. I'm sure I shall be happy here."

With a wry grin over this, Lucy wondered where her own sleeping quarters were, and how soon she was likely to get to them.

About to leave the room, she was startled by a whisper from the other corner.

"Mrs. Crabtree gone yet?"

"Gone?"

"Gone. Died."

"What makes you so sure she's going to die?" Lucy snapped.

"Matron won't take any pains to save *her*," Mrs. Chiddock whispered with assurance. "Not after Alice kicking her blessed puss-cat like that. 'Sides, they was having terrible words last night. Heard 'em myself. Alice was very bad in the night—she slept in here, see—she asked me to go to matron for something to make her better. You go yourself, I said, *you* were the one said I took cheese off the trolley."

Spiteful old hag, Lucy thought.

"So she went upstairs to matron's room. *That's* not allowed, says I to myself, there's bound to be trouble. Sure enough, a few minutes after I heard 'em at it, hammer and tongs. You know you're not allowed up here, says matron, couldn't you wait twenty minutes till I come on night rounds? I'd a bin dead by then with this pain, says Alice, your evening rounds wouldn't a done me much good then, would they? None of your impertinence, my lady, says matron, or you can whistle for your medicine. Oh, I couldn't help laughing. You mark my words, matron won't take any pains to keep *her* alive."

Removing herself without regret from these ghoulish opinions, Lucy carried a load of bed linen downstairs and stuffed it into the Bendix. Shortly afterwards Mrs. Marsham appeared looking harassed.

"Make a pot of tea for me and the doctor, could you, while we finish the inoculations? We'll be down in five minutes or so. I expect you could do with a cup yourself."

"I would prefer eggnog," Adnan called softly and authoritatively over the banisters, "that is, if Miss Lucy knows how to make it?"

"Sure I know," muttered Lucy going to the pantry for eggs. "Certain you wouldn't like a four-course meal while I'm at it?"

However, on reflection eggnog seemed a good idea; she was hungry herself but too tired for solid food. She found eggs, milk, and a simple but efficient electric mixer like a power corkscrew; Mrs. Marsham, no doubt because of the unreliable labour force at her disposal, had equipped her establishment with all the most superior mechanical aids; there was a deep-freeze room, a self-cleaning oven, an infra-red grill, an electric scrubber, polisher, potato peeler. Lucy wondered how often they all went wrong.

"Eggnog, aha, delicious—she really does know how to make it!" said Adnan, materialising in the kitchen doorway. "I suppose you would not have a drop of cognac to put in it, dear Mrs. Marsham?"

Without replying, Mrs. Marsham unlocked a cupboard and brought out a bottle of Martell.

"Would you like some?" she said to Lucy. "I must say you've been a big help this evening. Don't know how we'd have managed without you." The words were civil enough but her tone and her eyes lacked warmth; she's the sort that hates to be under an obligation or beaten in an argument, Lucy thought; won't ever admit she could be wrong.

There was a thump and a groan from upstairs.

"If that's old Mr. Cordwainer fallen out of bed again—" Mrs. Marsham exclaimed angrily, "I'll really give him what-for this time." She ran up the stairs, the light of battle in her eye, brisk as if she were just beginning the day.

"Wonderful woman," remarked Adnan, sipping his eggnog.

"*How* glad I am that I am not married to her. Even as only one of the four wives permitted by the Koran she would be a pain in the neck."

He glanced sidelong at Lucy for her reactions to this, but she, having finished her own drink, was silently stacking crockery in the dishwasher.

"Dear Miss Lucy, I appear to be under a cloud. Why is that, tell me, pray." Placing his hand on his heart he sang softly,

> "I am under a cloud,
> Bloody but unbowed,
> Yet five times to the girl I cry
> Why, dear Lucy, tell me why?

"I hope you catch the Wordsworthian reference? When I came to the north of England I was careful to read up on all the appropriate literature! Sweet Lucy, child of nature, tell me how I have displeased you?"

"When I got back this afternoon I found that my aunt had left the dentist's hours before. I couldn't find her for ages and I was terribly worried about her."

"Now, how could I have known how long Fawcett would take?" Adnan asked reasonably.

"Also you said it would be quite okay to leave my car in Market Street, whereas in fact the police towed it away, and I had a lot of trouble and was lucky not to be fined."

He burst out laughing.

"Alas! Humble apologies! Now I see why I am in the rogues' gallery along with the rapacious uncle who wishes to grab all the paintings and stop paying the pension—what is his name, by the way?"

"The same as mine—not that it seems any concern of yours. Why do you ask?"

"My father—a man of great financial acumen—in the old days he would have been a Pasha—bought me some shares in an American firm called Culpepper's Pharmaceuticals; they continue to rise and I am very happy about them. Would that be your uncle's concern?"

"Yes, that's Uncle Wilbie." Lucy grinned a private grin into the bowels of the Splashmaster.

"Please turn this way when you smile; I do so admire the diagonal incisors! And also tell me what you are smiling about? I suppose the uncle's firm is so prosperous because it peddles heroin grown by poor exploited Turks?"

"I don't know about the heroin—though, as I do know my uncle, I wouldn't be a bit surprised."

"Then why the smile? Share this piece of irresistible humour with me—think how hard I have been working, how much I need cheering!"

Untrustworthy Adnan might be, a self-seeker, a dark horse, but there was no doubt that he would also be the person to appreciate an item of information that had caused Lucy exquisite amusement when she learned it by chance a year ago; her only frustration since then had been that there was not a single soul in whom she could confide it.

"Oh well, it's just—my uncle, you see, is so very respectable, he lives a lovely executive and golf-playing life and my aunt is well-born and knows the right people and my cousin knows even righter people and is scheduled to marry some Rockefeller—"

"So? All this is admirable—I see nothing to laugh at."

"All this admirable propriety is based on the immense sales of a little article called the Hymen Holsterette."

Adnan exploded with laughter.

"H.H.! I see! No wonder this worthy man now wishes to launch out as a collector of the arts. And do the aunt and cousin know on what their prosperity rests?"

"Goodness, no!"

"So how did you discover?"

"Oh, some business acquaintance of my uncle's that he hadn't seen in a long time happened to meet him once when he'd had to take me in to Boston to get my eyes tested, and addressed him as H.H., and my uncle shut him up pretty smartly. Those aren't my uncle's initials, so they kind of stuck in my mind. And when I picked up the information from a boy at summer camp that this particular article was called a double-H, it all clicked into place."

"You have no real proof, however?"

"Oh yes I have, because then I pretended I knew all about it to Russ—to my uncle's personal assistant, and he was annoyed —and kind of scared too—said I'd better not let Wilbie find out I knew or there'd be real trouble."

"So you did not?"

"No. Not that he could do anything."

Adnan shook his head at her.

> "They followed from the snowy bank
> Those footmarks one by one
> Into the middle of the plank
> And further there were none!"

"Lucy, Lucy, your talent for finding out about things is liable to get you pushed under a train one of these days unless you keep it in check. You are too shrewd a girl for your own good, I sadly fear! While you are resident in this establishment I should particularly warn you—"

Mrs. Marsham came back into the kitchen, rolling down her immaculate sleeves.

"Still here?" she said, not very hospitably, to the doctor. "I thought you'd have gone already. They're all settled now. But you'll be up in the morning early, to see Mrs. Crabtree?"

"Yes," he said sighing. "She might make it. She has a tough constitution, that one. Have you given me back the box of B-serum?"

"It's by your bag there."

"Ah; thank you. I will say good night then. Good night," he said formally to Lucy, and walked out through the hall with his rapid, assured step. The front door slammed and they heard the Alfa roar off down the drive.

"Do you want me to spell you on night-nursing?" asked Lucy stifling a yawn.

"No thanks. I have my son staying upstairs, he'll give me a hand if necessary. Come along and I'll show you your room. It's in one of the cottages, I'm afraid; with all the quarantines I haven't a single room free in this house. We might as well go round in your car; bring your bag."

Lucy was not pleased at being put in a different building from

Aunt Fennel but saw there was no help for it. Guided by Mrs. Marsham she drove round to the rear of Wildfell Hall and on across the park for a couple of hundred yards to a cobbled stable-yard.

"That one is your cottage," Mrs. Marsham said. "The next is the gardener's; the third is empty at present. I've made up a bed for you in the top front room. Come over in the morning at seven, will you? Can you wake or would you like to be called? There's an internal phone."

"I can wake normally, but it's been a long day; I guess you'd better call me, thanks."

"Very well. You can keep your car in the yard here. Would you mind leaving your lights on just till I get back to the house? I forgot to bring a torch. Good night."

While Mrs. Marsham walked swiftly back along the footpath Lucy went upstairs and investigated her new quarters. The cottage was small, two up and two down, similar in layout to High Beck; the furnishing was sketchy but adequate, and a tiny bathroom had been squeezed in at the head of the stairs. Looking out of its window into the yard below she saw a man walk into the headlight beam; he turned and looked towards the open door of Lucy's cottage, then followed Mrs. Marsham towards the big house.

Lucy stared after him in blank astonishment.

Utterly unlikely though it seemed, and despite the fact that she had last seen him in Boston, three thousand miles away, and knew no reason why he should suddenly turn up in Yorkshire, she would have been almost ready to swear that the person following Mrs. Marsham was her Uncle Wilbie's assistant, Russ McLartney.

She went downstairs, automatically switched off her car lights and locked up, bolted the door of the house, washed, and fell into bed. Outside on the moor she could hear owls calling.

Russ—it didn't make sense. Then could Russ be Aunt Fennel's Other One, her nightmare pursuer? No; ridiculous; besides, at the time when Miss Beatrice Howe had fallen to her doom, allegedly pushed by That Other One, Russ had been glumly escorting Aunt Rose and Corale on a trip through the Florida Everglades.

Russ, That Other One, Adnan with his warning: "Lucy, Lucy,

you are too shrewd for your own good. While you are resident in this establishment—"

Too shrewd? Dear Max, I can't make head or tail of it. Too complicated. Too many things to worry about. I'll never get to sleep Lucy thought, burrowed her face into the pillow, and slept.

IX

"You are slurring that phrase," Benovek said. "Take it once more from the top F."

Lucy hit the top F, hit it again, and yet again. It continued shrilling in her ear. "Foot off pedal," she thought, "we're coming to a bend, better change down."

The shrill note persisted and, surfacing reluctantly from her dream, she reached out an arm for the telephone which stood by her bed.

". . . Taking her time about answering," said Mrs. Marsham's voice, "as you're going that way, Harold, carry the thermometers round to the patients in those two rooms, would you? I'll be along directly, tell them."

"Hello?" said Lucy out of her fog.

"Oh, there you are, Miss Culpepper. Are you awake? When you come over to the house, could you bring a roll of rubber sheeting that you'll find in the dairy next to the gardener's cottage? It's on a shelf wrapped in brown paper next to the—"

Mrs. Marsham's words were interrupted by a man's voice calling from farther off.

"Mother! Better come in here."

"What's the matter?" The matron evidently had her head turned from the receiver but still held it; Lucy could hear the tick of a clock and, somewhere nearby, a cat mewing.

"She's gone."

"Who?"

"The old one."

"Oh—excuse me, Miss Culpepper," Mrs. Marsham said hurriedly into the receiver. "Come over as quickly as possible, will you, with the sheeting. There's a great deal to do."

"Okay." Lucy rolled out of bed and put on robe and slippers. Did *gone* mean dead or run off? And who was the old one?

She dressed at speed, tugged a hasty comb through her hair, washed in the tiny bathroom, ran downstairs, and let herself out into the stable-yard. The moorland air smelt cool, with a tang from the large trees, pines and monkey-puzzles, that separated the stable-quarters from the main house. Which was the dairy? There were several doors. One led to a shed full of plant-pots and garden tools, another to a garage containing a white Rover, very mud-splashed. A third outhouse had a wide slate shelf round three walls; this must be the dairy. Here Lucy found and identified the rubber sheeting.

Odd, she thought, stowing the roll, which was too heavy to be carried far, into her own car and starting up, odd there was such a lot of mud on that Rover, we haven't had any rain for over a week. Perhaps it was driven from some other part of the country? Or hasn't been used since the last spell of bad weather—when was that?

Thinking back she recalled the thunderstorm on the day she had first come to Appleby; for a little while the rain had been so heavy she had been obliged to park. But since then it had been dry, unusually dry, the locals said, for the time of year. Today, however, the sky was overcast and threatening; good thing I got Aunt Fennel moved yesterday, Lucy thought. Even if she doesn't want to go out, at least here when it's wet there will be room to stroll around indoors.

Lucy had imagined that, once installed just outside Appleby, the old lady would wish to go on walks, to revisit old scenes or call on old neighbours, but Aunt Fennel had calmly refuted any such notion.

"I'll stay indoors at present, thank you, dearie. It's a lovely big house, I'll be able to get plenty of exercise walking about the hall-ways and passages. And I'll have the good air and be able to see the moors through the windows. And That Other One would never dare try to get into a big place like Wildfell Hall, with so many people about; I'll be quite safe, so long as I stay inside."

Well, it was to be hoped that Mrs. Marsham didn't have any inflexible rules about outside exercise every day for the inmates, or there would be trouble, Lucy thought, parking by the back door and going in through the kitchen; in a contest of wills she had a notion that Mrs. Marsham and Aunt Fennel would be about equally matched.

In the kitchen she found Emma Chiddock, who boarded at reduced rates in return for some housework, briskly fumbling about, putting knives and spoons and napkins on a trolley.

"That you, Miss Culpepper?" she said, peering in Lucy's direction. "Matron said to go upstairs as soon as you got here, and take the rubber sheet with you."

She came closer to Lucy and hissed in a meaningful undertone,

"What did I tell you? Old Alice Crabtree passed away in the night. Didn't I say she would? Poor soul—it's a wicked shame, if you ask me—I reckon she would a lasted for a good while yet."

Lucy was surprised, and rather remorseful, to see tears on Mrs. Chiddock's wrinkled cheeks.

"I'm so sorry—I didn't realise you were so fond of her," she said diffidently.

"Alice Crabtree and me have been friends ever since we was at school. Oh, we used to have our little differences, but that didn't mean I thought she ought to be *put away*—"

"Is that you, Miss Culpepper?" the matron called down the stairs. "Bring the big kettle of hot water up, will you, and put on another. Emma, can you get on with making the toasts for the breakfasts?"

A window halfway up the stairs looked out over the front portico. As Lucy passed this she saw a man walk round from the side of the house, raise the bonnet of an estate van that stood there, and peer inside. It was the same man she had seen last night. But in daylight his resemblance to Russ was less marked; he was taller, fairer, with features less fleshy; his hair rose in a quiff; he looked like some kind of bird, maybe a snipe? Even so, the likeness was considerable; an odd coincidence.

Dear Max, you would enjoy Wildfell Hall. Somewhere, quite soon, in a room containing a few instruments of torture, I am sure to find an old-fashioned cabinet of ebony and gold, which, being only secured by massy bars and a padlock, I shall, after a few efforts, succeed in opening, and discover a photograph of myself as a child, a whole pile of mysterious laundry lists, three executioners' aprons, two winding-sheets, and a shroud.

The shroud brought Lucy back sharply to the thought of Mrs. Crabtree's death; she went on upstairs in a more sober frame of mind. As she crossed the landing she heard the bonnet slam and the van start up and drive away.

"Was that my son leaving?" asked Mrs. Marsham, appearing and receiving the kettle. "What a nuisance; I was going to ask him to do a couple of errands in the village for me before he went. Oh well, perhaps you could later on, Miss Culpepper; it's useful that you have a car."

"When will your son be back?" Lucy inquired, as they made beds; she was still curious to get a closer glimpse of him.

"Oh, he doesn't live here; he just came over for a few days to give me a hand. He's an osteopath; has a practice in Birmingham, so he can't stay very long. It was handy having him here last night, though; several of the measles patients were quite restless, and we had one old lady pass away; Dr. Adnan thought she might."

"That's too bad."

"Oh, you get accustomed to deaths in an old people's home," Mrs. Marsham said indifferently, whipping a mitred corner of sheet into place with professional skill, "after all, it's what they come for, isn't it? Run down now and fetch the other kettle, would you, Miss Culpepper? Oh, and could you put these specimens on the desk in my office as you pass? And then see to the breakfasts."

Feeling slightly blank, Lucy took bottles and kettle. Mrs. Marsham's outlook and her own appeared to be so dissimilar that there could be no contact; it was hardly worth making an effort to communicate. Anyway, she evidently doesn't *want* me communicating with her, Lucy thought. Depositing the bottles on the office desk she noticed a framed newspaper clipping; it was from the *Kirby Advertiser* and showed an uncompromising picture of Wildfell Hall, arches, pillars, stone balls, portico, and all; inset in the column of print underneath was a photograph of Mrs. Marsham and the piece was headed "Ex-Air Hostess S.R.N. to run new old folk's home at Appleby." A memory clicked into place and Lucy realised why Mrs. Marsham's features had seemed faintly familiar at their first encounter; of course she must have seen this article, without taking special note of it, while stacking piles of old newspapers in Uncle Wilbie's attic. Perhaps there had also been a picture of Mrs. Marsham's son, perhaps this had made Lucy imagine the resemblance to Russ? But no, the more she thought about it, the more she felt that the resemblance was real, just one of those inexplicable similarities.

By now the elderly inmates, such of them as could manage it, were up and hobbling downstairs in hopes of breakfast; querulous Emma Chiddock seemed to have set the tables and made toast fairly capably despite her poor vision; Lucy hastily brewed up a cauldron of instant porridge.

"Eggs, too, we always have," Emma said fussily, "always an egg for breakfast here. Ah, she's a hard woman, that Mrs. Marsham, but she do see we have a good breakfast, that I will say. Not but what I'd fancy a bit of bacon for a change instead of everlasting eggs, eggs, eggs."

"Boiled or scrambled?"

"Scrambled, scrambled. Lots of 'em with bad eyesight can't manage a boiled egg, see; you serve the scrambled in those plastic bowls and they eat it with a spoon. And you beat up the scrambled egg with this—"

She reached up myopically and located the electric beater hanging on its hook; with the sureness of habit she plugged it in, broke eggs into a bowl, and began rapidly beating them while Lucy found an enormous skillet and set it on the Aga.

"Wonderful gadgets they have now," said Emma, passing the bowl of yellow froth to Lucy and pressing the release knob of the beater; the corkscrew attachment shot out like a javelin and buried itself up to the hilt in a loaf of bread.

"Hey, you want to watch it with that thing!" Lucy exclaimed, somewhat startled. "You only just missed me! Hold it pointing down over the sink another time, or you're liable to stick somebody in the gizzard."

"Wonderful gadgets," droned Emma, paying no heed to Lucy, lovingly washing and drying the beater attachment; she replaced it in the head section and hung it up on its hook again. "Is the egg ready then? That's good; I'll go and ring the breakfast bell."

She hobbled off; it was plain, however, that she had after all taken notice of Lucy's words for as she went she muttered, "Yes, and there's some folks as would be all the better for sticking in the gizzard if you ask *me*."

Next minute a brazen clangour worthy of the Abbot of Aberbrothock broke out in the hall; Emma was plainly putting all her vindictive feelings into the breakfast summons.

During the bed-making period Lucy had found time to slip into Aunt Fennel's room and make sure the old lady was all right, peacefully propped on pillows, gazing out at the grey-purple stretch of moorland visible beyond the grounds.

"Yes, thank you, dearie, I slept beautifully; the air here certainly suits me much better than all that smoke and fog down in Kirby. Disturbances? No, I never heard any. But then I had my hearing aid out, of course! I'm feeling quite rested, so I'll get myself up by and by, after breakfast; just you bring me a bowl of porridge and a cup of hot water; I'll put some of my own camomile in."

This Lucy did, when taking breakfasts to such of the bed patients as were capable of eating.

"Delicious," sighed Aunt Fennel, dropping a handful of yellow dust into the water, from which a bitter reek instantly arose. "It's months since I was able to enjoy a real cup of camomile."

Darting away to her other duties, Lucy hoped that Mrs. Marsham would prove accommodating about Aunt Fennel's fondness for herbal concoctions. Dear Max, it's no use, I'm not certain in my mind about Mrs. Marsham. Efficient she undoubtedly is, eggs for breakfast, warm bed-clothes, all very good, but *kind*? Old Emma's mutterings about her love-hate mate we can discount —or can we? Measles plus pneumonia would be quite enough to finish off most old ladies—but on the other hand it would be extremely simple to hasten somebody's end in such circumstances. Adnan did say Mrs. Crabtree was tough, though. Well, Adnan will have to come and sign the death certificate, won't he, he'd speak up soon enough if there was anything phoney? Or would he?

She ran downstairs to cast an eye over the scrambled-egg eaters, who were chomping away contentedly enough, seated at their red-topped tables, napkins tucked under chins, eyes fixed on vacancy as they applied themselves seriously to what was one of the most interesting activities of their day. Outside the large windows a steady rain streamed down from the slate-coloured sky, and the mixed conifers heaved and thrashed raggedly; inside Wildfell Hall seemed peaceful and cosy, but with a threatening whiff of insecurity about it, like the hopeful warmth of the sun about to be engulfed by a thundercloud.

Having dealt out second cups of tea and dollops of marmalade, Lucy bolted down a saucerful of scrambled egg herself, and then went up to ask what she should do next.

"Help me with bed-baths; Mrs. Thwaite's Ann said she'd come in at ten and wash dishes."

Mrs. Marsham yawned; for the first time in Lucy's short acquaintance with her she looked tired; her face was greyish-pale, her eyes red-rimmed.

"It was a wearing night; I'll just take my contact lenses out," she said. "Eyes are sore; had the lenses in for about twenty-four hours."

With a finger she stretched out the corner of each eye in turn, blinking over the palm of the other hand, then carefully tucked the resulting two shirt-button-size lenses in a small gilt box, and put on a pair of horn-rimmed glasses which made her look all at once older and more intelligent. Lucy suddenly wondered if she had been under-estimating Mrs. Marsham.

"Don't the lenses ever fall out by accident?" she asked.

"Only if you get dust in your eye and rub it. I don't wear mine in dusty, sandy places; but they're good for this sort of work because they don't get steamed up."

Mrs. Marsham seemed, perhaps because of her fatigue, more talkative than usual, and Lucy was glad of it; she would have been embarrassed to give the elderly patients their bed-baths in a dour and uncommunicative silence. When asked by Mrs. Marsham how long she had been in England, where she had lived before, she politely answered the trivial questions with a brief sketch of her life-history and connections.

"Boston? How interesting. I've never been to America. But you say that your uncle came from somewhere round here originally?"

"Well, no, from Liverpool, actually, but his family had come

from here, and of course my great-aunt lived in Appleby; Uncle
Wilbie used to come back here visiting as a boy."

"And his name is Culpepper, the same as yours? Does he remember Appleby quite clearly? What sort of age would he be?"

"Oh—late fifties, early sixties, maybe. He had always kept in
touch with Aunt Fennel; she sent him some of her embroidered
pictures. He wants me to try and get hold of some more," Lucy
said, thinking Mrs. Marsham in this more approachable mood
might be a source of information, "but Aunt Fennel seems to
have given them all away when she quit her cottage. Would you
happen to know anyone in the village who might have one and
be inclined to part?"

They were washing aged Mr. Cordwainer at the time; as Lucy
gently scoured into his thin old armpit with a soapy sponge, he
unexpectedly remarked,

"Nay, you'll be lucky if you get anybody in the village to part
with old Miss Culpepper's Bible pictures."

"Why is that?" Lucy carefully dabbed dry the bit she had
washed and proceeded to his ribs, which were covered with an
impressive measles rash.

"Don't you go tickling me now, lass, or I'll be obliged to wriggle
and all yon soapy water'll get spilt. Why, everybody in the village
believes as those Bible pictures bring luck; Mrs. Thwaite's dad
had a big win on the pools when the old lady gave him one, the
Holroyds sold their bull for a lot more than they expected to, and
Mary Coxwold got fixed up with Lenny Thorpe, which most folks
didn't think she'd ever bring off. I don't reckon you'll find anybody that's willing to let you have one."

"I wonder where Dr. Adnan got his?" Lucy said. "He's got about
a dozen; he said people had given them to him."

"Those as didn't believe in luck, maybe. But he must ha' come
to the end of 'em. He was asking all over t'village last summer,
but no one else was willing to part. Oh, and o' course the doctor
got four all at once when they auctioned off Sam Thorpe's stuff
—tractor fell on Sam and all his nevvies and nieces is in Brazil."

"A tractor falling on you doesn't seem like good luck," commented Mrs. Marsham drily.

"'Twas, though, because he'd been putting off paying his in-
come tax for months; letter after letter the Revenue sent him; and

then he never had to pay it at all!" old Mr. Cordwainer said triumphantly, putting out two arms like sticks of celery for his pyjama sleeves. "After old Miss Culpepper died—"

Lucy gasped. "Miss Culpepper! But she's here! It was the other old lady that died, Miss Howe, surely?"

"Well, whichever on 'em it was that died; most folk couldn't tell them apart. They looked alike, and they didn't use to come down to t'village much. Anyway, as I was saying, when one of 'em died and t'other moved away, some folk went up to t'cottage hunting for more pictures. But Colonel Linton had cleared out the lot."

"Which was Miss Culpepper's cottage?" the matron asked.

"Up the beck—all on its own. Has anyone ever suggested that it was haunted?" Lucy asked Mr. Cordwainer.

"Not as I know on. It's yon public convenience that Colonel Linton will have is haunted."

"Oh really, what rubbish!" Mrs. Marsham said impatiently, but Lucy asked,

"What by?"

"Why, by t'old lady o' course, the one who died. The colonel said he met her ghost there, moaning and wailing and bawling out that she'd been shoved to her death by one o' they summer trippers that comes up to Appleby expecting historical relics and cream teas for half a crown."

"Was she really shoved to her death?"

"Bless your heart, no. Twas just one o' t'old colonel's fancies when he'd had a few of his Highland Bluebells."

Lucy wondered what a Highland Bluebell was, but they had finished Mr. Cordwainer and the matron was already waiting by the next bed, glancing at her watch.

"Old Mr. Cordwainer seems a lot better today," Lucy said.

"They always are when the rash comes out. Can you finish off here, Miss Culpepper, I think that's the doctor arriving. And when you've done, could you go to the village—the shopping-list is on the kitchen table."

"Do you mind if I just see to my aunt first?" Lucy had been hoping for another word with Adnan, to ask for an explanation of last night's cryptic warning.

"She's perfectly all right—she won't mind waiting till you get back," Mrs. Marsham said impatiently. "I just put my head round the door, looking for Emma Chiddock, and she was still asleep."

Since Aunt Fennel did, in fact, often enjoy a short nap after breakfast even in Mrs. Tilney's uncomfortable parlour this seemed reasonable; when she had done the last bed-bath Lucy glanced in on her aunt and, reassured that she was indeed sleeping, ran down, picked up the shopping-list, and drove to Appleby.

Deciding, after she had done Mrs. Marsham's errands, that she was entitled to ten minutes for her own business, she parked little PHO by the haunted lavatory and walked up to the old parsonage.

This time Colonel Linton answered promptly when she rang the bell. He was plainly suffering from a notable hangover; his eyes looked liable to roll out at any moment; but in other respects he seemed tidier and more collected than on Lucy's previous visit, perhaps because it was earlier in the day.

"*Now* what?" he growled, peering at her with difficulty, but the growl seemed a formality, merely his accustomed manner of talking, rather than specifically directed animosity. Then his face changed: wrinkled out sideways into an eldritch but rather touching smile. "Why, you're little Cathy! Little granddaughter Cathy come back to see me!"

"No, I'm not little Cathy," said Lucy, foreseeing endless complications unless this misunderstanding were scotched right away. "But can I come in and see you just the same?"

While he still squinted at her doubtfully through half-closed eyes, she edged her way past him and crossed a dark flagged hallway into an equally dark dining-room where the sombre glint of gold frames had caught her eye. She was not disappointed. A whole batch of ancestors had evidently been removed from their frames and at least a dozen of Miss Culpepper's pictures substituted for them. The effect, in the gloomily furnished Victorian room with its huge expanse of mahogany table, was magnificent; the pictures gleamed and sparkled on the walls like glow-worms seen in a dusk-filled thicket. Lucy drew a sharp breath of pleasure and began to move slowly round, identifying them: Jacob and the angel playing tug-of-war with a ladder; a family piece, Jacob, Esau, Leah, and Rachel, conversing in front of an amazingly sequinned sunset; Daniel with some bright-eyed lions; Moses, Aaron, and a serpent; David, Saul, and a harp—

"If you aren't little Cathy," demanded Colonel Linton, "who the devil are you? What's your name?"

"Culpepper."

"Oh, *well*. Why didn't you say so? That accounts, of course. One of Great-aunt Cathy's children, Bell Earnshaw—*she* married a Culpepper. That explains the likeness. You could be two peas in a pod. Here, look—"

He turned and began rummaging among a pile of canvases without frames which had been stacked casually in the great empty hearth.

Really I've had enough of likenesses, Lucy thought. Any more peas-in-a-pod stuff is going to be a bit too much of a coincidence.

But then it occurred to her that of course, in a remote, cut-off place like Appleby, where even during the first half of the twentieth century inbreeding was the rule and few people moved away, where almost everyone was related to everyone else, likenesses would be common enough. Probably I'm a second cousin twice removed of his little Cathy and everyone else in the village.

But that doesn't account for the resemblance between Russ and whosit—Harold Marsham. *They* could hardly be cousins—Russ told me his family came from Ireland.

"There!" said Colonel Linton. He rubbed the canvas he had selected with his sleeve, and put it down on the dining-table. "That's her—Great-aunt Cathy Earnshaw—Linton was her maiden name, of course. See the likeness for yourself!"

Lucy could. It was like looking into a mirror; except that the girl in the portrait had long hair tied at the back with a ribbon, and a couple of ringlets.

"Even to the buck teeth!" said Colonel Linton triumphantly. "You're not a good-looker, my girl, but you're a proper Linton, proper sprig of the old tree. Well, well, well! Come into the kitchen and celebrate—the sun ain't quite over the clothes-line yet, but this calls for a Highland Bluebell."

He took Lucy's arm affectionately and piloted her into a warm, cluttered room where a couple of hens were nesting in majestic Victorian hatboxes in front of the coal stove.

"Saves going out to the hen-house for eggs," Colonel Linton explained. He then disconcerted Lucy very much by pouring a small tot of whisky into a jam-jar and adding a generous quarter-pint of methylated spirit.

"Is—is that a Highland Bluebell?" she stammered.

"That it is, midear. Invented it myself," said the colonel, absently swigging half of it.

"In that case I think—I mean—do you think I could possibly have milk in mine, instead of methylated? I have to drive, you see," Lucy explained cunningly.

"*Milk?* I don't think there's any milk in the house, midear. You could have an egg," the colonel said, casually thrusting a hand beneath a hen and fetching one out, "there's nothing to touch a raw egg beaten up in whisky if you suffer from Irrawaddy stomach, as I do."

"My stomach's okay at the moment, thanks. I guess I'll just take my scotch with a little water, if you have that?"

When she was accommodated with a drink—mildly surprised to see water come from the tap—and Colonel Linton had mixed himself another Bluebell, he said,

"Now, what can I do for you, my dear? Pleasure to help anyone so like Great-aunt Cathy."

Lucy explained yet again about Great-aunt Fennel and her pictures. The colonel listened attentively, mixing himself another drink midway.

"So you see if I could get hold of a dozen—even half a dozen—of those pictures and sell them for her, I have a notion it might make enough money to see her comfortable to the end of her days."

"Very good plan, my girl—splendid scheme. Don't deny I'll be sad to part with my lot—must confess I kept the pick for myself when she told me to give 'em away—but of course I'll be glad—hup!—excuse me, very high pollen count this autumn—glad to help. Glad to see your aunt again, too—used to be great cronies when we were young. Even proposed to one of 'em once, which one was it now? Anyway—hup!—that's an old story. Wouldn't leave her friend—devoted to one another, they were. Dill and Daff. Even looked alike—way people get to resemble their pets. Or vice—hup!—versa."

"Did you see Aunt Fennel after Miss Howe died?"

"No, didn't see her. Sent a note, asking me to deal with pictures.

Nasty business, that was. Pushed into the dene by a foreign tripper—daresay he was drunk after all those herbal brews the old ladies used to do for tourists—people will swallow anything on holiday. Ever tried Irish coffee, by the way? I do it without the cream—using scotch, of course. It's just about elevenses time—how about a drop now? Let's see, what's all this stuff in the kettle?"

The kettle appeared to be full of ants' eggs.

"Please don't bother," Lucy said hastily. "Is there really a ghost in the glen?"

"Heard it dozens of times. Sounds like an owl. Shows she must have been done in, doesn't it—ghost not paid by the council to haunt—hup?"

"Could I bring Aunt Fennel to visit you?"

"Delighted, midear. And what about the pictures? Want to take them now?"

He started towards the dining-room, carrying his fourth Bluebell.

"I guess perhaps I'd better fix up crating and transport first," said Lucy. "Maybe I could come back tomorrow? I don't think it would be a very good idea to take them to Wildfell Hall—"

"Where?"

"Wildfell Hall—the old people's home. Aunt Fennel's lodging there now and I've got a temporary job—"

"Clear out!"

Lucy had not believed that people could literally go black with rage; she had thought this to be a figure of speech. Now she saw that it could really be done, for Colonel Linton had done it. His face was fearsomely suffused, his eyes were like blood-blisters.

"Mean to say she's staying there—you've got the gall to come here—hup!—and tell me you've taken a job there—hup? The name of that place, I'd have you know, is not some tuppeny-halfpenny piece of tosh out of romantic fiction but APPLEBY OLD HALL! Now—clear out!"

Without conscious process, Lucy found herself outside the front door, vibrating from top to toe as if someone had swept a thumb across all her strings. The door slammed in her face.

Too bad, she thought, I forgot the Old Hall used to belong to him; at least I didn't realise it meant so much to him. That was stupid of me. Shame, just when things were going so well. Dear Max, we sure buggered it up that time. But will he remember, if I go to see him another day? He seems fairly disconnected. Maybe there's a chance he'll forget this visit—it would be worth another try, anyway.

If he does remember, she thought, it's an argument for getting Aunt Fennel away from Wildfell Hall.

A vague project had been forming in her mind. As a first step she went to call on Fiona Carados.

"Hi. How's the baby?"

"Oh, he's super. Come and see. He's put on two ounces, and learned to smile, and grown a whole tuft of hair."

Lucy studied the baby who seemed, to her ignorant eye, exactly the same as he had two days ago.

"He's not a bit like his father."

"No, thank God! What I ever saw in that little drip—"

Fiona stretched her arms, in immense relief, it seemed, at being free of male entanglements. She was almost too large for the tiny room; today she wore a bulky, natural-coloured Irish sweater over ploughmen's corduroys. "One of my many consolations is that I shan't now have to read the poor child his father's ghastly books."

"Oh, then he *is* the Robin Carados who writes all those children's books? I'd wondered about that."

Lucy had seen them in the Kirby W. H. Smith's where she bought her wrapping materials: shelf after shelf of brightly coloured thin red and green and blue books, price three shillings each—*Tom the Trawler, Douglas the Destroyer, Larry the Lifeboat, Fred the Ferry, Bill the Barge, Sam the Schooner, Percy the Punt, Dan the Dinghy.*

"Yeah," said Fiona, "that's him. He was just getting his ideologies sorted for *Ned the Nuclear-powered Submarine* when we broke up. And do you know what was the last straw? Why he insisted on stowing me in this hideaway, far from the madding crowd? It was because it wouldn't do for *his* saintly reputation as purveyor of high-moral-tone nautical slop for the kiddies to be sullied. Someone in the middle ages referred to woman as a sack of dung, didn't they? Well, that's how bonny sweet Robin really thought of me, and in the end the message got through."

"What did you think of him?"

There was a silence, and then Fiona laughed. "I won't plug poor little Bub's subconscious full of wicked words; don't they say that everything you hear before three months sticks tighter than glue?"

"I expect he hears it anyway, whether you speak it or think it," suggested Lucy. "Why didn't you and Robin get married?"

"Oh, the publicity of a divorce wouldn't do for someone in his exalted position; honestly, it was like associating with royalty. I expect really he just wanted to eat his cake and have it; that's the usual, isn't it? He's back with his wife now; she's quite rich. Want a drink?"

"No thanks, I already had one. I've been visiting Colonel Linton."

"The old boy at the vicarage? He's rather a sweetie, isn't he? I've met him once or twice when I take the bub a walk up the glen; he likes the noise the water makes."

"Water?—I shouldn't think it's quite his—oh, you mean the baby. Have you had measles?"

"God; yes; when I was fourteen. Why?"

"Are you still looking for a way to earn some cash?"

"Yes, it's getting quite crucial, actually. I was thinking I'd have to go back to London, only I'd have to sell the pram to raise the fare, and it doesn't seem likely anyone in Appleby would want it."

"How would you like to come and give a hand at Wildfell Hall? That's where I am at present. They've got a crisis: measles epidemic and next to no help."

"I thought you looked a bit washed-out and peaky," said Fiona. "Sure you won't have that drink? No? Well it might be quite a lark, I suppose; that's the old folk's home, isn't it, not the retired clergy place? But would the old battle-axe who runs it have *me*? I've seen her about the place; she looks like a tough Jane."

"I guess she'd take on Fanny Hill right now, if she'd do the work."

"I'd need to find somewhere to park young Oedipus Carados; measles wouldn't be the best thing in the world for him. But I daresay it could be managed. All right, I'm on, if she'll hire me. What's the form? Shall I put on my black bombazine and come to the back door?"

"I'll suggest it to Mrs. Marsham this morning, shall I, and then call you up. Are you on the phone?"

"Do me a favour! Phone? In Appleby? I'll call you, from that lovely public post office. When's a good time?"

"About five, I should think, when the old things are having tea."

"Right. And thanks. Meanwhile I'll organise a sitter. Maybe your old colonel would oblige."

"Not if you tell him where you're working," Lucy said, grinning, and told the tale of her previous call.

"So you didn't get your pictures? What a pity. Why do you want them?"

"They might fetch a good sum, my uncle thinks. He planned to make a fortune out of them—or show the art world he's an unacknowledged genius at spotting talent—but I plan to see any proceeds go to make Aunt Fennel comfortable."

"Like me to see if I can wheedle any out of the worthy villagers? You can't have a lot of time at the moment to go canvassing from door to door."

"No, I ought to be back right now; Mrs. Marsham will probably think I've absconded with the housekeeping. Yes, I guess that's a kind thought; thanks very much."

"I'll expect a commission on every one I collect," Fiona said calmly. She walked out with Lucy into Appleby High Street. An overalled figure, vaguely familiar, veered erratically past on a rusty bike and waved to Fiona, who waved back; after a moment's thought Lucy identified the figure as Clough, the man who had been knocked down.

"Is he all right again?" she said.

"Clough? As much so as he's ever likely to be; he's a bit simple. Heart of gold, though; he helped me when I had a rook stuck in my chimney. That was another of dear sweet Robin's little misdemeanours; he knocked Clough off his bike and didn't wait to see if he was all right."

"Oh, did Robin do that—are you sure?"

"Well, of course, being Robin, he never admitted to it, but it figured; Clough said he was hit by a white car, and it was just around the time Robin was here last; that day you turned up."

"Yes; I remember. Oh, there's Adnan," said Lucy, looking along the rain-swept village street.

"He's a funny one, the little Turk, isn't he? Has he asked you to join his harem yet? Well, he will. Oh, excuse me; I hear Oedipus squeaking. Call you tonight." Fiona vanished indoors.

The Alfa drew to a splashing stop beside Lucy.

"Dear Lucy Snowe! So we meet again."

"Have you come from the Hall?" Lucy drew her duffel coat round her; the rain was beginning to penetrate.

"Indeed I have; I even saw your aunt. She seems very happy. Perhaps you were right, after all, to move her."

"Tell me, what did you mean last night when you said I should keep my talent for finding out about things in check while I stayed at the Hall?"

"Did I say so?" He looked vague. Today he wore a bottle-green blazer with two bronze buttons over a deep-collared terra-cotta shirt and white silk cravat; he carefully flicked a small speck of lint from his lapel.

"Yes, you did."

"Oh well, I suppose I meant merely that Mrs. Marsham is not a lady who will permit interference with her matronly ways; she would soon send you packing if you did not toe her line. But then, I think you do not plan to stay long in any case?"

"What about Mrs. Crabtree's death?" said Lucy abruptly.

Adnan looked startled and reserved; his mussel-plum eyes hooded themselves.

"What about it?" he repeated.

"Was it a natural death? Did you sign the death certificate?"

"Good heavens, my dear Miss Lucy, today you are seeing bogies in every bush! Naturally I signed the death certificate, and, yes, it was a natural death. To die of measles and pneumonia mixed at age eighty-three is in no way remarkable, I assure you. I go now to arrange for an ambulance to fetch this poor old lady to the undertakers."

"She hadn't, for instance, been injected with that anti-measles vaccine which had to be withdrawn because it was giving people heart attacks?"

"My dearest girl!" He shot a glance up and down the village street. "You ought to be writing scripts for television, you are wasted in a tranquil little out-of-the-way place like Appleby-under-Scar! No such dark elements played any part in the poor old lady's death, I do most earnestly assure you! Any part whatso*ever!*— But I am keeping you standing in the rain, which is unpardonable. Good-bye for the present; we are sure to meet frequently while the epidemic runs its course."

The Alfa shot away, in a fountain of mud and exhaust.

Lucy, by now fairly damp, ran back to where she had parked little PHO and drove rapidly back to Wildfell Hall. On the way she listened to a recital by Denis Matthews, who was playing numbers 7 to 12 of Book One of the 48 Preludes and Fugues; half her mind listened with serious attention, contrasting his rendering with that of Benovek; the other half was occupied with trying to come to some, any conclusion, about Dr. Adnan. Did he speak the truth ever, occasionally, often, always? She had no means of deciding.

Dear Max, it will be a darn good thing if Mrs. Marsham okays the notion of having Fiona Carados come and help out. Maybe Adnan is right and I am seeing bogies in every bush. But Fiona seems a down-to-earth character; we'll see what she makes of it all. She's not likely to imagine things. Though I've a notion she could have been wrong about Clough; it needn't have been Robin who knocked him down. What about that white Rover? Who drove that? Harold Marsham? Or Mrs.? No, couldn't have been her, she was back at the Hall when it happened.

Mrs. Marsham herself appeared at this point—Lucy was unpacking the stores. Far from being annoyed at the time Lucy had taken, the matron was in an unusually amiable frame of mind, congratulated Lucy on her suggestion of enlisting Fiona's help, and told her that, as Mrs. Thwaite's Ann was making lunch, she, Lucy, could have an hour off.

"Thanks; in that case I'll go and see how Aunt Fennel's getting on."

Lucy ran upstairs and found Great-aunt Fennel pottering peacefully in her bedroom.

"It's so nice here, dearie," she said happily. "Nobody comes and tells you that you ought to be downstairs in the parlour. I do like this place! The bathroom's perfectly sploshous—big!—and Mrs. Chiddock says there are three or four others—people don't come banging on the door all the time. Basins in the bedrooms, too!"

"Would you like me to wash your hair and give you a manicure, Aunt Fen? I've got a bit of free time."

"That *would* be nice, dearie. I'll get out the lettuce shampoo."

While Lucy was washing the old lady's thin, fine white hair, her mind suddenly threw up a memory which the word *sploshous* had evoked: we were having a picnic by some stream near a station. I can remember water and rocks and a feeling of completeness; *every*body was there who mattered. Does that mean mother *and* father? I suppose so. He—father?—had a harmonica and played on it. Somebody—Aunt Fennel?—said, "That's a sploshous tune! Play it again."

"Was my father musical?" she asked suddenly.

"He was never taught to play any instrument," Aunt Fennel said. "But, yes, dearie, he had a natural ear; could always pick out a tune on the piano, or sing a second part. It was one of the nicest things about him—of course your mother loved it. She was musical too."

As usual Lucy had a sense of much left unsaid. She would have asked another question but at that moment a massive ginger cat jumped in through the window from the balcony and leapt confidently onto Aunt Fennel's bed.

"Hey, be off with you!" exclaimed Lucy, and tipped the cat out of the window again.

"Don't you let matron see you doing that!" warned Emma Chiddock, who came in at this moment.

Aunt Fennel was staring after the cat with a faint frown on her gentle brow.

"That cat keeps making me think of Taffypuss," she murmured. "Poor Taffypuss got killed by a fox—or so Dill said; she wouldn't let me look at the body; said it would upset me. She got Colonel Linton to bury it."

"Much better," agreed Lucy. "That was sensible of Dill. Look —here's a proper hair-dryer. Every mod. con. Anyway, I'm sure Taffypuss was a lot nicer than that fat over-fed animal."

"Bloody cat come in the window again," said Goetz.

Harbin was on the telephone. "You'll fix it then," he was saying. "Yes; well; you have the address. Green Morris estate wagon, CRU 299P. Something simple; act of God stuff. I leave it to you.

No rush—unless he starts acting suspiciously. Yes, keep him tailed. What's that—how much longer am I staying here? A month, maybe—couple of months. Stoker's getting the place in Palma fixed up? Right. Then you'll be in touch—good."

He put back the receiver.

"What's the idea, having him done?" said Goetz.

"I don't like loose ends. People who can talk."

He turned round, saw the cat, and said, "Get that animal out, or there's liable to be another act of God, here and now."

Goetz giggled.

"I found an old bow and arrows out in that ornamental summer-house place by the shrubbery," he said. "The cat'd make a nice target, wouldn't it—soggy fat brute." He grabbed it—his hands sinking inches deep into its thick shaggy fur—carried it to the window, and shot it onto the roof, the cat meanwhile struggling and emitting a sort of whining snarl. "Come on, Baby Brother, my ducky; you aren't wanted here, that's for sure."

"Baby Brother," muttered Harbin. "Judas, what a name. In any case, what were *you* doing out by the summer-house?"

"All right, all right, keep calm! I'm a legal citizen, I haven't escaped from anywhere, I can go where I like."

Harbin looked at him for several moments in silence. His pale stare unnerved Goetz, who muttered defensively,

"Anyway it was after dark, pitch dark it was! When you were watching telly night before last; I suddenly felt I'd go crazy if I didn't get a breath of air. Nobody saw me, nobody, I swear!"

"You do realise," Harbin said with controlled quietness, "that if anybody who knows about us sees you, they'd just naturally put two and two together and work out that I'm in the neighbourhood too? You do realise that? It's not going to be necessary for me to fix up another act of God?"

Goetz was frantic. "Look, honest, nobody saw me, but okay, I won't do it again, if it worries you so. But shan't I half be glad to get away from this goddam morgue! Anyway, if you're worried about people putting two and two together, how about Linda? I don't notice you fixing up any acts of God for *her?*"

"She's wanted to run this place, isn't she," Harbin said reasonably. "Time enough to tidy up Linda after we leave. Anyway she's changed her name and it was all years ago; no need for anyone to connect her with that business. Besides—"

"Watch it," said Goetz suddenly. They could hear footsteps on the landing outside the closed door. Goetz quietly shot the new brass bolt. A moment later there were three taps; relieved, he opened the door and Mrs. Marsham came in with a tray of food.

She looked less calm than usual; her hands shook a little as she put down the tray, and there was the hint of a flush on her prominent cheekbones.

"I believe I've got something," she said.

"Mince again!" Goetz peered at the food disgustedly.

"On what?" Harbin's pale eyes met those of Mrs. Marsham.

"On Fred."

"Old one-track Linda," sighed Goetz, helping himself to a large portion of the mince and starting to gobble it. "Don't you ever think of anything but your lost love?"

Harbin said, "What have you got?" Mrs. Marsham helped him to food, but he did not touch it; he moved his gloved right arm restlessly.

"This Culpepper girl, the one who's just arrived with her aunt; she had an uncle called Wilberfoss Culpepper who emigrated to America about twenty years back from Liverpool; family originally lived in this village."

Harbin sat looking at her in silence. Goetz, however, burst into a guffaw, and nearly choked on his mince.

"Wasn't she the one you didn't want here? Pardon me if I laugh, but that's really rich, that is!"

"Where is the uncle now?" said Harbin.

Lucy answered the telephone when it rang, as Mrs. Marsham seemed to have disappeared.

"Fiona speaking. How's the epidemic?"

"Running its course. Mrs. M. says your coming here is a fine idea and when can you start?"

"Tomorrow if she likes. Mrs. Thwaite at the post office is going to mind young Oedipus. And I can probably hitch a lift up in the mail van."

"Grand. We'll see you then. I'd better ring off now—I was in the middle of dealing out the mince."

As she hung up Lucy suddenly remembered with a pang of guilt that she had promised to call the police and tell them if Aunt Fennel turned up. She had never done so. She darted back to the dining-room, where the old people were patiently waiting, doled out mince and vegetables on to plates, and then returned to the phone.

"Is that Kirby Police Station? Oh, my name's Culpepper—I was in your office yesterday reporting that I'd lost my aunt. Well— I've found her again; I'm just ringing to tell you."

"When did you find her, miss? And where was she?"

Feeling abashed and guilty, Lucy related the circumstances of Aunt Fennel's recovery.

"And why did you not report the matter sooner, miss?"

"I'm terribly sorry—what with one thing and another I guess I just forgot," Lucy said humbly.

"You've given the police a lot of unnecessary trouble, miss. We've put out search calls and made inquiries and added her name to our Missing Persons list—"

"I'm sorry, I'm really sorry! There's a crisis going on at the moment, you see, with a measles epidemic where we are now—"

"Where is that?"

"Appleby Old Hall—Wildfell Hall old people's home."

She could hear him repeat the words as he wrote them down.

"Very well, miss. Thank you for calling. But do remember that if you waste our time with false alarms we aren't so likely to believe something's wrong another time."

"No, I do see," said Lucy, thinking, You weren't exactly falling over yourself to believe me yesterday, friend. "Well, thanks a lot. I do know how busy the police are."

"Anyway she's not likely to come to any harm at Appleby Old Hall."

Lucy hung up and turned to find that Mrs. Marsham had come into the office.

"*There* you are, Miss Culpepper. They are all waiting for their pudding; I couldn't think where you had got to."

"Oh gosh, I'm sorry," said Lucy, wondering why the matron suddenly seemed so annoyed; damn it, the old things hadn't been left for more than four minutes, they could hardly be finished yet; "I'll go and see to them right away."

X

"Dill and I used to do this for each other," Aunt Fennel said comfortably. "When you're old, you know, dearie, it gets harder and harder to reach your feet. That *does* feel nice."

"It must be frightful," said Lucy, trying to imagine the helplessness of not being able to cut one's own toe-nails. She carefully pumiced a corn, anointed it from a mysterious little bottle of dark green celandine lotion, and laid in place the small cotton-wool shield with a hole in the middle.

"My corns have never bothered me though," Aunt Fennel went on, "but Dill's used to give her a lot of trouble. Specially in the summer when we did the teas."

"Did you do a lot, Aunt Fennel?"

"Quite a few at week-ends, dearie. We had a 'Teas' sign, down at the bottom of the beck, and of a Saturday or Sunday we'd have a dozen or two, quite often; Dill's baking was so good, you see, people got to know and came back. That was how That Other One managed to come to the place."

Lucy sat back on her heels and regarded the old lady with interest, but she did not ask any questions. During the ten days since she had come to Wildfell Hall, Aunt Fennel, apparently feeling more secure in this large, well-appointed place, had been slightly less unforthcoming about That Other One, but questions were still liable to make her close up and lose confidence.

"He came along pretending to be one of those foreign tourists, wearing a little hat with a feather, and dark glasses and foreign-type shoes and accent—that was before I got so deaf, of course," she broke off to say quickly.

Lucy waited.

"Dill used to carry in the teas; we had three or four little tables in the parlour. I didn't always see the people. But I went in that time with more hot water and I saw him, sitting by himself. I know *that* face, I thought, though he's changed and has a beard and glasses, which he never used. But *he's* no foreigner. Even before he spoke I was certain in my mind because—"

There were quick footsteps outside the door.

"Postman's been; here's a couple of letters for you, Miss Cul-pepper," Mrs. Marsham said, coming in.

"Oh, is the mail strike ended, then?"

"Yes, it was mentioned last night on the TV news. I suppose it'll take them at least six weeks to get all the back-log sorted."

Lucy studied her letters with curiosity—who would have writ-ten to her? One was typed, with a York postmark; Aunt Fennel's bank, possibly? It looked uninteresting. The other, she saw, with a leap of the heart, came from Coulsham, Surrey, and was ad-dressed to her in an unusually beautiful handwriting, shapely and chiselled, if a little shaky.

She had an impulse to hoard it until she was alone.

"Here are your slippers, Aunt Fen; I'll just pour away the water and tidy up."

She whisked up bath-mat, basin, nail-scissors, towel, and file. Mrs. Marsham was putting clean linen into a large closet in the hallway.

"Oh, by the way," Lucy asked her, "have you heard when Nora's likely to be coming back?"

"Nora? Probably at the beginning of next week. Why?"

"Well—" Lucy was slightly surprised, "as my stay here was only temporary, to tide you through the measles and Nora's absence, and as the epidemic's on the wane and you've got Fiona now too, I imagined you wouldn't want me much longer?"

The matron seemed equally surprised.

"Please don't feel you have to rush off, Miss Culpepper! Your work is quite satisfactory"— *I'll* say it is, thought Lucy, fourteen hours hard every day—"and I'm sure *we* don't want to lose you, if you'd like to stay a while longer, until you are quite sure that your aunt is happily settled."

"That's very kind of you," Lucy said, deadpan. And quite a different tune from what you sang when the notion was first raised. Flattering, of course, but let's be honest, I'm not so dear to you as all that. What's the game now?

"Anyway, think it over," Mrs. Marsham said, smiling the tight smile which carved her thin cheeks into diagonal folds. "To be candid, I'd rather lose Mrs. Frazer than you—she is inclined to be just a *little* bit feather-brained."

Frazer, it had turned out, was Fiona's real name (the Mrs. was a courtesy appellation added by Mrs. Marsham and ungratefully received); Carados Fiona now rejected with scorn, saying that it reminded her of a part of her life she proposed to forget without delay.

"Oh well, if you're sure—" Lucy said vaguely. The vague tone covered an internal conflict: she felt a desperate urge to get away, to go south and make a start on her studies with Benovek, on her own life. Aunt Fennel seemed comfortable, well cared for, happy as a clam. But was this really a suitable place in which to leave her? If only one could be sure.

"You forgot my stockings, dearie." Aunt Fennel's tone was faintly martyred when Lucy returned to her. She put out a foot, like a child, Lucy thought, making a bid for attention the instant it senses the adult's interest has moved elsewhere.

"I'm so sorry, Aunt Fen. Look, here they are, nice and warm from the radiator."

"Who were your letters from, dearie?"

"I haven't read them yet," Lucy said defensively.

"Don't you want to look at them?"

It would be unkind to repulse this gentle persistence.

"I think one's from Benovek, the man who's going to teach me piano."

Aunt Fennel remained silent. It was one of her expressive silences; she had made it plain that she did not think highly of Lucy's choice of career. But perhaps this was just a rationalisation of an innocent possessiveness, a wish not to lose her newly acquired niece just yet?

"And the other one?"

"I don't know. It's from York. I might as well look, I suppose."
She pulled the envelope from her pocket, carefully reserving
Benovek's for future reading.

"It's from someone staying at the Royal Turpin Hotel—good
grief, it's from Uncle Wilbie. Who ever would have thought *he'd*
find time to come to England?"

Has he come to see why I haven't secured any pictures yet?
she wondered. Does he really set so much store by them? Or is
he determined to establish Aunt Fennel's status as an imposter
once and for all? Whatever he's come for, I bet he's up to no
good.

"Want to hear what he says?" She read aloud, her eye shooting
ahead, editing and abridging. "All neatly typed, he must have
hired a secretary—oh, I see, he says he has Russ along. 'Dear Lucy,
I got your letter . . .' hm, hm . . . 'I do not think Appleby Old
Hall sounds in the least a good place in which to leave her, these
private homes are often not at all well run and in any case it is
impossible to tell how a place so recently opened may turn out—'
humph! '. . . Obliged to visit England on business . . . contacting
firms in this part of the country . . . think it best if you bring
your great-aunt over to York to see me . . . discuss what to do with
her—' As if you were a parcel!" said Lucy indignantly. "You'll
have to tell him where he gets off—interfering so-and-so! He's
not going to shift you out of here unless you want—you like this
place, don't you?"

She was amused to notice that her sympathies had switched
round and were now strongly partisan in favour of Mrs. Marsham
and her smoothly run establishment.

" 'Russ McLartney is with me . . . suggest you ring and fix a
time to come . . .' hm, hm . . ." Lucy suppressed the final paragraph, which was an angry inquiry as to why she had not made
more progress in acquiring Aunt Fennel's pictures, what she had
done with the money given her for that purpose, why the matter
of identity had not been cleared up, and in general, what the hell
was going on? Signed, Uncle W. "Typical," said Lucy. She was
tempted to tear up the letter and throw it away, but he had better be phoned, at least. "Do you want to go and see him, Aunt
Fennel? Feel like a trip to York? Maybe he'll give us a champagne
lunch."

Aunt Fennel had been quite silent since Lucy opened the letter. It was as if her mind were preoccupied, very much elsewhere; and she hardly seemed to be attending. Now she said absently,

"See him? No, I don't want to see him, dearie. I'm quite happy here. I think this is a very nice place."

"You don't feel like an outing to York? Bit of shopping?"

"No, thank you, dearie. I never did think much of the shops in York."

"Okay. I'll tell him to go take a long walk off a short pier. If he wants to see you, he can come here."

"I don't want to see him at *all*, dearie."

"Who would?" Lucy agreed. "But one might as well be civil. I don't suppose he'll come." Unless lust for the pictures fetches him over, she thought.

Aunt Fennel's expression was still distant and withdrawn; she mumbled her lips together, and her eyes had the apprehensive look she had begun to lose since coming to Wildfell Hall.

"*You* can see him if he comes, dearie. I shan't. But you won't let him move me away from here, will you? Promise?"

Her thin fingers tightly gripped Lucy's. Miserable little bastard, Lucy thought, putting the poor old dear in such a fright again. He shan't upset her any more if I can help it.

"Don't worry," she said, "he needn't see you if you don't want. You can always retire to bed with a cold."

"That's a nobby idea; in fact I don't feel too well now; hearing from him has upset me. I think I'll have a little lie-down now."

"Yes, you do that."

Lucy helped the old lady into bed, crossly dislodging the repellent Baby Brother, who was asleep on the knitted patchwork. He yawned, stretched his gross body, and jumped out on to the portico.

"I do wonder if Taffypuss was really killed by a fox?" Aunt Fennel murmured, looking after him. "Didn't you say you saw a cat when you went to High Beck?"

"Yes, but surely it couldn't have been your Taffy. You said Colonel Linton buried him. This one was probably a stray."

"Suppose Colonel Linton was mistaken?"

"That doesn't seem likely. Now, don't you worry your head

about that—have a nice nap. I'll call you in plenty of time for supper."

Troubled by the old lady's rambling tone and dreamy, vacant air, she ran down to help Fiona prepare carrots for the evening meal.

"What's up? You look like Madame Defarge sharpening the guillotine."

"Just thinking about my uncle. He's arrived in England and making hell—wants to know why I haven't got any pictures yet."

"Just let him try getting them out of the good people of Appleby," said Fiona cheerfully. "Then he'll know. By the way, when I was exercising my powers of persuasion on Mrs. Thorpe, unsuccessfully, I'm afraid, I heard an interesting piece of gossip about Mrs. Marsham's son."

She glanced towards the door.

"Oh yes?" Lucy was inattentive, longing to get away and read her letter.

"He started training as a doctor, it seems, but got into trouble over some back-street abortion affair in Birmingham and had to give up. Now he has this osteopath's practice which, according to Mrs. T., is a highly shady business; she knows someone who has a friend who has a cousin who has a neighbour who has a daughter who's no better than she should be who went to him for you know what. All first-hand evidence as you can see."

Lucy stopped peeling. "That's a worry," she said slowly. "I wonder if it's on account of Harold that I've had this uneasy feeling about the place, that Adnan warned me off it? He'd know about a thing like that. Am I right to leave Aunt Fennel here?"

"Mrs. Thwaite did say that none of this had anything to do with Mrs. Marsham; she's as honest and jannock and hardworking a body as you could hope to find."

"Fiona," said Lucy abruptly, "I suppose *you* wouldn't consider looking after Aunt Fennel?"

"How do you mean, ducks? Look after her where?"

"Back at her own cottage—if she could be persuaded to go? It's a dear little place—" A dear *haunted* little place, Lucy thought, but Fiona was supremely unimaginative; if she did encounter a manifestation of the supernatural she would probably kick its shins and deal it a brisk blow with a hockey stick—"you could have your baby with you there, it would be great!"

"Well, I must say, I wouldn't mind," Fiona said slowly. "Your Aunt Fennel's a honey and a darling, I'd get along all right with her . . ."

"You see, it wouldn't cost any more than keeping her here— less, probably. And if she moved back to High Beck old Colonel Linton could be persuaded to part with his pictures. The main difficulty may be persuading Aunt Fennel herself to agree, but you're a big tough girl and she likes you—if she felt she'd be safe with you—"

"I'll think about it," said Fiona. "Really, it's not a bad notion. I don't think darling Mrs. M. and I are going to hit it off much longer, now measles are past their prime."

The carrots were done; there was only the fish to steam. Lucy escaped for five minutes and ran across to the stable-yard where little PHO was parked. Sitting in the driver's seat, she pulled Benovek's letter from her jeans pocket; there would just be light enough to read it.

The envelope was large, square, and white.

There should be a seal on the back, she thought, turning it over, with recollections of *Villette*. I ought to fetch my embroidery scissors and snip round it, carefully preserving it to put under my pillow. Pity people don't use them now.

There was no seal, but there was something else which did catch her eye; a large ginger cat's hair, sticking out from under the sealed flap. Odd; very odd, Lucy thought; it looks exactly like one of that revolting Baby Brother's hairs; but how would it get *under* the flap?

She gave it a tweak; the hair stayed firmly in place.

There were always cat-hairs on Lucy's jeans, because Baby Brother, whether welcome or unwelcome, rubbed vigorously against any human leg he encountered and shed fur in handfuls; Lucy found a hair on her trouser-leg and compared it with the one under the envelope flap. They seemed identical.

Has that goddam Mrs. Marsham been reading my mail?

The idea made her burn with fury, but it seemed the only explanation. She wished she still had Wilbie's envelope, to recheck and see whether that, too, had been tampered with, but unfortunately she had tossed it into the kitchen stove.

At last, with a feeling as if greasy fingers were on her arm, jeering voices whispering behind her back, she opened the envelope, prising it up with a pencil so that the cat's hair remained gummed to the flap.

Dear Lucy,

Julius Writtstein, who visited me last Wednesday, was immensely impressed by your aunt's picture and says that if there are more, and if she is agreeable to the idea, he would be glad to handle them for her at his Mayfair gallery. I may say that Julius is not at all in the habit of making such a suggestion after seeing a single sample of an artist's work, so this is an offer to be taken seriously, as I am sure you will appreciate. Can you let him know as soon as possible how your aunt feels on the matter (I will get my secretary to put the gallery's address at the bottom) and, if she approves, send him all the pictures you can lay hands on. Julius did not commit himself to the question of prices at this stage but, quite honestly, if you or she can produce ten or twenty canvases like the one you sent me, I think that your mind may be relieved of financial anxiety about her from now on.

You are right, I love the picture! I look at it all day. And your letters give me inexpressible pleasure. But you should lose no more time in those northern parts—there has been too much delay already. Make haste back to my piano!

                                                        Max B.

With a start, Lucy glanced at her watch and realised that she had been sitting in the car reading and thinking about this short letter for twenty minutes. Guiltily, she tucked it back into its envelope, and was about to move when she saw somebody leave the little grotto-summer-house among the conifers and make for the Hall, not crossing the open tract of rough park grass, but skirting furtively round by the belt of evergreen shrubs. Dusk was thickening; a great owl coasted by on moon-coloured wings. Lucy could not distinguish the man very clearly; he was short, and carried something under his arm—golf club? Fishing-rod? Perhaps it was Harold Marsham come back? No, too short for Harold, too fast-moving for Clarkson, the gardener, who had a pronounced limp. In a moment he reached the door that led by a back stair to Mrs. Marsham's flat, opened it, and disappeared.

Maybe she has a boy-friend, Lucy thought. Though it would be a bold fellow who'd take her on. Honestly, though, this place is beginning to spook me; I just hope Fiona and Aunt Fennel agree to my plan, I'm sure that would be the best arrangement.

She hurried back to the kitchen, where Mrs. Marsham was helping Fiona serve up steamed fish with mashed potato and carrot.

"My uncle's staying in York," she said abruptly before Mrs. Marsham could ask why she was late. "Will it be all right if I phone him after supper and go over to see him tomorrow afternoon?" I bet you know that already, you hag, I bet you read his letter.

"Of course you may have time off if you wish," Mrs. Marsham said smoothly. "But why don't you invite your uncle to come here? I'd expect he would like to inspect the place where Miss Culpepper is staying."

"Well, I will; thanks; but he's over on business and may not have time."

Aunt Fennel ate very little supper, Lucy noticed. The old lady's attention kept wandering; she would pause, with a spoon halfway to her mouth, and fall into a worried abstraction.

"Don't let your rice pudding get cold, Aunt Fen dear!"

"I keep thinking about Taffypuss," Aunt Fennel said apologetically. "I keep wondering if, after all, he's still up there at High Beck, half starved, with no one to look after him. I do wish you'd slip along after supper, dearie—it wouldn't take a minute, in your little car—and see if you can see him. If it is Taffy he'll have a big black A mark in the middle of his forehead."

This seemed such an unreasonable request that Lucy was quite dismayed. Had the news of Wilbie's advent so upset Aunt Fennel that she was becoming slightly senile?

"It'll be dark now, Aunt Fennel," she said gently. "Supposing I take a look tomorrow?"

"Very well, dearie," the old lady sighed. "I'll be off to bed then, if you really can't go this evening?" She gave Lucy a slightly reproachful look, and made her way slowly upstairs.

"He's in York—if it *is* him." Mrs. Marsham put down the tray. Goetz peered under the metal dish-covers.

"Steamed *fish*—for the Lord's sake! Can't you give us anything better than that?"

"Is he going to come here?"

"I don't know. The girl's going to call him—she wants to go and see him. I said ask him here."

"Good. When's she going to phone?"

"Any time now."

Harbin took off the extension receiver and laid it down. They sat listening. Presently they heard a crackle, and a voice.

"Royal Turpin Hotel—can I speak to Mr. Wilberfoss Culpepper . . . Uncle Wilbie? Lucy speaking. I got your letter."

"Hel*lo*. Princess. How's our little highness?"

Mrs. Marsham drew a snapping breath.

"I'm okay, thanks. I gave Aunt Fennel your message, Uncle Wilbie, but she's not keen to go to York, so I guess if you want to see her you'll have to come here."

"That's not at all convenient, Princess." As usual he sounded injured and put-upon. "In fact I don't think it can be managed; Russ and I are up to the ears in conferences. This is ridiculous! It's essential we should all meet and have a chat."

"Sorry," said Lucy. "I'm prepared to come over and see you tomorrow if you want. But Aunt Fennel won't be budged. Says she's happy where she is and no wish to move."

"How do I even know she's who she says she is?" he demanded angrily. "Can you bring a photo of her?"

"Oh really, Uncle Wilbie! What would that prove? When did *you* last see her? Anyway I've no camera. I'll come over and see you tomorrow afternoon about five. Okay? See you then."

"Hey, wait, Lucy, what about the pictures?"

"Tell you when I see you."

"What's this about pictures?" Harbin demanded when Lucy had rung off.

"Oh, some nonsense. When the old lady was living at home she used to do paintings all mixed with embroidery and patchwork and give them away to people—there are lots in Appleby—and it now seems the Culpeppers think they might be saleable, and want to get hold of them all. That sounds like Fred, doesn't it; he always liked to grab anything that might turn out valuable."

Harbin nodded slowly in agreement.

"Do you think that *was* Fred?"

"Well—American accent, of course. But then he would, after twenty years there. It could have been Fred. It was like his way of talking."

Harbin nodded again.

"Pity he won't come to this place. I wonder why? Could he know you were here, Linda?"

"He wouldn't know I'd changed my name."

"I'll ring Crossley; ask him to get a snap of this guy."

Goetz sniggered. "He wants a snap of his old auntie, you want one of him—it's like those royal marriages. Everyone acting coy."

"Harold could go and look at him," Mrs. Marsham said. "He'll be in York tomorrow."

"Harold won't—"

"Won't what?"

"Won't know him."

"He could get a picture."

"No need to worry Harold; I'll get Crossley on to tailing him. And maybe we ought to get hold of some of these pictures?"

"Why?" said Mrs. Marsham. "What use are they?"

"Bait, maybe."

Goetz laughed again. "It's really just that he doesn't want Fred to get them."

"Who has them?"

"Oh, most people in the village. And Adnan, the doctor in Kirby. But it's a trouble getting people to part, it seems."

"I don't mind going to some trouble for Fred."

"Nor does Linda, do you Linda love? What'll you do, give him a cold bath, like the old girl who wandered up here?"

"Fred's *my* pigeon," Harbin said. "Just you leave him to me."

Mrs. Marsham shrugged and went out.

"That's another angle," Harbin looked after her thoughtfully. "I don't want her interfering; Linda's getting a bit dictatorial in her old age. Maybe she'd better have a day off; two birds with one stone." He reached for the telephone again.

Lucy started for York in a drenching and purposeful rain; summer had turned to autumn. Leaves hurried from the wind-battered trees in great flocks; the whole upland countryside looked abused and bedraggled.

On her way she had the luck to catch a five-minute fill-in before the afternoon concert: Max Benovek playing Scarlatti sonatas.

Darling Max, if it weren't for the thought of you in between times, I swear I'd go frantic. Wilbie's being just as cussed as ever, and Aunt Fennel's decidedly queer today; I'm worried about her. Can it be that she really isn't Aunt Fennel, and Wilbie's arrival has put her in dread of discovery?

It was quite agreeable to go in out of the wet into the opulent Turkey-carpet and potted-palm atmosphere of the Royal Turpin Hotel—until she saw her uncle, just the same as ever.

"Hello, Uncle Wilbie, hi, Russ."

"So now, Princess dear, just tell us the whole story, will you?"

"Not much to tell, really," said Lucy.

She looked across the tea-table at smiling, pink-faced little Wilbie, hating him just as much as always. Seeing him again made her realise how life had changed for her since leaving his home. Her love for funny old Aunt Fennel, her love (yes, all right, wise guy Adnan!) for Max Benovek had introduced her to a new region of experience, and she was most profoundly reluctant to make a present of any part of this to Uncle Wilbie, grinning at her with plump malice, munching on buttery crumpets, reducing everything to plot and counter-plot, cheat, scheme, or be cheated.

"So where are all the old girl's pictures?"

"Scattered all over the village. Nobody will part; they are thought to be lucky. Adnan, the doctor who looks after the old people at the home, he's got nine or a dozen. But he won't part either. Well, he did offer me one."

"Big of him. Where's he live?"

"In Kirby."

"I'll get after him," said Russ.

Lucy started to speak, and checked herself. Adnan was a tough proposition; she was not concerned about him, he could take care of himself. But she decided not to mention Colonel Linton. He was a nice old boy; besides, he was Lucy's preserve.

"And what about the old girl's identity? You're still honestly not sure? How d'you know she's not Miss Howe?"

"I think she's just as likely to be Aunt Fennel pretending to be Miss Howe pretending to be Aunt Fennel."

"Why'd she do that, for pete's sake?"

"I don't know," said Lucy. "Sometimes I get the idea she's not sure now herself which of them she is. She thinks somebody killed her friend and now wants to kill her."

"Sounds crazy to me," said Wilbie. "Any chance of getting her into a mental home?"

"Good heavens, *no*; she's not in the least crazy," said Lucy, keeping calm with an effort.

"Well, Princess, you've made a pretty fair balls-up of everything, haven't you," Wilbie said genially.

Lucy exploded with temper. "I like that! I found her, didn't I? I got her out of that ghastly old drunk's house and fixed her up in a decent place where she's happy—"

"And what about the pictures? And what about the cash? I suppose you spent *that* on this amazing jalopy I see parked outside?"

"The cash is here," said Lucy angrily. She slapped down a pile of American Express cheques. "All except ten dollars which I'll pay you when I get my wages from Mrs. Marsham."

Wilbie whistled. "So! Where did the car come from then?"

"She found it in a wood," suggested Russ, who had kept silent during this exchange. Lucy, studying him from time to time—yes, he really was amazingly like Harold Marsham except for the difference in colouring—found his ironic eye always on her, which annoyed her still further.

"Max Benovek gave it to me, if you want to know!"

"*Really?* That's the guy who's going to teach you piano? The character who's dying? That was mighty decent of him—wasn't it, Russ?"

"He doesn't sound all that dying to me," said Russ. "He must have liked your playing an awful lot."

"Wonder what he expects in return for the car?" said Wilbie. "I mean—we all know our little Princess is quite a *genius* on the keyboard, but this seems quite unusual—or does he deal out sweet-pea-coloured automobiles to all his lady fr— pardon me, his lady pupils?"

My goodness, he does loathe me, thought Lucy, meeting Wilbie's twinkling little eyes over the greasy crumpet-plate.

Hating him so much herself, she should not have been surprised at the power of the hate he felt in return, but it still came as quite a shock. The fact that she had won Benovek's approval seemed to have intensified Wilbie's feelings against her to the point where they were almost beyond his control.

"I'm not staying here to be sneered at," she said furiously, pushing back her chair. "I've told you all I know, and you know where to find Aunt Fennel if you want her. I'm off." She slung her duffel coat over her shoulders and marched out into the downpour.

"Hey, Lucy, come on back!" called Wilbie in annoyance, grabbing up his watch from beside his plate and starting after her.

"Oh, what's the good?" said Russ calmly. "She won't come back. You shouldn't have needled her about the Benovek guy. It certainly does bug you that she's the only member of the family with the creative streak, doesn't it? Too bad Corale's such a dead loss."

"You keep your opinions to yourself," said Wilbie angrily. "If you want to be useful, look up this doctor's address, what's his name, Adnan. And hire us a car—something with a four-wheel drive and good tyres and plenty of room in back.— What's all that commotion outside?"

"Car crash," Russ presently returned to report.

"It would be too much to hope that our little Lucy was involved?"

"Afraid so. Truck overturned on some guy just as he was getting out of his car; it was loaded up with newsprint and he's still buried underneath."

"Oh," said Wilbie, losing interest. "That an evening paper? What's on at the movies?"

Lucy drove back to Appleby in a black rage, going much faster, overtaking more recklessly than was her normal habit. Just outside Appleby, however, she was obliged to slow to a crawl, for the travelling hedger was negotiating a particularly narrow stretch of lane at its maximum fifteen miles per hour and the driver could not or did not choose to let her by; very likely he could not hear her, for the tractor and the electric shears together made a formidable stuttering roar. At last he pulled in and halted at the foot of the track leading up to High Beck; Lucy angrily shot past and did not remember until she was halfway to Wildfell Hall that she had promised to go and look for a black A-mark on the stray tabby that roamed the glen.

"Oh hell," she thought, "I'll do it tomorrow. Aunt Fennel will just have to wait another day. After all the cat seems perfectly fit and well; probably has a high old diet of rabbit. Or maybe Colonel Linton feeds it."

The rage against Uncle Wilbie had exhausted her; she felt heavy and aching with it, hardly able to face the prospect of giving the old people their supper and shepherding them to bed.

Mrs. Marsham met her in the hall.

"Oh—Miss Culpepper. Thank goodness you're back."

Lucy's heart sank. "Is anything wrong?" she asked, observing Mrs. Marsham's pallor and distraught appearance. "Not Aunt Fennel?"

"No—no, it's Harold, my son. He's been in an accident in York, he's in the infirmary there, they just phoned me. I'd like to go at once. Can you see to things here? Adnan's coming either tonight or tomorrow—old Miss Copell's got a bit of a temperature."

"I'm so sorry—that's awful for you. Yes, I'll keep an eye on things—hope you have better news by the time you get there. Nothing special that needs doing?"

"No—just the usual routine. Oh, I seem to have lost one of my contact lenses—they're insured, as they're so tiny that once you drop them they're almost impossible to find—but if you should come across it, could you put it in the box on my desk?"

"Sure."

Mrs. Marsham hurried out through the kitchen. Lucy followed, and found Fiona stirring a massive cauldron of baked beans.

"Meals—meals—I must say, looking after just one great-aunt would be a nice change. Did you hear about Mrs. Marsham's son? Poor wretch—sixteen tons of newsprint fell on him—it took them an hour to fish him out. He isn't expected to live."

"Poor woman—how terrible for her."

During the evening Uncle Wilbie telephoned Lucy.

"Hi, Princess!" He sounded perfectly cordial; they might have parted that afternoon on the most dulcet terms. "Just ringing to tell you that Russ and I are shifting camp; going on to Kirby. To the Promenade Hotel there, if you should want to get hold of me."

"Oh really?" said Lucy coldly. "Tomorrow?"

"No, tonight. We finished our meetings in York and I got a sudden yen to sniff the ocean, found the Promenade had a couple of rooms, so we're just about to flit. Might look in on you to-morrow now we're so much nearer."

"Tomorrow's not very convenient for a visit," Lucy said drily. "The woman who runs the home has had to rush off as her son's been involved in an accident, and we're very short-staffed."

"I heard about the accident, it was on the local radio news; hap-pened just outside this hotel. Poor thing," Uncle Wilbie said cheerfully. "Oh well, if you don't want us tomorrow we might go up and take a look at High Beck cottage, for old times' sake."

"I thought you couldn't remember if you had even been there. Now you must excuse me; I've a lot to do."

Lucy locked the front and back doors, checked that the con-valescents were sleeping peacefully and that Miss Copell was no worse, and then dozed on a camp bed she had made up for her-self on the landing, since Mrs. Marsham, distracted by worry, no doubt, had locked the door leading up to her own quarters on the third floor. The night passed without event. Fiona had been obliged to return home to see to her baby, but promised to be back by ten in the morning, and Mrs. Thwaite's Ann had been persuaded to arrive at seven, with the milk. Eunice, the sulky girl from Kirby, also turned up, so routine went on more or less as usual.

"Did you go and have a look at the tabby puss?" Aunt Fennel asked hopefully when Lucy took up her porridge.

"Aunt Fen, I'm terribly sorry, I was late getting back and I didn't."

"Could you today, dearie, do you think? It *is* so much on my mind."

"Aunt Fen, love, I don't know if I shall be able today—we are pretty hard-pressed, you know, with poor Mrs. Marsham away. She rang half an hour ago to say her son is still in a critical state and she can't leave him."

Aunt Fennel treated this news with the inattention frequently accorded by elderly persons to details about individuals with whom they are not personally acquainted; she said pertinaciously, "I *worry* so when I think of that poor puss with no one to feed it. *Try* and go, dearie."

"I can't till the doctor's been, anyway."

The old lady was sitting in a bedside chair eating breakfast while Lucy straightened her covers; after a pause she said plaintively, "My right knee's rather stiff today, dearie. Do you suppose you'd have time to put on a hot compress?"

Really, they are like children, Lucy thought, sighing; if they can't get attention one way, they try something else. But this seemed a request that could not reasonably be ignored, so she said, "I'll do it at once, before Adnan comes," and hurried off to get hot water, lint, and Radiant Salts.

"Uncle Wilbie wanted to come here today, but I told him it wouldn't be convenient," she said, rubbing the knee vigorously.

"Oh well, that's a good thing then," Aunt Fennel said in something more nearly approaching her normal manner. She added thoughtfully, "I never did like either of those boys, but Wilbie was by far the worse."

Lucy's hands checked a moment in their rubbing; she was on the point of speaking, but did not.

"Both bone selfish, both dishonest, both lazy," Aunt Fennel went on. "How James could have had such a pair of sons! Nothing would stop them when it was a case of getting something they wanted. Wilbie was stronger than Paul, of course—"

"My father wasn't dishonest!" burst out Lucy.

"Oh, but he was, dearie." Aunt Fennel gave her a brief, vague glance, as if she had almost forgotten Lucy's presence. "Yes, just as bad as Wilbie, only not so clever with it. Well, I remember when he stole Wilbie's new camera and Wilbie found out—my goodness, *then* there was trouble. It always upset Wilbie terribly when someone else tried to cheat him, because he was such a sly one himself!"

"I don't believe you." Lucy's hands were trembling; she poured more hot water into the basin and picked up another piece of lint. "Anyway they were probably only children then—how old were they?"

"Then later on it was money, and to make matters worse they were both after the same girl, only Paul got her," Aunt Fennel went on dreamily. "Paul had the charm—girls never liked Wilbie—"

Lucy heard an echo of Wilbie's voice: "With all his faults, Paul was a dear lovable fellow—at least the girls loved him—"

It's not true, she thought. Aunt Fennel's just teasing me, because I wouldn't go and look for her cat. It's probably the thought of Wilbie in the neighbourhood that's put her in this funny mood.

"Paul was musical, too, and Wilbie was jealous of that, because he hadn't got a scrap of the artist in him. But Wilbie was the stronger, oh yes; Paul couldn't bear responsibility; he abandoned his wife and child, went to Canada and died. Whereas Wilbie's done well, I believe—"

Angrily, heedlessly, Lucy dipped the lint in the bowl, gave it a swift squeeze and dropped it on Aunt Fennel's knee. The old lady flinched.

"Oh, dearie, that's *hot!* It's far too hot. Take it off, quick!"

With a pang of remorse Lucy snatched it off and saw the red square that had begun to rise at once on the thin old leg.

"I'm sorry, Aunt Fennel, I'm terribly sorry! I wasn't thinking. I don't believe it's going to be too bad, though. Here, quick, I'll put a bit of salve on it," she added contritely. But Aunt Fennel shrank away from her hand.

"Never—never mind," she quavered. "I'll see to it myself! I'd sooner, thank you. You take away the basin."

She ignored Lucy's outstretched hand with the salve, and tottered with shaky dignity back to her bed.

"I'll have a little rest; that was rather a shock." And when Lucy followed to turn back the covers, Aunt Fennel, as if expecting another act of violence, retreated to her dressing-table, where she started rummaging in a drawer full of tubes and little bottles, casting one of her old distrustful glances at Lucy.

Oh, my goodness, does she think that *Wilbie* put me up to this?

"Please let me make it better, Aunt Fennel!"

"Don't bother, thank you," the old lady said. A bell rang. "Won't that be the doctor? Hadn't you better go, if Mrs. Marsham's away?"

Angry and unhappy, Lucy went towards the bedroom door. "I'll come back soon and see how you are," she said.

"Don't bother, thank you," Aunt Fennel repeated. She added, "If it should be Wilbie, say that I don't want to see him," and shut the door gently but firmly behind Lucy's back.

XI

"Brr!" exclaimed Adnan. "These Yorkshire fogs! A hot tot of egg-nog, dearest Miss Lucy, prepared by your skilful hand, would be most acceptable."

Lucy had been too busy all morning to take account of the weather. Now, glancing past him through the glass-paned front door she saw that thick, slow-moving coils of fog completely shrouded the park from view.

"But what is the matter, dear girl? You seem upset—agitated. The pulse and breathing are accelerated, cheeks flushed, the expression is discomposed—pray tell me what is troubling you? Are you having difficulties in Mrs. Marsham's absence?"

"No, no—I mean, it's not the patients. Old Miss Copell isn't any worse." She led him upstairs.

"No," he agreed, when he had inspected Miss Copell. "She is on the mend. It is not another case of measles—merely a feverish cold. We need not apprehend another Crabtree episode—though I must reiterate, dear Lucy, that your notions about misuse of measles serum are utterly unfounded. Try not to catch this cold though—you are not as strong as you like to pretend. Now tell me what has disturbed you?"

"Oh—" said Lucy reluctantly leading the way to the kitchen, as he seemed bent on eggnog, "it's too trivial. I had slight words with my aunt, that's all. It was entirely my fault, too."

"Tell Papa Mustapha all about it."

Quite without intending to, she found, as she beat up the egg-nog, that she was doing just that.

"Ah yes," he sympathised. "Very undermining, I quite agree. Very demoralising, to find that the father whose image you have set up on high all this time is in fact no better than the detested uncle. A most disagreeable shock."

"And the worst of it is," said Lucy, sipping her own eggnog and not looking at Adnan, "that I remembered something else. It's queer, I remembered it a couple of days ago, but I wouldn't *let* myself remember it completely. It was a memory of a picnic with my father, and it was a goodbye picnic, because he was going right away afterwards, catching a train that would take him to a boat. After we'd said goodbye to him, my mother picked me up and held me desperately tight; I can remember her saying, I don't know if it was to me or to somebody else, 'The truth is, Paul doesn't want us; he's only too glad to get away.' It's queer. I'd forgotten that."

"Why so? One does make haste to forget such episodes."

"No, but I'd remembered it once before; at a time when I was living with my uncle and overheard him saying he wished they could find somewhere else for me to live because I didn't fit in with them. I remembered *then*, and forgot again afterwards; isn't it amazing how dishonest one can be with oneself?"

"On the contrary, dear Lucy Snowe, it strikes me that you are a singularly honest and a particularly nice girl. In fact," said Adnan, glancing round to make sure he was unobserved and then rapidly kneeling down on the red-and-black quarry tiles, showing, for once, a remarkable lack of care for his mustard cavalry cords, "in fact, Lucy dear, I shall be very pleased if you will do me the honour to make one of the four wives allowed me by the Koran (though, alas, frowned on by the Turkish legal system). More I cannot say!"

More Lucy could not say either. She stared at him, dumb-founded.

"You are taken aback," he said, getting up as briskly as he had knelt, but not letting go of her hand. "Alas, you still hanker after this Benovek—a most romantic, unpractical aspiration I do assure you, dear Lucy! Now, please, I urge you, take time to consider my proposal carefully—take as long as you wish. I should so much enjoy escorting you back to Turkey! I am supposed to return at the end of this year, and to tell you the truth I do not in the least wish to go—but if I could carry *you* with me, so cool and sensible —like my very own leaf from the pages of nineteenth-century English literature—how lucky, how very lucky I should feel! A—a! Do not speak—I can see that what you said would not be to the purpose. Not to my purpose at any rate! Think it over. And I tell you what," he added magnanimously, "if you really feel you *must* go and sit at the feet of this Benovek, very well! Do that first, and then come to Turkey—I shall keep one of the four corners of my house prepared for you with WELCOME LUCY on the mat!"

He gave her his wide, flashing Mr. Jackson smile, and Lucy felt absurdly moved. She was trying to marshal her voice to thank him when they heard the telephone ring; Fiona came through from the front hall.

"It's for you, Dr. Adnan—your housekeeper. In Mrs. Marsham's office."

Presently Adnan reappeared, looking decidedly put out.

"Really," he said crossly to Lucy, "it is a good thing I had proposed to you before that telephone call. Apparently two men— one of them, doubtless, was your uncle—took advantage of thick fog in Kirby to break into my house and remove all your aunt's paintings. Paintings which I was proposing to make over to you as a bride gift. Now what an embarrassing predicament I shall be in—obliged to take legal proceedings against my future uncle-in-law. However, I absolve *you* of any part in the blame. Good-bye for the present. Think carefully over what I have said."

He marched out, leaving Lucy and Fiona regarding one another blankly.

"Well," Fiona said at length, "I told you he'd invite you to join his harem, didn't I? I was right, wasn't I? What are we giving the old trout for lunch—beef stew? Better get on with it—morning's half gone already."

"Sorry," said Lucy. "Such a lot's been happening. Pass that knife, I'll do the onions."

Fiona gave her a penetrating look.

"Have you got one of your heads coming on? You look like it."

"No, no," lied Lucy. "I'm just a bit worried about those pictures. It seems so odd."

There was a tap on the kitchen window. To their surprise they saw Adnan again; he beckoned vigorously to Lucy, who went out by the back door and round.

"This is a pretty thing to find!" he said.

He was pointing to something pale ginger in colour that lay at the base of the rhododendron shrubs beyond the gravel sweep. With astonishment and revulsion, Lucy, going nearer, saw that it was Baby Brother, the marmalade cat, lying dead, spitted clean through by a long arrow.

"A nice thing for one of the old people to discover," Adnan repeated disgustedly. With his foot he edged the body of Baby Brother out of sight, under the bush.

"But, good heavens," said Lucy in horror, "never mind about discovering it, one of them must have *done* it. How frightful. Everyone here disliked the cat, but I didn't realise any of the old things was as paranoid as that. Lord knows what Mrs. Marsham will say when she gets back—she absolutely doted on the beast."

"Lucy," said Adnan earnestly, "this Wildfell Hall really is not a good place for you or for your aunt. I do not like this occurrence at all. I do not like it following on the accident to Mrs. Marsham's son—"

"For heaven's sake! What's it got to do with that?"

"The police do not think that it was an accident. The truck driver has never come forward. The circumstances were odd. Now look, will you oblige me in this? When Mrs. Marsham returns, take your aunt, take that stalwart Fiona Frazer, and migrate to the aunt's cottage, where you will be peaceful and undisturbed. Will you do that?"

"And leave Mrs. Marsham without help?"

"I'll send up a nurse to look after them."

"There's no furniture in the cottage," said Lucy tiredly.

He swore. "Allah give me patience. I'll send up a van-load first thing tomorrow! Then will you?"

"I'll think about it. I really will! Now I must go in—there's a terrible lot to do."

"I must say," said Adnan gloomily, "Fate has not looked kindly on the moment I chose to offer you my heart." He kissed Lucy's hand, climbed into the Alfa, and drove away, going much more slowly than usual.

A heavy shower of drops fell on Lucy from the trees above. The fog was condensing and turning to rain.

She went in and helped Fiona with the stew.

The white Rover edged its way cautiously through drenching invisibility.

"Watch it," said Harbin. "This is where you knocked the cyclist into the ditch. We don't want any more mishaps like that."

"All right, all right, I'm watching it. You're a fine one to talk. It's just mad for you to come out—that hand would nail you at once."

"No one's going to see us in weather like this."

"If you ask me, *he'll* never go out in weather like this. Why should he?"

"Greed. He wants those pictures. He thinks there are some at the cottage. And he wants to have a look at the old aunt."

"Well, she's back at the Hall. We'd have done better to stay and keep an eye out for him there. Spit him with an arrow." Goetz grinned to himself.

"Oh, have some sense!" snapped Harbin. "We could hardly do him there, right on our own doorstep. After Crossley's balls-up in York we don't want any lines leading to Linda. Besides, I haven't waited all this time just to shoot an arrow through him. He's got to know why it's going to happen. He's going to realise what it's like to lose a hand, to lie helpless and know you're done for and that somebody's going to be laughing at the fix you're in for the next twenty years."

"Easy now," said Goetz. He peered through the streaming windscreen. "Here's the village. Not exactly like Hampstead on bank holiday, is it? And remember, we still don't know for sure that it is Fred."

"No?" said Harbin. "It has all the hallmarks of Fred. Fred in his solid gold waistcoat calmly walking out of the wreckage and going off to catch another plane to the New World; dear lovable Fred always on the look-out to take his chance. He's champion at taking a chance, Fred, but he's stupid when it comes to calculation. I've a feeling in my bones it's Fred, and this time he's going to come to grief."

"This must be the stream," Goetz said presently. "There's a track up either side, Linda said. One goes to the parsonage and church and stops short; t'other goes on to a footbridge you cross to the cottage. This must be it, but we can't drive up; something's parked right in the way. Damn the rain. Can you make out what it is?"

Harbin opened the side window and looked out. "It's a tractor," he said. "No one on it. Find somewhere to stow the Rover out of sight. We'll walk up."

"In all this bloody rain? Charming!" said Goetz bitterly, but he left Harbin and went on to park on a wide verge beyond the end of Appleby. Harbin waited for him, sheltering under the eaves of the public lavatory.

"Did you see who just went up the lane?" he said when Goetz joined him.

"Frankly no," said Goetz shivering. "It could be Ho Chi Minh for all I care. All right, who?"

"If I'm right," said Harbin, "the best bit of bait we could wish for."

Fiona rang the bell for lunch, while Lucy served up the beef stew and dumplings.

"Solid English fare," she observed, returning to push the trolley laden with plates. "Leave some for us, Luce, I'm starving, and you look as if you could do with a bit of protein. How's the head?"

"Okay. Is Aunt Fennel down?"

"No, she isn't, as a matter of fact. Want me to go and give her a shout? She's probably up in her room; she often sits upstairs till lunch-time."

"I'll go," said Lucy. "I've finished serving."

She was in Aunt Fennel's room, looking blankly at the tidy bed, when Fiona called from downstairs, "Lucy! Phone for you!"

"Oh, not Uncle Wilbie *again?* I suppose he's ringing to say he can't come out in this weather and insists on my bringing Aunt Fennel to Kirby—just let him wait till he hears what I've got to say to him."

She ran downstairs in a dangerous frame of mind and picked up the receiver.

"Yes?"

"Lucy? Lucy Culpepper?"

"Speaking!"

"Max Benovek here."

"M-Max?" she stammered. "You? I m-mean, hullo!"

"How are you?"

"I am okay. How—how are you?"

"I am okay too. When are you coming to play my piano? How is your aunt?"

"I'm not sure," she began.

"Well, listen, I have a piece of news. You know the green Eden picture you sent me?"

"Yes."

"I told you Writtstein saw it. He photographed it too. Now he has found someone who wants to buy it and has offered a thousand pounds after viewing this photograph. What do you think of that?"

Lucy gulped. "You're not going to *sell* it?"

"What do you take me for? I said it was not for sale of course—unless you would like me to do so?"

"No—no, of course not. It was a present. —A thousand *pounds?*"

"Pounds. This madman says he will pay as much for others, if they are as beautiful. Perhaps he is not so mad? You and I agree that he is not? So will you be able to send some other pictures quite soon? And then the great-aunt will be nicely fixed up and you need worry about her no longer, but can come and get down to Beethoven, which is what you should be doing at this moment, instead of ploughing about Yorkshire, disarranging other people's lives."

"Oh, Max, I've made a horrible mess of it all. I begin to think I should have left Aunt Fennel at Mrs. Tilney's in peace, instead of dragging her to this Wildfell Hall place."

"I begin to think so too, from what you write in your letters. Well, listen, how about planting her back in her own cottage with this Fiona person, who sounds a sensible girl, to look after her? Would that work?"

"Yes—yes, that's just what I'm hoping to do!"

"We think alike in numerous ways. That is fine, then. And Writtstein will send a representative to do some collecting—you will be surprised how he will persuade people to part with pictures when they hear what he will pay—so don't worry about that aspect any more."

"There's a Colonel Linton who has a lot. But listen—Dr. Adnan's have all been stolen, I have a horrible feeling my uncle's taken them."

"Your uncle? He is in England?"

"And how! He's staying in Kirby, threatening to come here."

"Upsetting for your aunt. And for you."

"Oh, Max! She's gone!"

"Gone? How do you mean?"

"She's been acting rather oddly—rather childishly—for the last couple of days. This morning I—I got impatient and behaved badly to her and that scared her, I think—and now she's vanished. Her outdoor things—her coat and hat are gone, and she's nowhere about the house—I'd just discovered this when you rang."

"Have you any notion where she could be?"

"Yes; yes I have. She had kept asking me to go to her cottage and look for a stray cat I'd seen there."

"So you think she might have gone there herself?"

"I'm afraid she might. But Max, it's pouring with rain—I ought to go after her at once. Goodness knows how long she's been gone—it could be two or three hours."

"Should you ring the police?"

"They'd be pretty sceptical, after last time. No, I'd better just start at once. Oh *Lord*, though, I've just thought: Uncle Wilbie might be there, he said he might go to the cottage today. The last person she'd want to meet."

"Yes, start at once, Lucy. I do not much like the sound of your Uncle Wilbie myself. Can you take somebody with you—Fiona?"

"No, she'll have to stay and keep an eye on everyone here."

"The doctor?"

"He's probably in Kirby now, telling the police about the theft of his pictures."

"Well, listen, Lucy. If I do not hear from you within an hour and a half that you have found your aunt and all is well, I shall ring the police myself—what is their number in Kirby?"

She told him.

"Right, then, off you go. Take the little car, wear your duffel coat—"

"Yes, yes!"

"And ring me directly you find her, understand?"

"Yes I will, Max."

"In any case," he said, "you must find her before seven, for there is a recorded recital of me then playing the Goldberg Variations which I should wish you to hear. Okay?"

"I know; I'd marked it already."

"And, Lucy?"

"Yes?"

"Take care," he said. "I can't do without you very well."

"All right, I'll take care. Good-bye for now."

"Good-bye."

Nice to be out walking in rain once more. Rain rather heavy, but road so familiar; must have been this way hundreds of times, thousands of times, coming home from High Tops, from picking bayberries or juniper or boghean, fern or ragwort or broom tops. Dill would be walking along too, taking turns with heavy basket, or at home with fire and tea ready; oh Dill. Never mind, that place really not bad, may get accustomed to it in time, good air, grass outside windows, own familiar country. Own cottage would be better still, if only could eliminate worry about That Other One. But how? And now worry about Taffypuss. Can't really be Taffypuss, can it? Almost sure, *almost*, that Taffypuss died, but never having *seen* him dead, can't be utterly certain. Keep thinking about him, dreaming about him. Suppose That Other One came to High Beck and hurt him? Can't bear the idea. Different with Dill: her poor stiff hands reaching out of stream; dreadful, but at least a certainty. Whatever she went through, now she's safe; happy; can't be harmed any more. Suppose that would be true of me, if That Other One did get me? Safe at last. Queer, never looked at it that way before. Will have another think about it in a minute when over the top of this little rise; need breath for breathing, not thinking. Rain coming down very heavy, now; one thing, have good thick outdoor shoes on Lucy child made me buy in Kirby. Worried, very worried about Lucy child. At first didn't know whether to trust, such a queer light and jangling sound coming from her like something out of tune. Then tuned, came clear, trusted her; happy, very happy, like own child, like with Dill. Paul's child, queer when you think of Paul. But he had that music in him, must have had something good about him. Then with Lucy child suddenly trouble, light went murky, out of tune, as if infection caught from That Other One. She'll get over it again, won't she?

Village now. No one about, rain pouring down, beck will rise fast if this goes on. Specially as weather coming down from moor, probably been raining there all night. Have to hurry, get to cottage in case beck rises over bridge. Lucky no one in village, weather too bad, neighbours might fuss, worry, try to keep me from going up. Suppose Lucy child will worry when finds I'm gone? Wrong to tell her about her father, upset her. Good little thing really, not like him, more like her mother, more like me. Will tell her so when see her next. Only a little thoughtless sometimes. Should have gone to see about Taffypuss for me, must have known how worried I was.

Track off to High Beck. Two men pass me, going quick. Strangers? Don't say anything. Know every bend, tuft, rock in this path. Taffypuss would always come down to meet us hereabouts. Hazel bushes, mountain ash, holly.

Lucy child fretful because of that piano man, perhaps? Would have to meet him before deciding whether trustworthy. Foreigner. Better if she stayed with me and Taffypuss, all three happy together.— Now, where were we, thinking about death, that's right. Not much of a problem really; really, maybe, no problem at all.

Here's ash stump; not covered yet, so bridge will still be clear. Beck very high, foamy, beautiful dark brown peat-coloured water, dark red-brown like garnet stone. Rushing along, rocks in middle all covered, only showing at sides. Track steeper than I remember —was it always so steep? Have to stop and take breath. Hedge-cutting tractor parked up there, foolish place to leave it, Lenny Thorpe always lazy about taking back to barn. Inconsiderate if we wanted anything delivered to High Beck, van couldn't get up track, but suppose everyone knows cottage empty now. Past old parsonage on opposite bank, kind Edward Linton, pity he took to drink, wonder why? Past church, opposite bank turns to cliff, then round bend in dene. Past tractor, two men sitting in cab, queer, suppose waiting for rain to stop, having lunch maybe. No one I know. Nod to them. Same two men who passed? Strangers, they don't nod back. Now, climb up on to wooden bridge. Slippery slats. Hold tight to wet wires either side. Water rushing along underneath like dark red ink. Across bridge, very slow, very careful. Down stone steps. Now climb up to cottage. Call. Puss? Puss? Taffypuss? He doesn't come. But then, wouldn't expect cat to be out in all this rain. Probaby sheltering somewhere, in shed, under bush. Better go into cottage? Wait for rain to stop? But what about That Other One? Suppose he came? Not likely he'd come out in such weather? Anyway, hadn't we just decided not afraid of death? Not afraid of death, no, but awful sudden fright of being grabbed, pushed, throttled—yes, can't help it, still very much afraid of *that*. Now look—Dill would say—one thing at a time? Mightn't be so bad? Anyway, while we're thinking, getting very wet. Let's get under porch roof.

Undo coat, dress, find key in little bag. Queer, door not locked. Can Lucy child have left door unlocked that day she came? Not like her, Lucy child very careful, reliable on the whole. No, lock broken, somebody else been here, That Other One? Don't loiter in porch wondering, go in. Into kitchen. Nobody about. Dear, *dear* little house, sorry to have left you. Are you pleased to see me? No one in scullery or parlour. Upstairs? Taffy? Taffypuss? Downstairs again.

Oh . . .

"What now?" said Goetz.

"Tie her up," said Harbin. "Something in her mouth so she can't call out. Yes. Now fix her in the window-seat, looking out. Half a minute."

He walked outside, recrossed the swaying bridge, and halted by the tractor, turning to give the cottage a critical survey. Then he came back, saying,

"That's okay. You can see there's a person sitting at the window. Enough to make anyone curious. Can she move?"

"No, I've tied her to the knob on the shutter." Goetz giggled.

"There's a poem about something like this: 'The highwayman came riding, riding, riding, Along to the Dog and Duck, Where Bess the landlord's daughter, the landlord's black-haired daughter, Was waiting—'"

"All right, all right, have you finished? Hurry up, we'd better get back to the tractor."

"If you ask me," said Goetz, rather aggrieved, "I spent my time in jug a sight more profitably than you did, acquiring a bit of culture instead of brooding for eighteen years about my missing right flipper. Want a pull up? Lucky this tractor has an enclosed cab, otherwise we'd be getting pneumonia *and* pleurisy. Of all the places to wait—"

"Have you ever driven one of these jobs?" said Harbin.

"Sure. Easy. Easier than a car. All you have to remember is to keep on an even keel—they're top-heavy. Why? What's the idea?"

Harbin was frowning, peering through the downpour.

"Somebody else coming up the track. That's a complication. It isn't the one we want."

Lucy, seeing the tractor still parked where it had been last night, left little PHO down at the bottom by the haunted lavatory and walked up the track. The beck was shouting now in spate, a hollow tenor roar, quite different from its usually clear treble. Rain had increased to what must, surely, amount to a cloudburst. Can't bring the old girl back in this, have to wait in the cottage till it eases a bit. If she's there. Hope to God she is. Light a fire, maybe? I wonder if there's any dry wood in that wash-house place at the back? Still, the rain can't go on long at this rate.

She dragged the hood of her duffel coat well forward, sank her chin in the collar, and hurried past the tractor. Annoying place to leave it. Up on to the bridge. Good Lord, the stream was high; already washing over the transverse wooden slats. With so much water pushing against it the bridge was dragged downstream into a bow-shape that shook and swayed under the impact of great rolling eddies.

"Do I cross or not?" thought Lucy.

She stared up at the cottage on the opposite bank of the dene and thought she saw—but it was difficult to be sure through the cataracting rain—a white face at the kitchen window. She pushed back her duffel hood. Yes, surely that *was* a face—Aunt Fennel? —sitting at the window. Silly old juggins, she had got there and now didn't like to start back. Well, I don't blame her. I'm not a bit enthusiastic myself, however, here goes.

Taking firm hold of the wire rail on either side she moved slowly, carefully, step by step over the jiggling, rocking, slippery slats, marvelling, as she had before, that the two old ladies could have used this insubstantial-looking affair as their only access to the village for so many years. I suppose they just stayed home in bad weather, eating own eggs, baking own bread. Must be stronger than it looks, I suppose. Frankly this rusty wire looks as if it were due to part any minute now. Wonder if the onus is on the council to keep it up, or who looks after it—does somebody splice in a new bit of wire from time to time? Oh well, at least I'm halfway acr—

Behind her she heard a strand of wire snap; the resonant twang was audible even above the rush of the stream. The slats underfoot parted on her left and tipped sharply downstream; instinctively, Lucy dropped to her knees, putting most of her weight on her hands grasping the wire rails.

The left-hand rail gave.

It pulled away from the post on the farther bank and, flying back, struck Lucy in the face. She was swung violently backwards against the right-hand rail, but only for a second; the water, grabbing at her back, threatened to force her under. The bridge was now hanging at a crazy tilt by one rail and one wire; Lucy, up to her waist in water, struggled to turn round and face the cottage, clinging with both hands to the right-hand rail. The sag of the bridge was such that it was going to be like climbing a ladder to get to land.

Duffel coat off, too heavy, if it comes to swimming. Swimming? this beck is only a foot deep as a rule. Ten feet at least now, or I'm the Prince of Wales's fiancée. Kick shoes off too; try and curl your toes over the edge of the slats, there's no other way to grip.

The second wire holding the slats in place parted; this time there was no sound, for it broke under water; but the remaining section of the bridge under Lucy's feet sank and vanished.

I'm done for, she thought, swept under, still hanging on to the last wire rail. She felt it snap behind her and was whirled and rolled by roaring mounds of brandy-coloured water, filling her eyes like blood, swamping and smothering her. Something struck her, a tree or rock, she felt the wire bite into her hands but clung on frenziedly, kicking out, swimming on her back, her side, her front, as the wire thrashed and the water buffeted. Now I know what it feels like to be a salmon, I always hated watching Wilbie battle with some fighting, gasping creature—

To her astonishment she hit the bank, one shin crashed painfully against a rock, her toes dug among stones. She thrust herself upward, still hanging on to the wire which, apparently, was still moored to its post. Her head came above water. She found a foothold-rock and crawled out, coughing and shaking, rubbing beck-water from her eyes.

Dear Max, that was quite a little adventure. I'm really sorry Adnan wasn't here, he'd surely have had himself a whale of a time. Even better than the Big Dipper. What times we live in. Proposal before lunch, nearly drowned before tea. Now I come to think, I haven't *had* any lunch, wouldn't have minded some of that beef stew.

Now then.

Is that Aunt Fennel at the window? You'd think she'd wave or come out? And those men in the tractor—why, for God's sake, didn't they do something, instead of sitting there watching me drown?

Wondering where her duffel coat would come ashore, Lucy started to drag herself up the bank.

Fiona came to the front door of Wildfell Hall, looking harried.

"Yes?" she said. "Who did you want to see?"

"Well, both my niece and my aunt, I guess." Wilbie gave her a winning smile. "And both called Miss Culpepper, as it happens."

"I'm afraid you're out of luck," Fiona said briefly. "Neither of them is around."

"Really? Are you sure?" He looked patently disbelieving. "Would you mind just having a look, to make certain? Surely they wouldn't have gone out in this weather?"

She gave a bleak glance past him at the teeming rain.

"Just the same they have. Your aunt was discovered missing at lunch-time, so Lucy went after her. That was about three-quarters of an hour ago; but we don't know how long she'd been gone."

"Missing? She'd gone out on her own? Why didn't anybody see her and stop her? Have the police been informed?"

"Not yet; Lucy thought probably old Miss Culpepper had slipped back to her cottage. Time to get in touch with the police if she's not there."

"It all seems very careless," said Wilbie disapprovingly.

"Look, Mr.—"

"Culpepper—"

"I'm taking care of this place more or less single-handed at the moment with a couple of part-time girls; if you've any complaint to make, just wait till the matron gets back, would you? She phoned not long ago; she'll be back sometime this evening."

"No—no—that's quite all right, I'm not blaming *you*, my dear," he said hastily. "No, I guess I'll just nip along to the village; I expect little Lucy was right and the old lady went up to her cottage; she and Lucy will be sheltering there till the rain stops, most probably. So I'll go up too and give them a big surprise."

"I'm sure you will," said Fiona coldly. She shut the front door and returned to the kitchen, where Emma Chiddock had taken down the electric beater and was contemplating it thoughtfully.

"No, Emma, it is not scrambled eggs for tea. Sardines on toast. You're getting a thing about that beater. Put it away, for goodness sake, and fetch out the tin-opener. Mrs. Marsham will be back after tea, and I don't want her to find the place all in chaos. Her son's died, poor woman."

"Oh her son's died, has he?" Emma showed no sympathy, in fact there was a note of satisfaction in her voice. "Maybe now she'll have some notion of what it's like when your best friend's put out of the world, sudden, just because she didn't lick somebody's boots. A taste of her own medicine wouldn't hurt Mrs. M. Eye for an eye, tooth for a tooth."

"Oh, do stop being so biblical, Emma, and give me a hand. I'm worried about Lucy and old Miss Culpepper."

"Shouldn't think we'll see *her* again," Emma said darkly. She picked up the tin-opener, but her eyes went back several times to the electric beater with its corkscrew attachment.

"Mighty odd," Wilbie said, returning to the hired Land-Rover. "The old girl's roamed out by herself and Lucy's gone after her, it seems. What a day to choose for a promenade! Girl who answered the door seemed to think she might have gone along to the old cottage, so we'll just nip up there and see. I must say," he added aggrievedly, "it's a damn nuisance the way she always contrives to wander off just when I'm in the neighbourhood; would have saved so much trouble if I'd been able to see her at that boarding-house place in Kirby."

"Telepathy, maybe; she kind of senses when you're close at hand," Russ said drily. He started the Land-Rover with a lurch that caused Wilbie to give him a pained look, and added reflectively, "However if she gets pneumonia and dies, you'll hardly complain, will you? That'd solve one of your problems."

"Why, Russ! What gave you the idea I wanted the poor old lady to die?"

"Well," said Russ, "for one thing, going to that bank in York and finding the old girls made wills in one another's favour. So whoever the pictures belong to, they don't belong to you, right? Whoever this old duck is, she owns the pictures, right? I've a notion those pictures are quite a bit more important to you than that piddling little annuity from Culpepper Pharm. And I've also a notion that something else is bugging you, that you're dead keen to get the whole thing sorted out and leave this country fast. Aren't I right?"

He shot a keen look sideways at his father.

"Well, and can you wonder? Who'd want to stay in this godawful climate?"

"It's just the climate? It isn't anything to do with that Harold Marsham?"

"Who the hell is Harold Marsham?"

"The guy who was squashed by sixteen tons of falling newsprint; there was a picture of him in this morning's Yorkshire *Post*. Son of the matron at the home. Not expected to survive."

"Why should I worry about him? I never even heard of him."

"Oh," said Russ calmly, "just because he was so uncommonly

like me. I wondered if he could be another of your little by-blows, dear old Dad? That's the track to High Beck up there, isn't it? Seems to be something parked dead in the middle, halfway up. We'll have to leave the truck here and walk."

"No, can't leave the truck here; too many nosy people about," Wilbie said hastily, looking up and down the deserted main street of Appleby-under-Scar. "No, I'll tell you what, Russ. There's a Water Board metalled track that leaves the village a quarter of a mile to the east, cuts up behind High Beck cottage, and runs on over the moor past the reservoir; it's quite a good short cut to Kirby. Couldn't do it in this weather in an ordinary car, it's not metalled the whole way, but we certainly can in that thing. Why don't you go along that way—you'll have to open a gate or two, and there are some cattle grids, but don't worry about the 'Private' signs, no one will be about in this weather—and I'll meet you up top; there's a little Ordnance Survey cairn where the path up from the cottage hits the track. Wait for me there."

"You seem to know this part of the country well for a guy who hasn't been back in twenty years."

"Oh, these parts don't change in generations," Wilbie said easily.

"Sure you wouldn't like me to come along with you and add to the family atmosphere?"

"No, don't you worry, Russ, boy; in many ways I think it'll be easier if I'm on my own. All I'm going to do is pass the time of day and see if the old girl *is* Aunt Fennel. No use in both of us getting soaked through," Wilbie said virtuously.

"But shouldn't we offer to drive them back to the Hall?"

"Have some sense. How could we, with all that stuff in the back? No, I'll see you at the cairn." Wilbie zipped up his gay tartan parka, pulled down the flaps of his client-watching cap, and set off briskly up the track. Russ, after a last doubtful look at his stocky retreating figure, turned the truck and drove eastwards along the Appleby village street.

Lot of water in that brook, Wilbie thought, striding uphill. Couldn't be handier conditions, really. Anybody might have an accident: steep bank, bad visibility, slippery steps, so easy to tumble down and hit your head on a rock. So what. The other one did it too, the place is still just as dangerous, isn't it? And if the old lady were to fall, of course our brave little Lucy would go in after her and *she's* got a dicky heart—it all adds up as if it had been worked out by computer. Suppose they aren't in the cottage, though? But they must be, where else could they be?

Hark to the stream; considerable lot of water coming down there. Nuisance about trouser legs getting wet.

And he thought resentfully: What a lot of trouble to dispose of an old lady who ought to have died a long time ago. Anyone would think I had nothing better to do than drop all my other commitments and come trailing over to England; it's always the way.

Want something done properly, you have to do it yourself. Wilbie has to see to it. Wilbie Culpepper. Wilbie the winner. Will be finally recognised as having more to him than anybody realised. Wilbie will show them. As for little know-all Lucy, with her bare toes and her threadbare jeans, setting herself up for an expert on art, princess of culture, squinting through her hair and despising me, like some scrawny supercilious little bird with her snide remarks and her offhand ways, as for that capsy little brat, just wait till I let her know—

He came up to the tractor, passed it without particularly regarding it, and went on to stand in outraged disbelief by the broken bridge. It's bust. Can't get across. That's rubbish, there must be some way across. House and church on that side farther down, you reach them by going back to the village and up the other side of the stream. Yeah, but then there's that bit of cliff in between. Path from the back of the cottage up to the moor? Sure, but that's three miles round, take me an hour, meanwhile Russ wondering where the hell I've got to. How long's the bridge been broken? Maybe old Aunt F. didn't get to the cottage either. In which case, where is she?

He stared at the bridge; dangling slats, strand of wire trailing downstream, might have been broken five minutes or five hours ago. Stared at the cottage; its little dark windows stared back at him impassively. Might be someone inside, might not. Well, if they are in there, they are cut off; yet, but they won't starve, Lucy can walk up over the moor, down the Water Board track for help, and anyway the beck will go down in twelve hours or so.

I can't stay here twelve hours though.

He turned, moved away indecisively, trying to think of some plan, and came face to face with Harbin.

"Hullo, Fred."

Wilbie stood motionless, except that his round head on its bull neck tipped slightly backwards as if his gyro control had shifted a point or two. He licked his lips slightly, then said, "Excuse me," and made to move past Harbin. But the pause had lasted too long.

"Oh no, Fred," Harbin said. "You know who I am."

"Sorry, no idea. Look, I'm in a hurry—"

"You don't remember Flight 507, Liverpool to Boston? You were the drinks steward, wearing a canvas corset with thirty thousand quid's worth of gold slung round your waist in three rows of dear little pockets. Don't you remember that, Fred? You must have a rotten memory."

"*My name's not Fred!*"

"Now I remember that trip so well, because that's when I lost my hand," Harbin said, and took a step forward.

Wilbie's nerve broke, he made a jerky movement to one side, and then saw Goetz looking down at him from the cab of the tractor.

"I like your American accent, Fred. Tell us, then, what did you spend the cash on? Set yourself up in a nice little business, did you? Funnily enough, you know, it's not the thirty thousand I begrudge; it's just this." He shook his empty sleeve. "It was those years in jail while you were living it up. I've thought about this meeting quite a lot."

Wilbie saw that there was no escape downhill past them, so he turned and ran up the track. No footsteps followed. For a moment of wild optimism he thought that perhaps they had intended to do no more than give him a fright; then he heard the tractor start up with a grinding roar that drowned even the stream's voice. Glancing haggardly behind, he saw the tractor begin to move; he also saw his niece Lucy run out of the cottage and stand at the top of the steps, staring across the brown, tossing water. Her face was very white, her clothes were soaking. She called something, he could not catch the words.

"Lucy!" he shouted. "Get help!" He knew she would not be able to hear him with the stream and the tractor; anyway, what could she do? No phone at the cottage. She's a witness, though, he thought; now they know she's seen them they can't really do anything to me.

But he knew this was not true. They could and they would. Desperately, he ran on uphill, slipping and stumbling on the wet rocky track.

Lucy went back into the cottage, sat down by Aunt Fennel on the window-seat, and put an arm round her.

"God knows what's going on, but I don't like it one bit. Were those two men in the tractor the ones who tied you up, Aunt Fen?"

"Yes, dearie."

"But who are they?"

"I don't know." Strangely, Aunt Fennel, who should have been terrified, was not; although very exhausted she seemed quite serene, even cheerful. "Do you know," she confided, "it wasn't as bad as I expected, being jumped on. Doesn't that show you should never worry about things beforehand? Though I was glad when you came and untied me, of course, dearie. What's happening now?"

"Those two men are chasing Uncle Wilbie up the hill. Do you know why they are after him?"

"No, dearie. I daresay they have their reasons. It won't do him any harm to have a good fright."

"I guess plenty of people have reasons for chasing Wilbie." Lucy tried to control her chattering teeth; the cottage was bone-chillingly cold. "Aunt Fen, please tell me—is Uncle Wilbie That Other One? Do you believe that it was he who killed your friend?"

Aunt Fennel peered out of the window, as if to make quite sure that Wilbie was out of sight. The tractor had vanished round a bend in the track and its roar had been replaced by the voice of the stream. What was happening farther up the hill? Lucy shivered again.

"You see, he always had that habit at meals, even as a little boy," the old lady said irrelevantly. "He was so greedy—it was as if he wanted time to stop while he was eating. What do you suppose they'll do to him, dearie?"

"I don't know—and quite honestly I'm scared to think. Why should they grab you and tie you up? Didn't they *say* anything?"

"One of them said something about a tethered goat. The other was talking about someone called Bess."

Lucy shook her head. She was too tired to try and understand it all.

"We oughtn't to stay here," she said. "If—if they do anything to Wilbie—if they come back—" Looking down at the windowsill she saw a small, gleaming lens in the dust. Idly, she pushed it with her finger.

"They can't reach us here, dearie, with the bridge broken. It was wonderful *you* got across."

"The stream might go down again. Anyway, we're both wet and cold and you haven't had your lunch—"

"We could light the fire," Aunt Fennel suggested hopefully. Lucy shook her head.

"No matches. I've looked. And all the wood's soaking. No, we mustn't stay, Aunt Fen."

"But suppose Taffypuss comes back and we've gone?"

Oh damn Taffypuss, Lucy thought wearily. Her wet clothes were dripping on to the granite flags. She squeezed Aunt Fennel's hand.

"We'll come back another day to hunt for Taffypuss. You could even come back and *live* here if you liked, Aunt Fennel. Fiona says she'd come and look after you."

"That *would* be nice, dearie! So long as That Other One was dealt with, so he couldn't come and try any of his wickedness. It is such a dear little house, isn't it?"

With Aunt Fennel in it, Lucy realised, High Beck had lost its aura of anguish. She was what the house had wanted.

"But I'd much rather *you* came and looked after me, dearie —if That Other One was safely out of the way."

"I'm going to be learning the piano—remember?" Lucy said gently. "But I'll come and visit very often."

Aunt Fennel preserved a reproachful silence. After a while she said, "Anyway I don't see how we can leave, dearie. I'm far too tired to walk three miles over the moor."

Lucy said, "But didn't you tell me there's a kind of sheep track along the cliff to the church and Colonel Linton's?"

"But that's so steep, dearie, and it'll be slippery as glass after all this rain. We'd never get along it!"

We've got to, Lucy thought, slippery or no. She longed just to curl up in her wet clothes on the window-seat, to lean against Aunt Fennel and shut her eyes, regardless of cold, to doze and wait, in the silent little house, wait in hopes that help would finally arrive. After all, Max had said he would ring the police in an hour and a half. But would the police immediately come to High Beck? No, they would go to Wildfell Hall first, but they might not do that for several hours, if they had other calls to deal with; several hours spent in sopping clothes in an unheated stone kitchen might well be the death of Aunt Fennel. Besides, what about those two men and Uncle Wilbie? Should not something be done about them?

No, we must leave, Lucy decided, and she said, "I'm going to have a look at the sheep track. Back in a minute."

The rain was still driving steadily down. Although it would be several hours to dusk, the light was bad; a kind of heavy, saturated gloom hung in the dene, and the tree-grown cliff looked dark and forbidding. However, when Lucy climbed along one of the terraces of the neglected garden she found a wicket-gate and a narrow little path, rabbit runway rather than sheep track, which disappeared through tangled growth along the steep bank. Well, at least there are plenty of bushes to grab when we slip, Lucy thought.

She went back to the cottage.

"Come along, Aunt Fen, love. At least climbing will warm us up. I think we can make it. Honestly, if you wait here much longer, you'll catch your death."

"I'm much happier staying in my dear little house," Aunt Fennel said piteously. And she added, with one of her occasional devastatingly intuitive shafts, "I expect you're anxious to get back and listen to some concert, are you? Why don't you go on ahead, dearie, and then presently you can bring your car up the Water Board track with some matches and dry wood. Or wait till the beck has gone down. I'd much rather stay here. I'm not a bit afraid any more."

Lucy said, trying to be patient, "Aunt Fen, I simply can't leave you here on your own! And it's probably only about ten minutes' climb along to Colonel Linton's—then we can sit and dry off in his nice warm kitchen and he can phone Fiona, who'll be worrying about us." She slipped a hand under Aunt Fennel's arm and gently but firmly hoisted her to her feet. "Come on, love—that's the way. Think how pleased Colonel Linton will be to see you."

Very reluctantly Aunt Fennel let herself be steered to the door.

Dear Max, it's perfectly true I do want to get back in time for your Goldberg Variations. But also, surely what I'm doing is for the best?

Russ glanced at his watch for the twentieth time. What in heaven's name could the old boy be doing? If he was seizing the chance to polish off Great-aunt Fennel—as Russ strongly suspected—he was taking a devilish long time about it. Was he slicing her up piecemeal? And what was happening to Lucy?

I'll give him ten minutes—fifteen, thought Russ. Then what'll I do? Suppose a Water Board official comes up to make sure the reservoir's not overflowing, and asks what the hell I'm doing here? I do not like that prospect at all.

He glanced uneasily behind him along the raised track on which he had parked the Land-Rover. The reservoir showed no signs of overflowing, but it was plainly over its usual high-water mark. It lay behind him, a great pewter-coloured lake, stretching for a couple of miles in either direction, sullen-flat, except for the tiny stalagmites of water that rose to meet the forest of rain coming down out of the sky. In front of Russ the land fell away eastwards; on his right stood the little cairn marking some Ordnance Survey point.

Beginning to be cold, Russ got down and walked along the concrete lip of the reservoir, which presently described a sharp curve, paralleled by the track, and rose in graceful steps to the beginning of the dam. Below the dam, a rocky, tree-scattered valley descended towards Kirby, and the track shot steeply down it in a series of zigzags. Hope Wilbie turns up before it gets dark, Russ thought, otherwise I'm going back and round; I don't fancy taking that track at night, in this weather.

He had walked back and forth between cairn and dam half a dozen times; was just turning away from the cairn when he heard a shout.

Pausing, he stared down the steepish path which led over the moor in the direction of Appleby. Somebody was running up it

—Wilbie? When the figure came a bit closer, he recognised the gaudy tartan parka. And something was following him, a darker patch in the general grey of the rain. Its pace was too slow, its engine too noisy for a car, it appeared to have some swinging extension out front—a breakdown truck? When it came closer he recognised the tractor with its hedge-cutting shear-mechanism. What the hell's going on? thought Russ, with calm objective interest. What's Wilbie gotten himself into now?

For the tractor appeared to be chasing Wilbie, veering from side to side as he tacked erratically up the hillside, keeping within snatch-range of him, every now and then making a grab at him with the shears—which consisted of two blades set against two dovetailing rows of rake-teeth.

Kind of teasing him, thought Russ. They could have caught him up and run him down long ago if they'd wanted to. So what's the idea?

Dropping behind the embankment out of view, Russ made his way back to the Land-Rover, which, where it stood, was concealed from the approaching tractor by a heather-grown hummock. He had noticed that the tractor was chivvying Wilbie, herding him as a collie urges a flock in one particular direction, away from the path, up the steeper hillside towards the lip of the reservoir. Russ quietly started his engine, got into gear, and waited. The chase was hidden from him now.

Suddenly he heard an appalling shriek—so high, so prolonged that it sounded more like a machine misused than any human cry. He heard the tractor change key and stammer in its roar; then it came into view, heaving up and on to the track that circled the reservoir. Wilbie was ahead of it, running lurchingly towards the dam. They haven't actually done for him yet, then, thought Russ dispassionately. He shot forward in pursuit.

The two men in the tractor were not expecting to see another vehicle, and the Land-Rover took them by surprise. For an instant it hung alongside, two wheels on the track, two on heather and scree, then it was past and cutting in sharply just where the water-edge curved and the track veered to the left.

The tractor swerved and tilted. "Watch it, you fool!" yelled Goetz, who was driving, to Harbin who, leaning over his shoulder, was operating the crane. Harbin, startled out of his usual impassivity by the sudden swerve, pulled the wrong lever, and the crane swung over and down to the left, fatally adding to the tractor's imbalance. The high, top-heavy vehicle teetered for a moment on the extreme lip of the great concrete bowl, then fell sideways down into the grey water and disappeared.

Russ missed the moment when this happened; having cut in, he had spun his steering wheel to the right and accelerated, to put himself between the tractor and Wilbie; it was out of his rear-view mirror at the instant when it overbalanced. When he looked in his mirror the track behind was empty; startled, incredulous, he looked again, jamming on his brakes, then stopped and stared at the reservoir in which huge black-and-steel concentric circles were shooting out, far across the water.

"Holy cow!" said Russ.

He ran the Land-Rover backwards to the torn spot on the bank where it had occurred, and peered down: nothing could be seen except a great dark crack in the concrete rim, running far down out of sight.

"Russ! Russ!" Wilbie's faint voice echoed along the bank; Russ jerked into forward gear again and ran the Land-Rover along to the dam against which Wilbie was leaning in a hunched position, holding one arm with the other; blood streamed down his parka. Russ looked at his right arm and then away again.

"Can you put a tourniquet on this?" Wilbie said hoarsely. "And then get me to a doctor fast."

Using a spanner, Russ twisted his scarf round the mangled arm.

"Who were they?" he inquired. "Old pals?"

Wilbie glanced behind him. The water was calm again, noncommittal.

"Never mind," he said. "For God's sake, just forget them."

"I dunno," said Russ uneasily. "Oughtn't we to report that we saw the tractor go in? It's cracked the reservoir bed; maybe all the water will escape."

"Someone will notice soon enough. Let's just get away from here!"

"Was it on account of that pair that you weren't keen to come to England?" Russ asked, helping Wilbie into the Land-Rover. Wilbie did not answer the question.

"Brandy in my hip flask," he muttered; tears, and blood from a gash in his cheek ran down his face. When Russ had found the flask and given him a swallow—

"Did anybody see you come up this way?" he asked.

"Not a soul." Russ had started up again and was driving with extreme caution down the zigzag track into Kirby.

"Nothing to connect us then. And I daresay Harbin wasn't the owner of the tractor—"

Wilbie stopped short, but Russ took him up.

"Harbin—that rings a bell. He was the escaped convict—the gold smuggler. Right? They reckoned his pal who was released last fall must have helped him escape. Oh, now I see the whole thing. You must have nipped over here for a quick visit from Stuttgart last summer while Rose and Corale were in Florida and before the first guy—Goetz was his name wasn't it?—was released. I've a notion you meant to get rid of old Aunt Fennel then—why? Maybe because she was the one person in England who knew your whereabouts? Or did you just want those pictures? Of course you didn't want to leave it till after Goetz was out and maybe looking for you. Am I right in guessing that you were the third member of the gang, the one who crawled out of that crashed plane and made off with all the loot? One has to hand it to you, Dad, you certainly seize your chances. In fact the only mistake you ever made was to push the wrong old girl in the river, was that it?"

"Oh God, Russ, stop talking and drive a bit faster, can't you?"

"So then everything was a mess; the old lady was maybe still alive, or anyway you couldn't be sure and if she was alive she was a link with you; she knew your address in America; and Goetz had come out of prison and might have some reason for connecting you with Appleby; evidently did; and all you could think of was to send over little Lucy to sort matters out. That wasn't smart; you'd much better have sent me."

Wilbie was silent. Suddenly he realised how much he hated Russ. God, and I'm saddled with him for life now, he thought. Why do my kids turn out so badly? Puny little Lucy's the only decent one of the bunch with any guts; shame she wasn't mine—

"You realise we can hardly go along to this Doc Adnan's surgery with a crateload of stolen art in back," Russ said.

"There's a first-aid place on the front promenade," Wilbie said.

"Right opposite that big underground car park. I noticed it this morning. You can go there."

"Okay. I guess this is Kirby now. And thank God. My arms are just about wrenched out with nursing this monster round those bends."

Wilbie said nothing. He sat holding his arm, grey, sweating, but calm; things aren't working out too badly, he thought.

XII

"Pictures by an old lady patient, half embroidered, with bits of stuff stuck all over them?" Superintendent Nottall smiled sceptically. "They seem funny things to make off with—someone playing a practical joke, maybe? What would you value them at, Dr. Adnan?"

"Well, I *gave* the old lady fifty pounds apiece for them," Adnan replied moderately.

Nottall dropped his ballpoint and gaped at the doctor.

"*Fifty pounds* apiece? You're joking?"

"I am aware that I got them at a bargain price and was hardly playing fair with the poor old person, but what have you—I am only a hard-up general practitioner, I am not a Rothschild." Adnan carefully rubbed one of his bronze buttons and flicked a ruffle into place. "One must be thrifty where one can."

"I think you must be clean round the bend," Nottall muttered, making a note. "A dozen pictures, owner's valuation six hundred pounds. Subjects?"

"Christian mythology. Bible pictures."

"Any suspicion as to who might have made off with them?"

"Yes indeed."

Nottall's telephone rang. He picked up the receiver.

"Switchboard. Superintendent, there's a Mr. Benovek on the line, calling from Coulsham, Surrey, who wants to speak to somebody about a Miss Culpepper—could you take the call?"

"Benovek?" Adnan looked up, startled. "He's ringing about Miss Culpepper?"

"Hello?" said Nottall. "Kirby police here. Can I help you?"

He sat listening. His blank expression intensified. Presently he said, "And what value did this expert place on the picture? I *beg* your pardon? And you say you have reason to believe the old lady has been missing for several hours?"

Adnan looked at him sharply.

"The niece has gone after her and has not returned? Are you aware, Mr. Benovek, that this old lady was reported missing once before, and that time it turned out that she had simply gone to sleep in someone's car—yes, yes, very well, we'll look into it. I'm afraid we're short-staffed at the moment, though—we've been having exceptionally heavy rain here and several roads are flooded—yes, we'll do what we can and ring you back as soon as possible."

He wrote down a number.

"Old Miss Culpepper's missing?" said Adnan.

"Wandered off again, it seems, and the niece has gone after her. Why this Benovek rings from Surrey to tell me this, I'm not quite clear. I'll just get someone to call Wildfell and check that she hasn't returned in the meantime." He did so. While they waited, Adnan said, "I had better get back to Wildfell Hall without delay. If the old lady has been wandering for long in this weather it will be a miracle if she survives. And little Lucy is not a strong girl." He glanced at his watch.

"Have to go the long way round to Appleby," Nottall said. "There's been a sudden outflow of water halfway down Cleg Hill; report just came in. It sounds like underground seepage from the reservoir. Worrying, that is, with the extra weight of water there must be up top right now; if it comes out in one place it might somewhere else. Anyhow, part of the Appleby road's washed away, you'll have to go round through Strinton-le-Dale."

"Then I shall be off." Adnan got briskly to his feet.

A sergeant came in.

"I've been on the line to the old people's home, superintendent; neither Miss Culpepper nor her niece are back yet."

"Like to go up there, Sergeant, and see what's happening? Want to go in the police car, Doctor?"

"Thanks, but I prefer to go in my own car. I know how reckless your police drivers can be!"

Lucy leaned against Colonel Linton's doorpost and pressed the bell.

Supposing he's out? Or suppose he remembers me and is still mad?

Presently the door flew open. Colonel Linton appeared, swaying slightly, and peered at Lucy with bloodshot eyes.

"Who are *you?*" he said truculently. "Third girl who's come pestering me in the last three weeks—first some stranger, then my own granddaughter, now you—what *is* this, some kind of Mass Observation stunt?"

"Could you come and help me, please," Lucy said. "I've got old Miss Culpepper on the other side of the wall at the top of your garden, and I can't get her over; she's wet and cold and very faint."

"Old Miss Culpepper? Thought she died. Sure it's not her ghost?"

"No, but it soon will be if she's left there much longer. Please come!" Lucy grabbed his hand; he came reluctantly.

A dry-stone wall divided the untended garden from the tree-hung cliff beyond, and a flight of protruding stone slabs had been set in the wall for steps. On the far side of the wall, on the bottom step, sat Aunt Fennel.

"God bless me heart, that's old Daff! Or is it Dilly? Never could be certain which was which after we all passed our mid-eighties. Whatever are you doing there, midear? Come down from High Beck by the cliff path—flighty sort of thing to do at your age? Why not use the bridge? Not much farther? Well, never mind. Here, you give us a hand, gel; I'll shove her up to you, you steady her there, that's the ticket?"

Colonel Linton clambered over the wall and, showing unexpected strength and dexterity, hoisted Aunt Fennel up to Lucy, assisting her on her way with a powerful waft of Highland Bluebell. Then he clambered back, and Lucy tipped Aunt Fennel down into his arms; puffing a good deal, purple-faced, but triumphant, he carried her into the house. Lucy, following, was relieved to find that he had taken her to the warm kitchen and placed her on a deep, high-backed settle.

"Never expected to be doing that, Daff midear—or is it Dill?" he said, panting. "Good as a honeymoon, hey?"

Aunt Fennel's eyes had been closed; she opened them briefly and gave a faint smile.

"Edward—fancy . . ."

"Now, if you have some blankets, Colonel Linton—and a tot of your egg-and-whisky mixture—not a Highland Bluebell—"

"Anything you say, midear."

He produced eggs, and some rather moth-eaten blankets, then tactfully retired while Lucy peeled off a layer or two of Aunt Fennel's numerous garments, discovering with relief that the rain had not penetrated beyond her petticoat.

While she was being wrapped in blankets a large tabby cat stalked in and lay down on the rag mat in front of the stove.

"There!" exclaimed Lucy. "That's the cat I saw at High Beck."

"That? *That's* not Taffypuss," said Aunt Fennel, much disappointed. "Not a bit like. Much bigger."

"Not Taffypuss? I should think not," said Colonel Linton, returning. "Don't you remember I buried poor old Taffy three-four years ago? Fox got him."

"Colonel Linton, are you on the phone by any chance?" Lucy asked.

" 'Fraid not, midear."

"Oh well, then I'll walk down and phone from the post office in a moment," said Lucy, leaning against the kitchen table. The room swayed, then settled. She felt as if she were still manhandling Aunt Fennel along that greasy, nightmarish little path, tippily overhanging the rock-filled gully. "I can get my car at the same time."

"As you wish; as you wish," said the colonel vaguely. He sat down by Aunt Fennel. "Now, Dill, midear, how are you feeling? Had your tot? Bit better, eh?"

"Yes thank you, Edward," she said faintly. "It seems quite homely to be here again. But I *am* disappointed about Taffypuss."

Lucy looked at her great-aunt in affectionate exasperation. Then she caught sight of the kitchen clock.

"Is that the right time, Colonel Linton? My watch seems to have stopped. And do you have a radio?"

"You filling in one of these BBC Listener Research forms?" he said suspiciously.

"No, it was just something I wanted to listen to."

"Oh, that's different! Test score, was it? In the dining-room, midear. Help yourself," he said, busily tucking up Aunt Fennel more comfortably in her fusty blankets.

Lucy wandered weakly into the dining-room and found a radio on the windowsill—a gigantic period piece with art-nouveau arabesques of fretwork all over the front, about eighteen different knobs, and a list of stations including National, Regional, and Droitwich. Mercifully it was already tuned to BBC band four; she switched it on and left it to warm, which it did at the speed of the tundra in the arctic spring. I ought to warm up too, Lucy thought, wrap in a blanket like Aunt Fennel; too tired just at this moment, I'll listen to Max first. Those two old things are perfectly happy in there having a lovely gossip.

She could hear the gentle counterpoint of voices from the kitchen; she sat down, facing Aunt Fennel's pictures across the huge expanse of dusty mahogany, and propped her chin on her hands. If only my head didn't ache so, and if I didn't have this curious pain as if my chest were jammed inside a square bracket, I'd be able to think; I've got to try and work out why those two men were chasing Wilbie, what was going on. So as to phone police about it. Phone Fiona about Aunt Fennel. Phone Max.

She looked up at the row of pictures. Jacob and Esau, Rachel and Leah, Saul and David, Moses and Aaron.

Curious, I never noticed before that each of Aunt Fennel's pictures was in fact double, one image superimposed on another. Like the cottage that day. Those two brothers now—Jacob is Wilbie, why didn't I notice that before? Scheming and smiling, planning to come out on top one way or another. And Rachel could be Aunt Fennel when she was young. David playing to Saul —he looks like somebody familiar—wonder who? I wonder if Aunt Fennel knows about this? That sunset, with the four figures, that is really something much more complex and mysterious—

They were all mysterious. She let her eyes drift along, from one enigma to the next, each more profound, subtle, and beautiful than the last. But I can almost understand them, if I had just a little more energy . . .

Dear Max, I can't wait for you to see them. If anything could put you back on your feet again, I believe they could. Dear Max . . .

". . . Six o'clock," said the announcer. "And now we have a recorded programme of the celebrated pianist Max Benovek playing Bach's Goldberg Variations . . ."

The orderly, jewelled music began to move out into the room.

More enigmas, Lucy thought. Hieroglyphics. No, a maze, a wonderfully worked-out maze in which every compartment leads logically to the next and yet you feel it is only one of an infinite number of possibilities . . . Soon I shall be able to see the whole pattern, which is in fact the same as Aunt Fennel's embroidered sunset. How extraordinary that is; I believe I've discovered something really fundamental. If this pain would ease up a little I could understand the whole thing . . .

Her eyes closed.

How can I get rid of Russ, Wilbie thought, letting his detestable son drive him through the maze of Kirby's back streets. It was lighting-up time; orange sodium flickered and dripped through the deluge. Police loud-speaker vans toured the town, bawling some announcement.

"What are they saying?"

"Can't catch. The accent's so thick in these parts. Power-cut, maybe? Or warning that there's an escaped convict in the region."

"He's thought to be in London," Wilbie muttered.

"Here we are." Russ pulled up by the first-aid post, but Wilbie, irritable with agony, said, "No—no. Go into the car park, Russ. This is a no-parking zone, we don't want the cops towing the van away. I can walk fifty yards, for God's sake!"

"Proper little hero," Russ said, spinning the wheel, running the Land-Rover down the slope. A red-and-white barrier arm rose to let them in and Russ found a space at the back.

"This inconspicuous enough for you? Come on then; better get you fixed up before gangrene sets in."

The sister at the first-aid post was horrified.

"Really you ought to go to hospital and have it X-rayed. All I can do is clean it up for you."

"No time to go to hospital," Wilbie said. "We're hoping to catch a plane in Liverpool."

"Mind you get it seen to as soon as you can. How ever did you do it?"

"Motor-mower jammed; tried to free it."

"Horrible, dangerous things!" The sister launched happily into a series of blood-curdling anecdotes about crushed feet and severed toes which saw her nicely through Wilbie's cleansing and dressing.

"You're abandoning the rest of the pictures, then?" said Russ, outside.

"Only for the moment. With Harbin and Goetz out of the way it'll be all right to come back soon." With Russ out of the way, too, he thought. And there's still Linda. But I can deal with her.

"What about the old lady? Did you see her? Identify her?"

"Never did. I guess she was cut off in the cottage with Lucy. Maybe they'll be rescued."

"Or maybe they won't, you hope?"

Wilbie did not answer. Russ started up.

It was at this moment that the weight of water, which had been forcing its way down from the reservoir through a fault in the limestone hill beyond Kirby, suddenly split the last two feet of concrete and burst out through the rear wall of the underground car park. Russ, glancing to his right before driving off, saw the wall beside him open like a dolphin's jaws and spew out water. Instinctively he jabbed down the accelerator, and the Land-Rover bounded forward.

"Christ, Russ, what happened?"

"I dunno, but we've got to get out quick."

Other people had the same idea. The water was up to their axles and more coming at a frightening rate. Russ made for a narrow opening between two other cars, both converging on the exit. There was not enough room; they all three jammed.

"Reverse, you fool!" yelled Wilbie.

"I'm trying to!" Russ battled with the gear-shift. Then he gave it up, jumped down, up to his waist in muddy, oily water, and ran.

"Russ! Wait for me!"

Wilbie cast an agonized look back at the load of pictures. All those wonderful treasures. Wilbie famous. Wilbie celebrated. Wilbie justified. No time. Have to leave them. He scrambled down, sobbing and cursing. "Russ! God rot you! Wait for me!" He was shorter than Russ; the water came up to his chest. He could see Russ ahead of him, a long way ahead, making for the heaving, hooting, churning tangle of cars that blocked both exit and entrance.

Wilbie pushed someone aside, tried to climb over a bonnet, slipped, started toiling forward again.

But it was already too late.

"Miss Culpepper hasn't come back since we rang you?" the police sergeant asked.

Fiona shook her head. "No, she hasn't. No message, nothing."

Adnan, standing behind the sergeant, saw Mrs. Marsham come out of her office and give them a strange, panicky glance.

"Police checking Miss Culpepper's disappearance," Fiona said.

Mrs. Marsham seemed to relax a little. But she was pale and strained, her glasses crooked, hair untidy. "You've no news of her?" she asked.

"Not yet, matron. We're just going along to inquire in the village."

"Can I hitch a lift with you?" Fiona said. "Time I was getting back to my baby. Mrs. T.'s Ann will be here in twenty minutes," she told Mrs. Marsham. "And I've cut all the bread-and-butter for supper, and Emma Chiddock's waiting to help you."

Mrs. Marsham nodded tiredly. Fiona climbed into Dr. Adnan's Alfa.

"I don't much like that woman, but she's in a bad way, poor thing," she said to Adnan. "Don't you think you ought to go back presently and give her a tranquillizer or something?"

"Yes, I will do this," he said. "Let us hope we find Lucy and the aunt at the cottage. Then I will go back with them and look after all three."

At the foot of High Beck Lane the sergeant's attention was attracted by a large white towel tied in an ostentatious manner to the parsonage gatepost.

"Who lives there?" he asked, pulling up.

"Colonel Linton."

"Seems as if he wanted to attract attention. I'll just inquire."

They watched him ring the bell and Colonel Linton open the door and talk. The sergeant turned and beckoned. Adnan joined him; Fiona followed inquisitively.

"The hunt is over; they are here," Adnan said.

"*Here?* Why hasn't Lucy phoned then? Where is she? What happened?"

Colonel Linton had embarked on a long and complicated explanation.

"Broken bridge . . . cliff path . . . amazing old lady, ninety-two if she's a day—or was it ninety-three . . . and my own little granddaughter Cathy . . . horrible sad about her . . . proper Linton . . ."

"Where's Lucy?" Fiona demanded again. They were all standing in the flagged front hall; Adnan moved into the dining-room.

From the kitchen they could hear Aunt Fennel's voice:

"It's been a nice visit, Edward, but I'm a little tired; think I'd better be getting back to that place, have a bit of supper and off to bed. Must be nearly supper-time. Where's my Lucy child?"

"That's why she didn't phone," Adnan said.

Lucy was sitting at the table, apparently resting, with her head pillowed on her arms.

"Just the way I found her an hour ago, with Record Rendezvous turned on full blast," Colonel Linton was explaining wretchedly to the sergeant. "Thought I'd best leave her so. But turned off the radio."

"She's not—she's not—*dead?*"

"I'm afraid so." Adnan touched her wrist. "It was her heart, without doubt. Silly, silly girl. She always would do more than she ought." As he looked down at her his dark mussel-plum eyes glistened with tears; he said very crossly, "And now I suppose *I* shall have to be the one to telephone this Max Benovek, and God knows what damage that is going to do if he had the same feeling for her that she had for him. Besides which there is this poor old lady; *you* will have to take charge of her," he said to Fiona.

"Yes; all right." Without more ado Fiona turned on her heel and walked into the kitchen.

"Aunt Fennel," she said, "I've got a piece of dreadful news for you, I'm afraid."

"What, dearie?"

"It's about Lucy. She's had a heart attack. I'm afraid she's dead."

Aunt Fennel looked up at Fiona, moving her head slowly. She took out her hearing aid, stared at it, and returned it to her ear. "Dead?" she repeated. "Lucy? Dead?"

"Yes, I'm afraid so."

There was a longish pause. The sergeant had gone back to the police car and was radioing for an ambulance; Colonel Linton gloomily shook up a whisky and methylated cocktail in a jam-jar, gazed at it, and poured it down the sink; Adnan gently checked the old lady's pulse and breathing.

She suffered this unresisting, almost unnoticing; presently she murmured as if to herself,

"Dead? Quite peaceful and happy then. Like Dill. Like Taffy-puss. *All right.*"

She looked up triumphantly at Adnan.

"All right?" he said. "Dear me, yes. And you're all right too. All set for a hundred, I should judge. You are a marvellous old lady, aren't you. What is your secret?"

"My secret?" Aunt Fennel looked up at him again, then beyond him at Fiona, at the sergeant, at Colonel Linton. "You mean, which of them am I?" She smiled to herself, a smile that her great-niece would have recognised. She said to Adnan,

"If I didn't see fit to tell my Lucy child, do you think that I would tell any of *you?*"